A night in a M............................ women to
satisfy, an elegant Victorian lady in a rowing boat
with a strapping sailor to attend to her sea legs, a
naked swimmer in the warm blue sea watched closely
by hungry eyes, a pert and pretty whore making
payment to her lawyer in the currency she knows
best, a jealous lover looking on as his curvaceous pro-
tégée writhes in the arms of her muscular stud . . .
these are just some of the intriguing scenes and
images from Eroticon III, a new sampler of the best
of erotic writing.

EROTICON III

Anonymous

Introduced and edited by J-P Spencer

NEXUS

A Nexus Book
Published in 1989
by the Paperback Division of
W.H. Allen & Co Plc
338 Ladbroke Grove
London W10 5AH

Reprinted 1990

Typeset by Phoenix Photosetting, Chatham
Printed and bound in Great Britain by
Courier International Ltd, Tiptree, Essex

ISBN 0 352 32166 0

CONTENTS

INTRODUCTION

Readers of the previous two books in this series of erotic anthologies will be familiar with the format of this present volume. *Eroticon III* presents a further sample of titillating writings composed by a variety of hands. However, the profile of the average pornographer does not change and it is reasonable to assume that all the authors whose work is included here are male mercenaries whose identities have been deliberately obscured. Followers of the series and readers knowledgeable in this field will recognise the obvious exceptions: Andrea de Nerciat the frustrated soldier/dramatist, author of *The Pleasures of Lolotte* and other erotic novels, who died miserably at the dawn of the nineteenth century after a period of incarceration in Rome's notorious Castel Saint Angelo; the Comte de Mirabeau, the great orator of the French Revolution and a hero of the people, who relieved the boredom of his own imprisonment by writing, among other erotic masterpieces, *The Lifted Curtain*; and, of course, the enigmatic 'Walter', Victorian England's most notorious libertine by virtue of his *My Secret Life*, the most exhaustive and exhausting sex diary in the canon of erotic writing. (The selections from *My Secret Life* that are given here, as in previous volumes, are from that portion of the work not available in the traditional British publishing territories.)

The pieces selected have been written exclusively

to sexually arouse the reader (and assessment of their worth, like that of sexual activity itself, is a purely personal judgement) but if one cares to look beyond the breathless coupling of the protagonists in the foreground, it is interesting to note the background settings that have been chosen. With one exception here those settings are European – from an eighteenth century French convent to a Turkish harem, from a sun-soaked Spanish beach to, inevitably and frequently, the boudoirs of Paris. Though the origins of many of these excerpts are American, only one selection is set in the New World – obviously the old one is considered to be more erotically inspiring!

This American selection is taken from *The Devil's Advocate* – also published in the United States under the title *The Sign of the Scorpion* – a novel with a mystery theme and a hard-boiled style that echoes Raymond Chandler. The central relationship in the book, between a cynical lawyer and the naïve young beauty who involves him in her search for her missing sister, is a fascinating example of a classic theme of erotic writing – the corruption of an innocence that secretly desires such corruption. The excerpt chosen here, however, is a set piece sexual encounter in the lawyer's fly-blown office – and innocence definitely does not come into it! For that the inquisitive reader must turn to the full-length novel – a course of action recommended, where possible, in every case. It is worth remembering that the excerpts chosen are simply samples of whole works and it is to be hoped that they will whet rather than satiate the literary appetite.

J-P Spencer

Eveline

After breakfast I wandered along the Parade. I watched the sea and the boats. One old boatman interested me.

'Go for a row, miss? Beautiful mornin', miss. Sea like ile. Launch her down in half a jiffy, miss. Pull alongshore and see the bathin'.'

The loveliness of the day tempted me.

'Which is your boat, my friend?'

'That's she, miss. Yon white one, with the red streak.'

'She looks a safe craft. Does she rock about much?'

'Lor' bless your sweet soul! No, miss! Why look at her grand flat bottom, and her fine run aft! She can travel too. She's got legs on her! You should have seen her at the regatta. Better have an hour's row, miss.'

I got into the boat. *The Locket, David Jones of Eastbourne*, was painted on the board against which I leaned. It was a nice big boat with good cushions in clean white covers. The old man pushed off and jumped in.

'You'll go past the machines, miss, o' coorse?'

'Anywhere you like, Mr David Jones. I have confidence in you. It is quite warm on the water.'

'Yes, miss. These are the ladies' machines. The gents' is further hup. We shall have to pass the ladies fust, but it won't take long.'

2

'Where are you going then, Mr Jones?'

'Why, o' coorse—past the gents. All the ladies goes past in my boat. 'Tis what they likes best—as is nat'ral. That's what they takes the row for.'

The old fellow grinned. He screwed up his face into a comical expression. He actually winked.

The boat did travel well, as the poor old fellow said. It only took ten minutes to pass the line of gaudily arrayed, tall, angular female figures, of squalling children and shouting girls bobbing about knee-deep with their 'flat bottoms and fine runs aft' presented seawards.

'What a number of people on the beach, Mr Jones!'

'Yes, miss. They allus comes there to look at the ladies.'

'I don't see very much to admire, but then perhaps it's because I'm a woman.'

'Jus' so, miss. You wait a bit. It's all right, I knows what the ladies like.'

Presently we passed the first of the men's bathing machines. Old Jones had pulled in closer.

'There we are, miss! Fine 'uns too among 'em today!'

I laughed—the idea was so crudely expressed. The fact was so evident that this was only an ordinary exercise on the part of the girls that I shook off the awkward feeling of restraint which troubled me. I looked boldly enough now. The men stood upon the machines with the doors open. They seemed to be employed principally in sawing their backs in a painful manner with bath towels. They were absolutely naked; their figures entirely and unblushingly exposed. Indeed when they saw me pass along with the old fellow they took special pains to exhibit themselves, their privates wagging proudly about in front.

'That's a fine 'un; ain't he, miss?'

I gazed in the direction in which the old man nodded his head as the boat glided by. I thought he even seemed to row slower as we passed. It was a tall man—white, handsome, well-developed—a patch of dark hair on his belly—a huge instrument of pleasure dangling between his thighs.

I held my breath. I noted the man well. I also observed the number of the machine—it was 33.

'Ah, he's a fine man, he is, miss, but he ain't half as fine a made man as what my son is. He's a sailor, miss, aboard of a big four-masted ship, he is, and comin' home tomorrow. He's been round the Horn to Valparaiso and he's been took very bad along of the Horn and the weather. He's been paid off today, and he's comin' down here to see his old dad again. I 'spects him by the first train. He's been ten months away, but he's bound straight here, for he's a good lad and nothing wouldn't stop him in Lunnon.'

'Dear me, Mr Jones, you quite interest me. And you think he would not stay to spend any of his money among the pleasures of London? He must be quite a model young man. I'm sure you must be proud of him.'

'I am that, miss. Not that he's much of a muddle either—he's fond of his old father, but he's fond of a pretty gal too. He'll be here tomorrow, then you can tell me if I'm right or not. Lor', miss, you should just see him pull these oars about. He used to make *The Locket* fly, he did! I fear I won't keep him here long. Not that he wouldn't go to sea again, but he'll get rid of his money among the gals here. They'll all be after him like they was afore.'

'What a sad thing, Mr Jones. Don't you give him good advice?'

'So I used to do, miss. But Lor' luv yer, what's the good; lions wouldn't hold him, miss, he's that hot when he gets ashore. I got the missionary to reason with him, but it wasn't no good. He went about just the same again. No, miss, wild helephants couldn't hold him.'

'I think, perhaps, if you removed him from such temptations; if you kept him to your boat-letting business now, under your own eye, you know, Mr Jones, don't you think that might tame him down a bit?'

'P'raps it might, miss, if he'd anyone to read and talk serious to him, but I don't know no one; and he's that quick and impatient—'

'You make me feel very much for your poor son, Mr Jones. I shall come round in the morning, and if he's there then I should be pleased to talk to him on his duty to his parents.'

'I've been a widderer these twenty year come Michaelmas, so there's only me to look after the lad. He's more fit to look after me now. There's one thing I likes about him. He don't drink.'

I had one of my headaches next morning. I have not always the remedy for them at hand. On this occasion I had left it in London. I thought the air along the sea front might do me good. After breakfast I strolled along the Parade to the far corner where Mr Jones—who, by the by, was not a Welshman but a native of Sussex—had his boat.

'Good morning, Mr Jones. I see you are an advocate of cleanliness. Your *Locket* looks splendid, after the scrubbing you are giving her.'

A fine, tall, young fellow, fair and freckled, with

his short curly hair shading his broad forehead, wielded a mop which belaboured the bottom and sides of the upturned skiff. His legs were bare to the knees. He stood like an old Northern Viking, a splendid specimen of the Anglo-Saxon race. The heavy bucket might have contained only waste paper from the manner in which he shifted it about, charged to the brim with sea water. He almost dropped it, however, as he turned and saw me. His mouth opened. He stood stupidly staring at me from behind his old father. I recognised the youth at once.

'Good mornin', miss. I don't know nothin' about no advocates, miss, but my son Bill is just a givin' her a rub round as we was a thinkin', the mornin' being so fine, I might see a young lady down for a row.'

He had a twinkle in his eye which conveyed a silent hope that the liberal fee he had received the previous day might be repeated.

'So this is your son, is it, Mr Jones? He must be of great service to you now you have got him.'

'Oh, yes, miss—he's a main stronger nor me. You should see him capsize that there butt all alone by hisself. Why a rhinersorous couldn't do it!'

The old boatman was brimming over with pride—satisfaction at recovering his long-absent son betrayed itself in every feature.

'You must be very glad to see your father again.'

'Yes, so I am, miss, and to find him so well and hearty. You see, miss, he's getting on now. It ain't as I'm so awful strong—it's that my old dad is a gettin' a bit shaky in his timbers, miss.'

There was something charming in the kindly smile, and the rough, yet tender, manner of the blunt young sailor towards the old man which made me look him over more attentively. He was certainly a superbly built young fellow. His bare arms and legs were furnished with a muscular development which is rare in these days of effeminacy. A vigorous, healthy life upon the ocean had served to enhance all his natural advantages. He was a man to my mind. My headache increased—I wanted him badly to cure it.

Between them, they turned the boat over again. It was a good substantial skiff. I had been used to boating with Percy as a child. I knew something about rowing. I used to astonish the girls at the *pensionnat* near Paris when we all went in a formal party down the Seine from Suresnes. It suited me now to pretend ignorance.

'I hope you will stop with your dad, and—and be a good boy. He tells me you are too fond of—of pleasure.'

My manner was demure. I flashed him one of my glances. He seemed struck. There is—they say—a Freemasonry in love. I say there is *more*. There is a magnetism in love which is conveyed from mind to mind—from brain to brain—from heart to heart, if you will—but there is a power, subtle and irresistible, which speaks more powerfully than words. 'I love you, I want you.' Such was the influence which flashed between us now.

'We sailors don't get too much pleasuring, miss—but I've been ten months at sea, shut up in an old box of a ship all the time, four hours out and four hours in—and that's about the size of it. My dad ain't the man to deny me a fair run ashore now I'm home again. I know how to take care of the rhino all the same, but I mean to stay some time with him now and I shan't trouble about shipping again yet awhile.'

7

There was a half serious, half comical air about the young fellow which showed he only partly believed in me. His keen blue eye followed me. He was noting me well from head to foot. He was distinctly struck with my appearance. Admiration was plainly, visibly written in his look. I read him like a book. I was a revelation to the young sailor. No doubt his appetite was sharp after ten long months at sea. I inwardly rejoiced. Meanwhile the boat was ready, the cushions in their places.

'If you've a mind for a row, miss, my son Bill will go with you and pull you about in the butt anywhere you likes.'

I got into the boat. They launched her down. Bill swung himself in over the bow. He backed her out from the smooth beach. Then he sat himself down facing me and began to row steadily away from the shore.

'I really don't know if I ought to trust myself all alone with such a gay young man as your dad describes you, Mr William, but after all he does not give you a bad character, though he does say you are somewhat—somewhat—what shall I say?'

'Oh, I know, he's a larky old customer, is my dad, and he thinks I'm not much steadier than he was when he was a young 'un. Which course shall we steer, miss—go along the Pevensey shore, or keep on out of the Bay a bit?'

'Let us get into deep water and right away from the sound of the noisy people ashore. How fast you row!'

He was pulling as if for a wager. We were already half a mile away, heading straight out to sea. He slacked a little as I spoke. All this time his gaze never left my person or my face. He was trying to sum me up. Speculating, probably, as to what sort of bedfellow I should make. He was very good-looking certainly. As he bent forward to his paddles, his loose shirt disclosed his broad chest covered with a fine sandy down. I felt impatient as I sat on the broad seat with a back to it. I faced him all the time. I sat cross-legged, my right knee over the left. As Bill pulled away at the paddles, my leg was jerked backwards and forwards. I took care he should have a good view of my feet and my stockings as well. I soon fascinated him. The black silk seemed a new sensation. He commenced to row still more unevenly. My leg moved in cadence. He could see at times up to my knee as the light breeze assisted his design. He was evidently getting excited. A strong lascivious expression extended itself over his features.

'So you have been shut up ten months on board ship, Bill? That must have been trying to a fine young man like you?'

I could not beat about the bush. I wanted him. I meant to indulge my inclination—to have him. It was no time to waste in mere sentiment—in childish trifling.

'I guess it was, miss. Never saw a petticoat for over four months. We were not allowed ashore at Valparaiso, only in the daytime. It's a queer hole for British seamen, miss; nothing but rows and robbery.'

'Poor fellow! But of course you have a sweetheart here?'

'Not I, miss. I only came home last night, or rather early this morning. I couldn't stop in London with the poor old dad here and he so old and feeble-like, so I jumped into the first train I could.'

'You are a good fellow, Bill. I like you very much.

What a long way we are from the shore now! I can't see the pier any more.'

'We're over two miles from Eastbourne now. See that light-ship there—that's the Royal Sovereign shoal.'

'How lovely it seems—how calm the sea is! We need not go any further out. You might not be able to get back, Bill.'

'I only wish I couldn't!'

'Why so, Bill?'

'Because I haven't had the chance to see a face like yours in all my life, miss! There—now it's out!'

'Oh, Bill! You don't mean that? Come and sit here and tell me all about it.'

I made room for him beside me on the broad seat with the backboard. The words 'David Jones' were quite obliterated by our figures. Bill took up a rope and began undoing the end into four separate cords. Then he got the other end of the same rope, and served it the same. I watched him. Then he put two ends together, the four cords of each end interlacing.

'Why Bill! What do you call that?'

'That's what we sailors call making a splice, miss—when it's done.'

'Do you ever think of being spliced yourself, Bill?'

'Sometimes, but sailors ought never to be properly spliced up, miss. There ought to be a slippery hitch somewhere. They're awfully true when spliced, but the gals ain't. They can't stand the long absences.'

'Can you make a slippery hitch, Bill?'

He laughed. We both laughed. I looked into his eyes. He returned my gaze. I put my hand on his thigh. He slipped his left arm round my waist. He

10

had dropped the rope now. We sat quiet a moment. The only sound we could hear was the low gurgling of the placid sea under the boat's bows and sides, as she lay idly rolling on the gentle swell.

'We are quite alone here, Bill—not a boat anywhere.'

He had white canvas trousers on, turned up to his knees. My hand stole along until it was suddenly arrested by something hard and solid between his legs which lay along the inside of his left thigh. I lifted my face up close to his. Instantly he kissed me on the mouth.

'Oh, Bill! Oh, you bad boy!'

He seized me tightly in his arms. He covered me with kisses. He pressed my bosom with his great sailor hand. I closed my eyes and suffered all.

'Make me a slippery hitch, Bill dear!'

He pressed me again tighter than ever. My fingers pressed his limb. It seemed tremendously thick and stiff.

'Ten months! Only think, Bill, how bad you must feel!'

His hand was already on my leg. As I spoke it moved further up. I opened my legs and let it pass. Meanwhile I deliberately unbuttoned his canvas flap.

'I want to look at it, Bill!'

'So you shall, my dear. It's a whopper!'

A moment later, a huge naked limb stiffly erect and throbbing with eagerness for enjoyment was in my grasp. His hand had already taken possession of the centre of my desires. His fingers maddened me. Without more ado, I pulled the big member into the warm daylight. It was a beauty! White and red, with a large soft top and hard sides—very long and awfully stiff. We rolled about together in this position as the boat answered to the undulations of the sea. It could not last so, however, and so it came to pass that I slipped, cushion and all, off the seat. Bill and I found ourselves on the floor-boards of the skiff with the cushion under us. I still retained my hold of his limb. He reached out and secured another cushion which he placed under my loins. Then he tilted me back. He pulled up my clothes. I am afraid I helped him. He took one look at my exposed legs—at my white belly. I saw for a second his big truncheon menacing me within a few inches of my thighs. Then he threw himself upon me. I was quite as eager as he was. I helped him to his pleasure. The lewd business was about to begin—the curtain was up—the actor and the actress were on the stage.

'Oh! Oh! Bill—you hurt! Oh! Oh! You're right into me! You're too big! You're—Oh!—Oh!—Oh! My goodness, Bill!'

Nothing stopped him. The young fellow had had a long fast. I was getting the full benefit of his abstention. He pushed his great tool into me to his balls. He never spoke, but he set his teeth together. He worked up and down, thrusting at me like a battering ram. In less time than it takes to relate he sank on my chest. I felt a sudden gush of hot seed. I knew that his pleasure had reached the climax. He lay discharging, until a flood of thick sperm deluged my interior. My own pleasure was supreme. He gave me no rest. Instead of withdrawing, he recommenced. A few thrusts, aided by the natural elasticity of my vagina, restored him to all his virility. He commenced another course. Oh, the impatient fellow! How he worked me!

'Oh! Bill, dear Bill! Go slowly—do it gently, Bill!

Oh, oh! You'll know the bottom of the boat out! Oh, my goodness! Oh!'

'Boat be damned!' was the polite rejoinder.

At last he got up. He adjusted his clothes. He wiped his smoking member. I raised myself on my cushions. I dipped my handkerchief into the cool sea-water and sopped up all I could of the tremendous overflow I had received. I made the best toilette possible under the circumstances.

'We can sail back easy. The wind is almost dead fair. Then we can sit together. Do you feel jolly now, my dear love?'

There was something that touched me beyond simple lust in this young fellow. There was an innate tenderness towards 'his gal,' to which they say sailors are particularly prone, just as one makes a pet of a dog.

I have heard of sailors at Portsmouth newly discharged from their ships and envious of married men who had found a ready-made progeny on their return, seeking to emulate them by hiring babies to carry up and down the Yard. I can quite believe it.

Bill set to work. In two minutes the mast was stepped; in two more the sail was hoisted and set, and the sheet, as he called it, hauled aft. The skiff sailed along merrily—too quickly I thought, as I sat on the cushioned floor of the boat with my head on the thigh of the young sailor who held the tiller. My restless fingers would not remain quiet. They sought their playfellow. Bill opened his flap. I pulled out his stiffening limb.

'Oh, Bill! What a big one! Do you feel any better now?'

'Why, yes, my lovely dear one, of course I do, and I'm damned grateful to you for the chance, miss. But

13

I wish—that I do—we were not going to part so soon. I should like to have you all night.'

'Oh, Bill! A pretty thing you'd make of me by morning!'

His limb rose again under the skilful touches of my nimble fingers. As I sat, my face was just on a level with his erect weapon. He held the tiller in one hand; with the other he caressed my neck and bosom. I bent forward. I examined minutely his splendid limb from end to end. I put my hand under and felt his testicles. I tickled him lusciously. I put the tip of the broad nut to my lips. I kissed it. I opened them—it entered. I sucked it. I rolled my hot tongue round the red head.

'Oh! Oh! Little lass! You are driving me mad, don't ye know! Stop a moment. Here, come stern on. I'll arrange all in the twinkling of a handspike. Now sit down between my legs. So! Oh, my God!'

He pulled me backwards. He had already raised my clothes. My buttocks were exposed to his salacious view. I settled myself down upon his thighs. I felt his thing pressing in between my pliant globes. The big knob was jammed between them. I put down my right hand. I placed his weapon between the moist lips of my little slit. I pressed down.

'Oh! Damn my eyes and limbs! My bowsprit's run you aboard, missy! It's right into you up to the gammoning! Oh, isn't it lovely?'

He seized me round the hips. He pushed home. With my left hand, I tickled his testicles. His big limb stretched me tremendously. I enjoyed it all the same. I shared his transports. I was mad with lust. I jogged up and down. My spasms came all too soon. I ceased moving. I could only moan now. Bill took up the movements. He pushed with fury.

'Oh, Bill! You'll upset the boat!'

'Upset the soup, you mean? There it goes! Enough for all hands!'

Truly the vigour of this active young sailor was tremendous. He had been ten months, remember, without copulation. His excitement, doubtless his enjoyment, was proportionate to the length of his abstinence. I was really glad when the boat's keel touched land.

A Gallery of Nudes

Casilda had sunk into a reverie. She even ignored her tepid little drink, and sat bemused, staring into space. I mentioned half a dozen restaurants by name, and pushed the evening paper, with the list of cinemas, in front of her eyes. But they were fixed, vacantly, on a point past my right shoulder, and when at last she spoke, I could barely catch the words, they were uttered so softly, under her breath.

'Yes, I do, too—I know what I'd like. It's over there in the corner. Daddy, buy me that.'

I followed her gaze the length of the bar. At the other end, facing towards us with an evidently keen interest in Casilda, sat a hulking, swarthy young dago in a flamboyant brown suit, with vastly padded shoulders and an air of almost insolent admiration. Casilda, I am sorry to say, was giving him very much the same look in return.

'You can't mean that seriously,' I exclaimed—as a statement of fact, not a question. For one thing, he sported the sort of moustache that might have been drawn with an eyebrow-pencil an inch below his nostrils.

Casilda merely nodded, but as an affirmative gesture it was all too definite. Any doubt in my mind was pure wishful thinking.

'I thought you said you didn't go in for gigolos,' I protested.

The girl gave a snort of mirth. 'Nor do I,' she

18

agreed. 'But I can have this one for free, I assure you—if you'll let me. And you could watch,' she added in the same quiet tone, scarcely above a whisper. 'Wouldn't that excite you?' Her face was set, almost sullen.

There was silence between us for a moment. I needed time to think, to ponder this startling proposition. Without a word I paid the bill, kissed her cheek and walked out, bowing stiffly to the baffled foreigner, who hastily returned my salute with joyful bewilderment.

Was he any less puzzled on the back seat of the car, after an unceremonious introduction as 'My toreador,' while we drove towards Chelsea, with Casilda, happy and tense, nestling against my shoulder, her hand on my knee? He had a smattering of English—enough to gargle polite assent when Casilda asked him if this was his first visit to London, but her next question—'Have you ever been kidnapped before?'—virtually drew a blank. 'Very pretty,' he assured us.

'Isn't he, though?' Casilda murmured, hugging my arm. 'He's a matador, you know,' she insisted.

'More like a picador, to judge by his looks,' I retorted. 'What are you going to do with this tough when you get him home?'

'The best he can,' said Casilda.

He chose whisky and accepted with alacrity an invitation from Casilda in French to be shown the house. I poured myself a big dollop of brandy, and settled down to read a couple of letters that the postman had brought. To this day I could not tell you what was in them. A few agonising minutes' wait was as much as I could bear.

They were not next door. She had led him off to

the spare room upstairs—which was very considerate of her. He was kneeling with his back to me
as I entered, his face pressed against her navel. She
sat, naked to the waist, on the high fourposter, with
an arm around his bull neck, twisting his greasy
curls. She took no notice of me whatsoever, and her
conquest, oblivious of all else but the free gift of this
magnificent body, did not even hear me come in. I lit
the fire for them, and slipped into an easy chair near
by to contemplate the scene.

He had evidently set about his business without a
second's hesitation. The square, exaggeratedly masculine shoulders obscured her lower half from view,
while his bent head was sunk in the hollow of her
lap, and blindly, with both brown, hairy paws
upstretched, he mauled, rather than fondled,
Casilda's breasts. The way the fellow manhandled
those sumptuous tits struck me as exceedingly rough
and uncouth for a Latin lover: he plucked and
tweaked and tugged at them, like some famished
urchin snatching oranges from a tree. Nevertheless
there was no sign of objection or complaint on her
part; she kept her mouth shut tight and made not a
sound, except for the fast, heavy breathing that
shook her whole frame more violently from within, it
seemed, than the harsh treatment to which this
clumsy lout was subjecting her shapely façade.

She did not budge or flicker an eyelid. Yet if she,
in rigid submission, might have withstood his bold
assault indefinitely, it was clear that the hotblooded
Spaniard could brook no further delay. Muttering
with impatience, the coarse creature sprang to his
feet and started to tear the rest of her clothes off. She
helped him then at once, promptly raising a docile
backside to facilitate the complete removal of her

rumpled dress and skintight panties, while she herself took off her fetching little suspender belt and
stockings. As she leaned forward to do so, she
suddenly, as I saw, undid his fly—and I too had the
same impulse of unrestrainable curiosity, though for
a different reason. What intrigued me was not Don
Juan's credentials, but the effect they would produce
on her. By craning my neck I caught a glimpse of her
face, which revealed an expression of such sad and
obvious disappointment that I probably let out a
delighted guffaw. He spun round on me like a tiger,
with eyes blazing fury at my intrusion. But his
beautiful big dark eyes did not interest me; his
erection did. It was rather short; not small, exactly,
but a funny, fat, stubby instrument—a replica of the
cocky young masher himself. His spitting image, I
thought. Thick, I'll grant you—exceptionally thick,
and to all appearance hard as marble.

Personally I am fairly large, even now, and though
of course comparisons are odious, I could sympa-
thise with Casilda for taking such a dim view of his
singularly unimpressive member. Certainly this was
not the doughty Toledo blade by which she had
expected to be smitten to the quick. It was stiff
enough to fit her sheath, and stout enough to fill it
adequately, but surely not long enough to pierce her
very heart, as she had hoped.

In any case, this queer little blunderbuss was the
last alarming weapon that our swashbuckling
Spanish guest could brandish at me as he advanced in
threatening fashion. I stood my ground, and
watched him with some amusement.

'Go away from here!' he shouted, pointing
towards the door. 'Madame and I will be alone.'

But Casilda rose up at that moment, like some

21

vengeful goddess clad in the imposing plenitude of her pagan nudity, and summoned the hound to heel. She clung to the sleeve of his chocolate suit, restraining him. 'No, no!' she cried. 'Quiet, Carlos!' It was an order, rapped out sharply in the tone you would employ to subdue a ferocious mastiff, and she accompanied it with vehement shakes of the head, which he could not fail to understand. He hesitated, scowling in my direction, but she gripped him firmly by the convenient handle she found within reach and clamped her mouth on his, silencing his ugly splutters of rage. Barefoot, she was considerably the taller of the two, though no match for him in strength. He flung her back against the bed—but she held on to his penis firmly, so that he fell sprawling across her where she lay.

'No, no!' she cried once more. 'Not like that— naked like me. 'Hurry—take all this stuff off, quick!'

Hastily he obeyed her, stripping at full speed. He was as hairy as an ape. With a shock of surprise, I noticed that his shoulders were in fact immensely broad—no less broad than his natty suiting had made them out to be. Like Casilda herself, the brute looked better out of clothes. He was admirably built, I have to admit—as strong as an ox, evidently, and well shaped, with a deep chest and narrow hips, although too hirsute and too short of stature to qualify as an Adonis. But the general impression was of good, young male muscle beneath the thick coat of black fur which covered him like a rug from his neck to his ankles. It was only his genitals that were not up to much, by contrast, with the rest of his sturdy physique.

Casilda eagerly scrutinised this classical virile type

while he undressed. Reclining between the pair of carved, slender posts at the foot of the bed, where he had thrown her, for all the world like a goalkeeper alertly awaiting the next exultant forward rush, and with her eyes still riveted on him, it was then that she made the lewdest gesture I ever beheld in a lifetime of debauchery. Slowly, deliberately she stretched her long, lovely legs as far apart as she could spread them, doing the splits in that lolling position, so that we both—he and I—were confronted with a medical diagram of the vulva, highly coloured and fully extended, as in a textbook for students of gynae-cology. Not content with this obtrusive exhibition of her secret flesh, she turned exposure into invitation by offering him the target of her parted lips which she held open with two fingers in an inverted V for victory—or vagina.

For him it was an explorer's survey of the promised land, a preliminary viewing for his approval of the savoury dish that he had ordered. For me it was a blow across the face, a sudden, stinging shock of jealous horror. Until then my emotions had been mixed, uncertain, mostly dormant, as though by dint of will I had contrived to keep my feelings, if not under complete control, at least in abeyance. Curiosity and a shameful, vicarious excitement had usurped my normal faculties, numbing the spirit of revolt in my brain like a narcotic. Now, realisation of the vile role that I had assumed, both as pimp and cuckold, seeped over me, and a sweat of anguish broke out upon my brow. I was enveloped in some foul nightmare when I heard Casilda cry in the same urgent, raucous tone of imperative, intemperate desire:

'Come on now, man—take me! Give it to me! I want you.'

Before the words were out of her mouth he was inside her. He hurled himself forward into the open breach that was presented to him, as a battering ram of old must have crushed triumphantly through the weakened ramparts of an enemy citadel, vanquished and abandoned under siege. The impact winded her, and she uttered a loud gasp as the weight of the gorilla's vigorous onslaught knocked the breath from her body. His grappling hands dragged at her hips, pulling her half off the end of the bed, as he clambered upward, thrusting and jolting against her, jabbing and jerking, but at the same time holding her pelvis suspended in midair, as though to prevent the force of his attack from carrying her backwards, lest he should lose the prize he had seized or risk diminishing the violent contact of their private parts. I studied Casilda's face at this juncture, as she was lugged bolt upright into a sitting position by her arms, which were clasped behind his neck. She looked stunned, bereft, flabbergasted. Her eyes and mouth were as wide open as her legs, and fixed in a dazed expression. Rocked and pummelled amidships, she was beginning now to pant and strain in a wild attempt to draw the man down on top of her, so that she might herself enjoy the act in comfort, prone beneath his lunging bulk but solidly supported by the bed and able therefore to reply on even terms and keep her end up. He had gained the initiative; with his feet firmly planted on the floor, he seemed solely concerned to take his pleasure of her surrendered sex without scruple for his amorous partner's physical need, but seeking only to press home his own advantage over an all too easy victim.

My heart leaped for joy when I saw what was happening: this brash little dago was manhandling

Casilda with the utmost rigour, he had roused her erotic instinct to fever pitch, he tupped her as savagely as a beast of the field—yet he could not satisfy her. He was using her merely as an object suited to his lustful purpose; but his very success in this selfish aim would prove a bitter blow to her— and she had asked for it. I was delighted to think that she was doomed to experience the direst disenchantment in my presence. Already I toyed with the idea of how I would upbraid her for this sordid and disgraceful display when it was over. If she was so wanton and so immoral as to hope that I might take the satyr's place, after he had finished with her, and carry on from where he left off, she would soon discover that she had made a big mistake. This was the end—I realised the fact with meridian clarity as I watched her lascivious antics in the arms of another man. I was through with Casilda Vandersluys for good and all. Directly after the fellow had gone, I would kick her out of the house. Or she could buzz off with him on her own if she liked—I didn't care.

Alas, how wrong I was! The mistake was entirely mine. I underestimated the dirty bastard—and the harlot who had picked him up, frankly preferring him to me, as casually as I might choose a whore in a brothel. She could not have guessed beforehand that he possessed such a small, stumpy tool which would scarcely fill the bill; but then neither could I foresee, at this initial stage of events, what stalwart use he would make of it, what fantastic feats of endurance the monster was capable of performing, how complete his victory would be, or what a shattering effect his persistence would have on so doughty an opponent as Casilda. She, I knew, was a tough nut to crack. I had marvelled at her reserves of energy and enthusiasm when she lasted through round after gruelling round with Helen. Keen as she was for the fray, Helen had not stood the pace to the finish with half so much in hand as the younger woman, who seemed wholly inexhaustible, ever ready to renew the engagement, gallantly impervious to fatigue. Casilda met more than her match in Carlos. His staying powers were incredible. Again and again he outlasted her, checking his own orgasm but making the randy bitch spend with increasing ecstasy each time, with longer, more profound, more exquisite spasms, by a delaying technique of extraordinary resilience which I never would have credited from hearsay.

Unfortunately for my peace of mind, it was not from hearsay that I learned the grim, incontrovertible truth of that young orang-utan's sexual proficiency. To my chagrin and disgust I was obliged to witness the revolting demonstration of his prowess untiringly exercised on Casilda's wracked but willing frame, as it appeared to me, for hours on end . . . I was in agony throughout, yet powerless to prevent it. The experiment was conducted under my nauseated gaze—but there was nothing that I could do to stop the unspeakable cad from screwing my girl to distraction . . . and at her own request.

He started by his sliding both hands under her thighs and tearing them apart still further; then, when he had wrenched her open like an oyster, he pushed her knees back, bending them outwards as supplely as a frog's, so that he mounted her as if to probe her guts upon the operating table. She protested feebly, but her long legs were crossed high around his loins while he gradually ploughed his way deeper into her and farther up onto the bed. Eventually he had her flat on it, and she got a chance to retaliate in kind, battling against him hammer and tongs, as he crushed her under his weight and pounded her with his stiff, stout, chugging piston. For a time, as though moved by clockwork, he stuck to the same steady, regular, relentless rhythm, which was neither fast nor slow but evenly stressed, a succession of short, sharp stabs for many minutes at a time—until, not heeding Casilda's cries but of his own volition, to please himself, he would alter the tempo and shift the angle and the manner of his strokes. These tactical changes, occurring at odd intervals, swept all before him and soon reduced Casilda to an abject state of unassuaged, amazed submission. All trace of restraint, dignity or pride was gone. She had what she wanted—a surfeit of it, lashings of cock, almost more of the sweet physic than she could stomach. Well and truly was she getting laid; he poked her, decidedly, as she had never been poked before. The devil's pitiless prong sparked the molten red volcanic fires that consumed her burning crater and licked her entrails like subterranean tongues of flame. Tied to the stake, she wilted in the searing heat while he kept her there dangling upon the brink of an eruption, yielding to the protracted torture which she craved, yet yearning for the coup de grace to snap the unbearable tension of her nerves.

What the occupying force lacked in size, its seasoned spearhead, diligently employed, irrevocably entrenched, made up by aggressiveness. He humbled her twice, without succumbing himself, without the slightest sign of exhaustion. Indeed he seemed annoyed by the readiness of her response, for on each occasion, as she neared the inevitable climax, he growled 'No, no, wait—not now, not yet!' when plainly she was incapable of obeying his command. Otherwise he seldom spoke, but uttered only a continuous series of guttural grunts while she, fainting in his arms, loose-limbed, tossing and floundering like a spiked fish, raved and moaned incessantly, repeatedly, through gritted teeth:

'Yes, oh yes, that's it, that's it, go on, yes, like that, go on, don't stop—ah yes, my God, dear God, don't stop, don't stop—you mustn't, oh Christ, now—ah—go on—more, more, oh please, no, don't stop, that's it—come on, you brute—oh God, yes, like that, damn you—ah, Jesus—you're killing me—go on, more—now, now, my God—I'm coming—I can't bear it—aah—now!'

They lay quiet, scarcely stirring for a while, but he did not withdraw. Hatred of them both sickened me; my knees were weak, escape or interference would be equally impossible, pointless; stricken with misery, anger and resentment, I retreated to my corner and slumped there, dosing my distress with brandy. The minutes slipped by. This disgusting farce had gone on long enough. Even Casilda must have had her fill by now, and more, by the sound of it. I must tell her southern stallion that time was up, that he would have to leave, he need not think I had invited him to spend the night.

I was somewhat fuddled, but I had come to this drastic decision and was just getting ready to throw the blighter out—when they began again. He started rodgering her once more, for all he was worth, and she of course responded straightaway, putting her back into it, grinding and groaning as gladly as before. She was in luck. I doubt if anyone, in all her rich and varied experience, had ever screwed her so thoroughly. She was beside herself. For a girl who disapproved of blasphemy in bed—as I remember she had told me—some of the obscenities which she uttered now were, to say the least, appalling. I was shocked and revolted. Filthy endearments mingled in her mouth with invocations of the Almighty, animal noises, and muttered insults. Her scarlet nails, like talons, clawed at the ruffian's hairy back, scratching the humped, muscular neck, digging with bestial passion into his neat, bobbing buttocks. He growled, but manfully bore the sharp pain for a time, then—suddenly infuriated—he grabbed her by the throat, as if to throttle her, and raising himself, struck her savagely across the face, a stinging blow, with the flat of his hand.

Her mad, agonised grimace did not alter. But to me it was an outrage that was intolerable, a typical example of caddish violence that called for instant, chivalrous, condign retribution. I must avenge this maltreatment of a woman, if not the honour she herself had trampled or the respect which Casilda no longer merited. In attempting to do so, however, I tripped—or the young brute hit me, I'm not sure which—and I fell heavily against the fender, knocking my head. Before I could pick myself up— perhaps I was too slow, being somewhat dazed—that scoundrel of a Spaniard pounced upon me, as I lay there defenceless among the fire irons, unable to move. Quicker than lightning, he had ripped off my tie and fastened my hands with it securely beneath me. I aimed a kick at his midriff, but a dressing gown cord was knotted tightly about my ankles. I was trussed like a goose! He had no difficulty in hauling me onto my knees and toppling me backwards into the chair.

Limp and dishevelled, Casilda sat watching us from the bed. Her chin cupped in both palms, she looked listless and remote, a picture of dejection. I noticed that she did not raise a finger to help me, nor did she say a word, she was too haggard and cowed. When he turned to her again, she dropped meekly back to receive him in the same supine posture as before, with broad smooth thighs lifted above her navel . . . I remember nothing else from that moment on, except an aching glare behind the eyes. . . .

When I came to, a long time later, the pain was still there but the Spaniard had gone. Casilda was bending over me, her naked bosom in my face, as she untied my wrists, having already freed my feet. Somewhat belatedly she showed intense concern for my condition, and fussed over me like a devoted nurse who arrives on the scene of a childish accident after the harm has been done. I eyed her with derision and distaste. True to the innate, uncaring harlotry of all her sex, she gave not the slightest indication of remorse, regret or even consciousness of the enormity of her offence. She had been having a damned good time; it was over now, and that was that. Surely (her manner implied) I could not be so unreasonable and churlish as to begrudge her a little fun once in a while? After all, I had not stepped in and prevented it. Quite to the contrary, I had allowed her a free hand, for which she was prepared to be duly grateful, so long as I did not go and spoil everything by electing to grumble about a mere peccadillo that was best forgotten. How could I be so tiresome as not to realise that *our* relationship was far more important, whereas this business with the lecherous Spaniard was just a passing fling?

I believe in the sincerity of her innocent attitude towards what had taken place. She did not give it a further thought. Such honesty, even in a flaming whore, should be accounted a virtue. But I could not look on it in that light. My love and loyalty, my every emotion, my own manhood had been spurned, insulted, trodden in the dust. Jealousy flooded my brain like a raging torrent. Casilda was calmly putting on her clothes. She drank a sip of brandy out of my glass, and offered me the dregs.

'I'm so sorry, darling,' she said—but I could not tell exactly what she meant by the remark: she might have been apologising for the mere dribble she had left me.

'How many times?' I asked, through my fatigue, in a voice that may have sounded either casual or surly. She cast a glance at me and understood the question.

'Five in all, I think,' she answered. 'But I lost count.'

Half dressed, she came and sat cross-legged on the rug at my feet before the dying fire, which she dutifully replenished with a shovelful of coal. She braced herself for a post-mortem—the errant schoolgirl or the housemaid expecting to be rebuked for breaking some valued knicknack.

'Do you know,' she said sadly, 'he only came twice? I always thought it was less easy for a man who is not circumcised to last out so long. One lives and learns.'

She had got into her stride. 'I must say he amazed me,' she added. 'But there it is. Phew! Give me an uncircumcised cock every time.'

I slapped her hard across the mouth, as he had done. The suddenness rather than the force of the blow sent her sprawling to the floor. She sprang up and faced me, spitting fury.

'You swine!' she snarled. 'You shit! How dare you? You filthy, drooling, dirty, impotent, goddam son of a bitch!'

There have been a few occasions in my life when I have lost my temper with some stupid woman—but never can I recall having been so shamelessly provoked, so wholly justified in the use of violence, as I then was by this crowing trollop. I will not deny that I enjoy a bout of playful flagellation now and again. I have spanked or whipped most of my mistresses at one time or another, for the fun of it. But this was different. I saw red. Her screeching abuse was more than I had bargained for. Strangling would have been too lenient, too quick a punishment for her, I felt. I snatched hold of her by the wrist and by the hair, I dragged her over to the bed, I clouted her again across the face and boxed her ears. She went on cursing me, pouring out a stream of shrill, inept invective against my righteous wrath when I left her there and rummaged through a chest of drawers downstairs for what was needed.

When I returned with a bamboo cane, she had not moved, but she fought like a wildcat to break away from my clutches, until I succeeded in turning her over by wrenching her arm round behind her back, while I knelt on her neck and other wrist, so that she was pinned face down upon the bed, the furious tirade muffled by the pillows, and able only to retaliate with kicking heels because I rolled the elastic knickers into a sort of rope or hobble binding the thighs tightly together, some little way below the bouncing buttocks. They leaped and shuddered and swung from side to side as I thrashed her with all my might, until the sound of her screams, muted as it was, could be heard above the whistling of the cane and the loud thud which signalled each stroke as if to count the crimson weals that marked the wonderful wide expanse of her arse in next to no time. I flogged her blindly at first, as I might have beaten a carpet— but the pattern of punishment, as it deepened and darkened in crisscross streaks, began to fascinate me, and soon I was drawing hieroglyphics in a methodical manner, with more art than sadism, on the taut, quivery canvas that bloomed like a peony. I decorated both cheeks equally with a design in purple, black and blue. When they opened with a supplicating, subconscious jerk, wincing apart as though split by a cruel swipe of my wand. I aimed a lengthwise cut along the smooth ravine itself, which shrank and shut again at once like the big, bulbous jaws of some strange, flustered sea monster. From her nape to her knees Casilda's back heaved, flinched, rippled and shook. It was a wind-swept yellow cornfield, poppy bright: bowed, tossed, flurried by the gale. It was an ice rink scarred by a thousand skaters' trails, a seething, swollen river lashed to livid turmoil at the storm's mercy. . . .

Mercy? She howled for mercy, but I gave her none. She could not escape; she must only endure. She should smart and bleed and faint, cringing and grovelling, while my wrath lasted. I flogged her till my arm grew tired. I relished her struggles, I joyed in her suffering, I got acute pleasure from inflicting extreme humiliation—where she would feel it most—on the incontinent flesh which she had yielded so readily, so wickedly, to another man in my presence.

I wish to emphasise again, however, that this

pleasure for my part was physical perhaps, but not sexual. Her tail excited me: I trounced it for precisely that reason, in reverse—to cure myself of its attraction, not because I was jealous of the promiscuous slut, but simply to break her hold over me, to settle our account, to call it quits, and to teach her a lesson. I would do no permanent damage to her naughty, burning backside; but if it ever forgot itself in the future, it must never forget me—the one lover who had missed his share of the lady's favours, yet had enjoyed her charms to his heart's content, by caressing them in his own special way. . . .

I let her go as soon as I was through—when I had lost interest in her wriggling, and felt she had been chastised enough. For me it was a sweet relief. I discovered that I no longer bore her any great grudge. It had simply had to be, and now it was done; I could rest easy, with the whole load of Casilda Vandersluys, a worthless burden, off my mind. It would be some time before she would care to flaunt her sorely bruised bum under Helen's nose or waggle it at any casual bedfellow, I reckoned—unless dignity mattered as little to her as decency. If she chose to make herself cheap, at least for a week or so, I'd turned her into a laughing-stock, highly coloured and comic; she could only indulge in intimacy at the risk of causing hilarity or actual ribaldry—and of providing me with a private joke in compensation. I flung the cane away across the room and fell asleep.

I do not know whether I awoke after a few minutes or an hour later, but the discomfort of wearing clothes prevented peaceful slumber. Casilda was still lying next to me, huddled on her side. I allowed her to doze on without interruption. She opened her eyes when I pulled the blankets over her and tucked her up for the night, but she did not speak or move, and her absent expression told me nothing of her feelings towards me. I undressed, tumbled into bed, and dropped off to sleep again instantly.

Daylight and the louder sound of traffic, or maybe the clatter of Mrs Howarth, the charwoman, barging about downstairs, gradually impinged on my consciousness and dragged me back to the realities of life which mankind coops for preference within four walls. But there was something else as well that I must have brought with me from the dreamless purlieus of a different, remote, forgetful world—a sense of serenity. I was awake, tranquil, refreshed—still drowsy, but peculiarly cheerful. Casilda lay curled in my arms, her head, a soft, fragrant nosegay of tousled chestnut tresses, on my shoulder. Assuming that she slept, I refrained with the utmost care from the slightest movement that might disturb her, even attuning every breath I drew to the tempo of her deep breathing. I conquered my intense desire to stroke and fondle the warm, firm, delicate flesh of the girl, lest my touch, however light, should rob her of the restful remedy that nature alone provides for rash extravagance.

So we remained, quietly locked in a tender embrace, for some time. But she, too, was feigning sleep, I realised, for when she stirred after a while, her hands glided with gentle stealth about my belly, caressing, fingering and finally clasping the emblems of power, the orb and sceptre of manhood, which she wielded silently but insistently until she was sure of me and satisfied with the result of her research, like the witch who knows that the love philtre she has brewed is infallible in its effects. Then she spoke. In a murmuring voice that was low but distinct I heard her say:

'You're a fool, Tony, you know. You were wrong. But—never mind. I don't care. I love you. I really do. Not only now. Before. Only, it'll be still better now . . . you'll see. I'll show you. I had to make you wait . . . this is going to be the real time. . . .'

From nowhere her mouth burst out at me, engulfing mine, pressed to my lips like a hot, ripe fruit that is cool, thirst-quenching, sweet to the taste. In the next instant her body, an uncoiled spring, slid under me, beneath me, length for length, limb against limb. Her arms and legs were entwined about my body like ivy around a tree. . . .

'There, my love,' she said. 'Fuck me. D'you hear? I'm telling you now—fuck me.'

I plunged into her and dug my nails deeply into her belaboured buttocks.

'Go on,' she repeated. 'Fuck me!'

I had the incentive, and her command—and her. From that morning Casilda was my mistress. For both of us the long delay was over—and, as we had known in our hearts all along, the prize was worth it.

The Lustful Turk

Pedro to Angelo

She is mine, soul and body. I have the delicious angel
safe in my secret apartments in the convent, where
uncontrolled I revel and feed upon her thrilling
beauties. She came to my fierce embrace a blushing
timid maid. Oh, Angelo, how delicious were the
moments spent in unravelling the gordian knot of
her coy chastity! How sweet to the ear was the soft
cry that announced the expiration of her virginity.
Angelo, (believe me when I write it), the very
moment I saw the parlour grating close upon the
lovely Mezzia on the afternoon she received the veil,
a prophetic spirit whispered in mine ear, 'She is
thine.' She is mine—only mine—wholly mine.
Nearly the whole of last night was I voluptuously
encircled by her wary limbs, her young budding
breasts rapturously beating against my manly
bosom, her glowing cheek fondly pressed to my
burning kisses. Night of exquisite rapture! May it
never be weakened in the tablet of memory!

As I predicted, Angelo, for her attempt to escape
from the convent, the austere Abbess of St. Ursuline
immediately called a chapter to try this lovely dis-
grace to our holy religion. Her friends were notified
of her infamous attempt, and in due time the trial
took place, in the presence of her father, brother and
other friends. Sister Sophia, the nun in whom my
young pupil had misplaced her confidence, was the
principal evidence against her. It appears before she

was excluded from the world an attachment had subsisted between her and a young nobleman, whose name was the only thing Julia had not acquainted Sister Sophia with. As he luckily escaped in the confusion of securing Julia, he has nothing to fear. The poor girl had no defence. The detection was too public. What she urged in mitigation of her fault not only incensed the Abbess more and more against her, but absolutely caused her father and brother to deny and abandon her to her fate altogether.

She publicly avowed that she was compelled to take the veil by her father and brother, and called on heaven to witness the truth of her assertion and protect her in her distress. Her father and brother fled the convent, venting curses on her, and she was condemned by the chapter to be buried alive. Oh, Angelo, how great was my joy at hearing this sentence. You are the only one of the order to whom I have communicated the fact of the existence of a subterraneous passage from my dormitory to the tomb of death in the convent of St. Ursuline. Guess with what impatience I waited the result of the case from Rome. The sentence of the chapter being confirmed, the following day was appointed for depositing the victim in the dreadful sepulchre. In the meantime I descended and conveyed by our subterraneous entrance a comfortable mattress and other conveniences, and I also cleaned out the dungeon of the filth and vermin, so that the tender girl should be able at least to sleep without interruption during the time I intended she should stay there; that you may be sure would be no longer than to make her thankful to surrender her person to my desires, to afford her an opportunity to escape death by starvation. I shall not disgust you with an account of the ceremony of

forcing this young creature down the marble jaws of
the tomb opened in the Ursuline Church. Suffice it to
say that a rope of sufficient length was fixed firmly
round her waist, then spite of her struggles and
screams, she was carried and held over the dreadful
opening, and then gradually lowered into the fright-
ful abyss, her cries making the church echo, until the
marble slab enclosed her, as it was supposed, from
the world forever. I had placed by the side of the
mattress sufficient provision to last her for a day,
intending to leave her to reflection for about two or
three days; by that time I had no doubt hunger and
fear would have so reduced her that to escape from
her horrid prison she would quickly submit to any
terms I should propose.

On the third day of her incarceration, after
vespers, I took my dark lantern and again tried the
subterraneous passage. On arriving at the secret
entrance of the tomb I waited a considerable time ere
I could ascertain whether she was awake. At last I
was assured she slept. With caution I opened the
door and silently approached the unconscious
sleeper. Removing the shade off the light by degrees,
I turned it on her face, fearing to awaken her by
letting it flash instantly on her. Poor girl! How evident was the inroad of care and despair on her lovely
countenance. She lay at her full length on the mattress, her head resting on her right arm, her beautiful
tresses playing in confusion over her ivory neck,
while the disorder of her veil only half concealed her
young delicious breasts. Her cheeks still retained the
evident traces of recent tears, and her slumbers were
disturbed with the horrors of her situation, for un-
knowingly she uttered, 'Oh, Father, save me!' her
whole frame becoming convulsed with the agony of

even her dream. I could bear this no longer, but shading my light, coughed loud enough to break the bonds of sleep. 'What noise was that?' exclaimed the poor sufferer. 'I thought I heard someone move. Oh, no, it was the deception of my giddy brain. Alas, there is no hope for a wretch like me!' I seized this opportunity and slowly uttered the word 'Hope'. A faint scream, evidently mixed with pleasure, followed my response. After a few seconds' silence, she exclaimed, 'Oh, pray do not play with my wretchedness! If there is anyone near do not drive to despair a miserable girl!' 'Help is nigh,' was my reply. 'But let not joy deceive you with hopes that may not be fulfilled; your release from death depends entirely upon your submission to certain terms.' 'Oh, for heaven's sake name them,' she cried; 'keep me not thus in agonizing suspense, say what I am to do to save myself from the dreadful lingering anguish of famine I now so powerfully feel.' 'Listen,' I replied, 'the only terms upon which you can be released from this den of horrors and certain lingering death, is the entire submission of your person to my enjoyment; this is the only way you can be saved.' At this moment I unshaded my lamp, and let it reflect full on my face. She could not bear the light, and covered her eyes with her hands, but she did not answer. 'Come,' I cried, 'time wears apace; you must be quick in your resolves, for if I leave this dungeon your fate is fixed forever.' Still there was no answer. I again covered the lamp and solemnly said, 'Well then, farewell,' and moved from her as if I was leaving the tomb. 'Oh, save me,' she cried, believing I was going. 'Well then, you consent to submit to my desires—to every desire or request I choose to make?' 'Oh, yes, any, everything; save me from death, I will submit to anything.' 'Then you are saved,' I replied, approaching and taking her in my arms. Her soft lips I drew to mine, and sucking her perfumed breath I sealed our contract. I now told her it was sometimes the case that the Abbess would cause the marble covering to be removed off the tomb to point out to any disobedient nuns the punishment that might await them, therefore her clothes must be laid immediately under the opening that they might be seen. Should such an event occur, the depth of the tomb would prevent any possibility of ascertaining whether she was in them, else an immediate search might be made in the tomb, and perhaps her retreat eventually discovered, in which case the power of the Church would drag her back to her punishment. I again uncovered my lantern, and could clearly see her modesty struggling with her fears. Therefore I told her there must be no delay made. 'Come, come,' I cried, 'we must depart this moment; you must yield to the necessity of plucking off your habit.' She trembled, and said she could not think of being naked, with a confusion which made her look on the escape she was about to make as scarcely a recompense for the shame she must undergo. No doubt she would have debated the propriety of it, but I peremptorily cut her short by beginning to get rid of her dress by degrees, getting off one thing, then another, until she was wholly stripped of everything. For the trouble I took in her toilet I rewarded myself as I proceeded. I laid her dress at full length on the ground immediately under the opening of the vault, so that they could be plainly perceived from above, and bore the appearance of then covering a body. I first fixed a handkerchief round the eyes of Julia, then taking her round the waist, led her out of the vault. In a few minutes she was safe in my private apartments, where a table well laid out with every kind of refreshment awaited her. Carrying her to the sofa by the side of the table, I gently laid her on it, and taking off the bandage from her eyes, with a loving kiss assured her of her safety. Although I well knew she must have been suffering considerably from hunger at the time, still I could not refrain from indulging myself with a few moments toying with her young beauties ere I permitted her to satisfy Nature's wants. It is true as I conducted her through the subterraneous passage, every part of her delicate body had been felt by my eager hands, but that you know, Angelo, was in the dark. Now I had her in my arms, every charm exposed to the broad glare of day. The unrivalled whiteness of her skin was increased by the black velvet of the sofa on which she was laid. Quickly my daring hand seized upon her most secret treasures, regardless of her soft complaints, which my burning kisses reduced to mere murmurs, while my fingers penetrated into the covered way of love. How transporting is the combat between coy modesty and new born pleasure. How delicious appear the first blushes of shame on the snowy purity of the virgin's bosom. Ah! Angelo, do you not envy my joys? Guess how I dissolved as my lips wandered over her sweet body! How soft were her cries of 'Ah!' and 'Fie!' then a bright falling tear, but it was the tear of pleasure. Then she tried (but in vain) to remove my hand, whilst her closed eyes clearly told of the soft languor gently creeping on her senses. I scarcely knew how to account for my not having at that moment exacted my recompense for saving her from the jaws of death. But I did not. I suddenly desisted, and raising her from the position I had held her in, drew the table towards the couch, desired she would assist herself to what she thought fit, and left the apartments. In my bedroom I had some fine chemises, one of which I brought her and assisted to put it on; it was quite large enough, but of course it was no defence to my curious hands, which I could easily slip to any part of her I pleased. However, I did not interrupt her during the repast, but attended to her wants, with the greatest care, forcing her to take two or three glasses of mulled wine, which was already prepared. As the cravings of her appetite were appeasing, mine were every minute growing more furious. Seeing she had finished, although she pretended still to be eating, I gently encircled my arm round her neck; I drew this soft, languishing sighing, and nearly fainting beauty to my bosom; then fixing upon her humid lips a long, burning kiss, I nearly sucked her life away. Whilst occupied in this sweet employment, I loosened the cord which kept the gown tight around me, and told her I then intended to reap the reward for the service I had rendered her.

The poor affrighted maid pleaded hard for a moment's pause, and weeping, strove to persuade me to spare her innocence—said much in defence of virtue's laws. But I took her into my arms, and then began the soft contention preparatory to the fierce fight. How delicious was the glow upon her beauteous neck and bare ivory shoulders, as I forced her on her back on the couch. With what joy as in the full tide of vigour I divided her swelling thighs. Quickly was the unspotted maid placed in that position which I vowed never to permit her to rise from until she had forfeited every claim on that name.

How luxuriously did her snowy hillocks rise against my bosom in wild confusion. Luckily she did not know what she was about to suffer. The confusion which seized her on my fingers again entering the cell of Venus for the purpose of introducing myself considerably favoured my proceedings. I felt its head between her lips and with a vigorous thrust strove to penetrate, but so cruelly tore her delicate entrance that she screamed, tried to escape, and effectually threw me out. Inflamed with lechery and rage at this repulse I swore by heaven if she again resisted I would convey her back to the tomb. Again I forcibly fixed myself between the lips of her yet untasted first fruits. I saw she was much alarmed at my rage and threats. It had a good effect; her fears lessened her defence. I then took every care to make my attack quite certain, and I began the fight of fierce delight, of pleasure mixed with pain. However enormous the disproportion between the place assailed and the attacking instrument I soon found it piercing inward; her loud cries announced its victorious progress. Nothing now could appease my fury—the more she implored grace the more I pressed on with vigour. But never was conquest more difficult. Oh, how I was obliged to tear her up in forcing her virgin defences! With what delicious tightness it clasped my rod of Aaron, as it entered the inmost recesses of till then virgin sanctuary. How voluptuous was the heat of her young body! I was mad with enjoyment! Her young breasts rising and falling in wild confusion fixed my caresses. Guess my state of excitement. I first pressed her ivory globes, then sucked them, and at last bit them with delight. Although Julia was much overcome with her suffering, still she reproachfully turned her lovely eyes swimming with pain and languor on me; at this instant, with a final energetic thrust, I buried myself up to the very hair in her. A shriek proclaimed the change in her state, the ecstasy seized me and I shot the inmost recesses of the womb of this innocent and beautiful child with as copious a flood of burning sperm as ever was fermented under the cloak of a monk, when—oh, marvellous effects of nature!— the lovely Mezzia, spite of her cruel sufferings, ceded to my vigorous impressments. The pleasure overcame the pain, and the stretching of her delicate arms clearly spoke that Nature's first effusion was distilling within her.

When somewhat recovered from my ecstasy, without giving up possession of my prize, I lay on her soft bosom contemplating the numerous beauties fate had thrown into my possession. A profusion of dark brown tresses flowed negligently in the luxurious curls below her slender waist; under her fine formed brows beamed the brightest eyes of ethereal blue ever created; her nose is Roman; her soft blushing cheeks imitate the rose; her teeth are like orient pearls, whilst her yielding, pouting lips are most admirably formed. But at that moment these delicious inhalers of our fondest impressments were terribly wounded, so boisterous had been my enjoyment of them. Her face is decidedly Grecian, her bosom, shoulders, and neck resemble the purest ivory. On running my eyes lower on her young snowy hillocks, I blushed to see the crimson marks which my teeth had left on those lovely orbs. Softly insinuating my arms round her neck, I drew her blushing face to mine, and after impressing a few soft kisses on her yet bleeding lips, anxiously entreated the sweet girl to pardon my cruelty, assuring her with the tenderest oaths that I knew not what I was about, so much had the maddening transports overpowered me. She replied not. I placed one of her beautiful arms round my neck. She suffered it to remain. Again from her pouting lips did I inhale luxurious sweets. Although I thought I had distilled my very existence into her, the life-inspiring suction completely reanimated my whole frame. I felt myself in as proud a state of erection within her as when I commenced her defloration; her young breasts heaving quicker, soft sighs, blushes, and tremblings sufficiently told that my prey also felt the return of my vigour. I determined the second enjoyment should amply repay her for all she had suffered, and began my movements with a caution and slowness which made her sigh with voluptuous ecstasy. It was now indeed that I, uncontrolled, enjoyed the lingering bliss, as by tender and ravishing degrees I forced myself up to the very quick within her. Scarcely mistress of her feelings, her yielding lips with delicious kisses joined more and more close to mine, blushes deeper covered her neck and blooming cheeks, her arms closely grasped me. By degrees my thrusts became quicker, but no complaints interrupted my joys. She panted with rapture; her limbs encircled me; she voluptuously heaved to my thrusts, while the wanton movements of her body and limbs, her ardent transports, her soft kisses, gave ample testimony of how quick the transition is from coy chastity to unrestrained luxurious enjoyment. In short I was as blessed as youth and voluptuous beauty could make me, until forced to retire from her arms to attend to my monastery duties. They were quickly dispatched, and after refreshing myself with a few hours, rest, I returned to my captive with recruited strength for the night's soft enjoyment. The smile of welcome was on her lovely countenance; she was dressed from a wardrobe I had pointed out to her, containing everything fit for her sex. With grateful pleasure I instantly perceived that her toilet had not been made for the mere purpose of covering her person, but every attention had been paid in setting off her numerous charms. The most care had been given to the disposing of her hair, whilst the lawn which covered her broad voluptuous breasts was so temptingly disposed that it was impossible to look on her without burning desire. She sprang off the couch to meet me; for a moment I held her from me in an ecstasy of astonishment, then drawing her to my bosom, planted on her lips a kiss so long and so thrilling, it was some moments ere we recovered from its effects. My passions were instantly in a blaze. I carried her to the side of the couch, placed her on it, and while sucking her delicious lips, uncovered her neck and breasts, then seizing her legs lifted them up, and threw up her clothes. A dissolving sentiment struggled with my more amorous desires. I stooped down to examine the sight! Every part of her body was ivory whiteness, everything charming; the white interspersed with small blue veins showed the transparency of the skin whilst the darkness of the hair, softer than velvet, formed most beautiful shades, making a delicious contrast with the vermilion lips of her new-stretched love sheath, the brilliant vermilion shell evidently heightened with the blood of her defunct virginity.

Tired of admiring without enjoyment, I carried my mouth and hand to everything before me, until I could no longer bear myself. Raising myself from my sloping position, I extended her thighs to the utmost,

48

and placed myself standing between them, letting loose my rod of Aaron, which was no sooner at liberty but it flew with the same impetuosity with which a tree straightens itself when the cord that keeps it bent towards the ground comes to be cut; with my right hand I directed it towards the pouting slit the head was soon in; laying myself down on her, I drew her lips to mine; again I thrust, I entered. Another thrust buried it deeper; she closed her eyes, but tenderly squeezed me to her bosom; again I pushed—her soft lips rewarded me. Another shove caused her to sigh deliciously—another push made our junction complete. I scarcely knew what I was about, everything now was in active exertion, tongues, lips, bellies, arms, thighs, legs, bottoms, every part in voluptuous motion until our spirits completely abandoned every part of our bodies to convey themselves into the place where pleasure reigned with so furious but still with so delicious a sentiment. I dissolved myself into her at the very moment Nature had caused her to give down her tribute to the intoxicating joy. My lovely prey soon came to herself, but it was only to invite me by her numberless charms to plunge her into the same condition. She passed her arms round my neck and sucked my lips with dovelike kisses. I opened my eyes and fixed them on hers; they were filled with dissolving languor; I moved within her, her eyes closed instantly. The tender squeeze of her love-sheath round my instrument satisfied me as to the state she was in. Again I thrust. 'Ah!' she sighed. 'The pleasure suffocates me—I die!—ah, me.' I thrust furiously; her limbs gradually stiffened, she gave one more movement to the fierce thrusts made into her organ; we both discharged together.

49

It will be of no use, Angelo, to give you any further description of my enjoyment of this adorable child, but the agonizing reflection that I must part with my delicious prize nearly drives me to distraction. During cooler moments I have explained to her the necessity of a separation, and pointed out to her the danger of her remaining in this country. The solemn assurance I have given her of her safety from the fangs of the Church have tended to comfort her. But then, Angelo, how can I force myself to part with so voluptuous a creature? Advise and counsel your friend.

Pedro

The Lifted Curtain

Translated from the French by
Howard Nelson

The following day, my father was given a letter which seemed to please him. After having read it a second time, he spoke to me.

'My dear Laura, it is time for you to have a governess. One is arriving tomorrow. Although she comes with the highest recommendations, I have to see her for myself to make my own judgment if they are exaggerated or not.'

I was totally unprepared for such news which, for some reason, greatly saddened me. Without knowing why, I was uncomfortable at her presence and I did not like her even before I had seen her.

Lucette arrived the day before she was expected. She was a big girl around nineteen or twenty with an opulent bosom, extremely white skin, a good but not unusual figure, a pretty mouth with carmine lips, and two perfect rows of enamel teeth. Immediately my preconception of her was changed. In addition, she had an excellent character, an abundance of gentleness and kindness, and a winning way. I was completely taken by her, and we soon became the most intimate friends. It was evident that my father was more than satisfied with her.

Envy and jealousy are strangers to my soul. Besides, what arouses the desire of men often is not our beauty or our merit. Thus, for the sake of our own happiness, it is wisest to let them alone and not to worry. More often than not their infidelity is nothing more than a slight fire that goes out as soon as it is lit. Consequently, it is folly to torment oneself about it.

Although I was not yet capable of reasoning in such a way at that time. I still felt no animosity towards Lucette. Besides, there was no diminishment in the signs of affection that my father bestowed on me. The only thing I perceived was his reserve when she was present but I put this down to mere shyness. Some weeks passed in this fashion until I finally noticed the attentions he was paying her. He never let an opportunity escape to reveal his feelings towards her. It was not long before I shared his sentiments for her.

When Lucette expressed her desire to sleep in my room, my father readily gave his consent. When he awoke in the morning, the first thing he did was to enter our chamber in which our beds were side to side. This arrangement enabled him to make advances towards Lucette while pretending that he had come to see me.

It was obvious that she was not rebuffing him, but she did not respond to his urgings as quickly as I would have liked her to, and I could not figure out the reason for her dragging feet. Loving my father as much as I did, I was of the opinion that everybody should feel towards him as I did. I could not help but chide her for her indifference.

'Why don't you like my Papa?' I asked her one day. 'He seems to have such warm feelings for you. I think that you are very ungrateful.'

She merely smiled at these reproaches, assuring me that I was doing her an injustice. She was right, for in a short time the apparent coolness vanished.

One evening after supper, we retired to a salon

where my father had coffee and liqueurs served. In less than half an hour, Lucette was sound asleep. At that, my father took me up in his arms and carried me to my room where he put me to bed. Surprised at this new arrangement, my curiosity was instantly aroused. I got up a few moments later and tip-toed to the glass door, whose velvet curtain I slightly pushed aside so that I could look into the salon.

I was astonished to see Lucette's bosom completely uncovered. What charming breasts she possessed! They were two hemispheres as white as snow and firm as marble in the centre of which rose two little strawberries. The only movement they showed was from her regular breathing. My father was fondling them, kissing them and sucking them. In spite of his actions, she continued slumbering. Soon he began to remove all of her clothing, placing it on the edge of the bed. When he took off her shift, I saw two plump rounded thighs of alabaster which he spread apart. Then I made out a little vermilion slit adorned with a chestnut-brown tuft of hair. This he half opened, inserting his fingers which he vigorously manipulated in and out. Nothing roused her out of her lethargy.

Excited by the sight and instructed by the example, I imitated on myself the movements I saw and experienced sensations hitherto unknown to me. Laying her on the bed, my father came to the glass door to close it. I saved myself by hastening to the couch on which he had placed me. As soon as I was stretched out on the sheets, I began my rubbing, pondering what I had just viewed and profiting from what I had learned. I was on fire. The sensation I was undergoing increased in intensity, reaching such a height that it seemed my entire body and soul were concentrated in that one spot. Finally, I sank back in a state of exhausted ecstasy that enchanted me.

Returning to my senses, I was astonished to find myself almost soaked between my thighs. At first, I was very worried, but this anxiety was dispelled by the remembrance of the bliss I had just enjoyed. I fell into a deep sleep filled with dreams of my father caressing me. I was not yet awake when he came the next morning to awaken me with kisses which I eagerly returned.

Since that day, my governess and he seemed to have a secret understanding, although in the morning he did not remain with us as he formerly did. Of course they had not the slightest suspicion that I was *au courant* as to what was going on, and lulled into a false security, during the day, they shamelessly flirted before retiring to my father's room where they remained for long periods of time.

With justice, I imagined that they were going to repeat what I had already seen, and my ideas did not go any further than that. Nevertheless, I was dying to view the same spectacle again. The reader can picture to himself the violent desire that was tormenting me. Finally came the moment when I was to learn everything.

Three days after the event I have just described, I took advantage of my father's absence to satisfy my burning curiosity. While Lucette was engaged in some task in another part of the house, I punctured a little hole in the silken curtain of the glass door.

I had not long to wait to profit from my stratagem. On my father's return, he immediately donned a flimsy dressing-gown and led to his room Lucette, who was in equally casual attire. They were careful to close the door and draw the curtain, but my preparations frustrated their precautions, at least in part. As soon as they were in the room, I was at the door with my face glued to the glass by the lifted curtain. The first person to meet my eyes was Lucette with her magnificent bosom completely bare. It was so seductive that I could not blame my father for immediately covering it with quick, eager kisses. Unable to hold himself back he tore off her clothing, and in a twinkling of the eye, skirt, corset and chemise were on the floor. How temptingly lovely she was in her natural state! I could not tear my eyes from her. She possessed all the charms and freshness of youth. Feminine beauty has a singular power and attraction for those of the same sex. My arms yearned to embrace those divine contours.

My father was soon in a state similar to his partner's. My eyes were fixed on him, because I had never seen him that way before. Now he placed her on the divan, which I could not see from my observation post.

Devoured by curiosity, I threw caution to the winds. I lifted the curtain until I could see everything. Not a detail escaped my eyes, and they spared themselves not the slightest voluptuousness.

I was able to perceive clearly Lucette stretched out on the couch and her fully expanded slit between the two chubby eminences. My father displayed a veritable jewel, a big member, stiff, surrounded by hair at the root below which dangled two balls. The tip was a scarlet red. I saw it enter Lucette's slit, lose itself there, and then reappear. This in-and-out movement continued for some time. From the fiery kisses they exchanged, I surmised that they were in raptures. Finally, I noticed the organ completely emerge. From the carmine tip which was all wet spurted a white fluid on Lucette's flat belly.

How the sight aroused me! I was so excited and carried away by desires I had not yet known that I attempted, at least partially, to participate in their delirium.

So entranced was I by the tableau that I remained too long and my imprudence betrayed me. My father, who had been too preoccupied with Lucette, now, disengaging himself from Lucette's arms, saw the partially lifted curtain. On spotting me, he wrapped himself in his robe as he approached the door. I hastily withdrew, but he raised the drape and discovered me trying to beat a retreat.

He stationed himself at the door while Lucette was dressing. Seeing that he remained motionless, I fancied that he had not noticed anything. Still curious to know what was going on, I returned to the curtain. My astonishment when I met his face on the other side can be imagined. I was thunderstruck with fright.

By this time, Lucette had her clothes back on. My father pretended that nothing was amiss. Reminding Lucette of certain errands she had to carry out, he dismissed her, and I was alone with him.

When he came up to me, I was trembling and pale with fear. But, to my great surprise, instead of castigating me, he took me in his arms and covered me with a hundred kisses.

'Calm yourself, my dear Laurette,' he comforted me. 'Who in the world could have inspired the terror I see in your eyes? You need have no fear, my darling. You know that I have never harmed you. All I ask of you now is the truth. At this moment, I want you to consider me a friend rather than your father. Laura, I am your friend, and I beseech you to be sincere with me. Don't conceal anything from me. Tell me what you were doing when I was with Lucette and the reason for your peeking around this curtain. If you are honest, you will not have any reason to repent. If you aren't, my warm feelings for you will vanish and you can count on the convent.'

The mere mention of the final word had always filled me with dread. What I had heard of the life in those retreats! I mentally contrasted life there to that with my father. Besides, I had no doubt that I had witnessed everything. Finally, from past experience, I knew the wisdom of avowing everything to him, and I blurted out the entire truth.

Each detail I told him and each tableau I retraced, far from igniting his wrath, was repaid with kisses and caresses. I hesitated, nevertheless, at confessing the new, delicious experiences I had procured by myself, but he suspected them.

'Darling Laurette, you still haven't told me all,' he remarked, as he passed his hands over my derrière and kissed me. 'You should not hide anything from me. Give me the whole story.'

With some reluctance, I admitted that I had imitated his friction movements with Lucette, which had produced in me the most wonderful sensations. Even though I got all wet from doing it, I had repeated it three or four times, always with the same pleasure.

'But, dear Laura,' he cried, 'seeing what I put into Lucette, didn't you get the idea of inserting your finger into yourself?'

'No, Papa, the thought never crossed my mind.'

'Don't try to deceive me,' he warned. 'You can't hide anything from me. Come over here so I can see if you are telling the truth.'

'Honestly, Papa, I have told you the truth,' I protested.

Using the most endearing words with me, he led me into his bedroom, where he stretched me out on a couch. He lifted up my skirt and examined me carefully. Then, slightly opening my narrow slit, he tried to penetrate it with his little finger. The screams from the pain he was causing me made him stop.

'It is all inflamed, my child. Nevertheless, I recognize that you have not lied to me. The redness undoubtedly is due to the friction you committed on yourself while I was with Lucette.'

Now that I had lost my fear, I even told him that I could not obtain the pleasure I was looking for. The sincerity of my mouth was rewarded by a kiss from his. Then he lowered it, and with his tongue, tickled a certain spot that made me squeal with delight. I found this kind of caress new and heavenly. To bring my raptures to a peak he produced that member I had seen before. Involuntarily, I took it with one hand, while with the other, I opened his robe. He made no objection. I regarded with admiration and fondled that joyous instrument that I had seen disappear into Lucette's interior. How pleasing and unusual it was! From the first moment I touched it, I instinctively realized that it was the originator of pleasure. It went up and down in rhythm with the movement of my hand, which covered and uncovered the skin of the tip. Imagine my surprise when, after several moments of this sport, I saw gush out the same fluid that had flooded Lucette's thighs. As the last drops oozed, I noticed that he was trembling all over. I was happy that I had given a pleasure which I partially shared.

When I released my sticky hand, he resumed his

previous game with his tongue. I was dying of an ineffable bliss. I was suffocating, but he continued.

'Dear Papa, stop it!' I pleaded. 'I can't stand it any longer.'

I fainted in his arms.

From that time on, everything became clear to me. What I had guessed before became a certainty. It seemed that the instrument I was touching was the magic key to understanding. Because of that organ, my father became even dearer to me. And my sentiments for him were returned in like measure.

He led me back to my room, where my governess appeared a few moments later. I did not have the slightest idea of what he was about to say to her.

'Lucette, from now on it is senseless to watch our step with Laura, for she knows everything.'

Then he repeated to her everything I had related to him and showed her the curtain. She appeared very disturbed, but I threw my arms around her neck, and my embraces, along with the reasons I gave her, quickly dissipated the embarrassment she had evinced. Kissing us both, he told Lucette not to leave me out of her sight. He left, returning an hour later with a woman who, as soon as she was in the room, made me completely disrobe and took my measurements for a sort of garment, the form of use of which I could not guess.

When it came time to go to bed, my father put me in Lucette's bed, admonishing her to keep an eye on me. Once again he departed, only to return a few minutes later and crawl in the same bed with us. I was between the two of them. My father held me in a tight hug. Covering with his hand the space between my legs, he prevented me from putting mine at that spot. I took his instrument, which surprised me because it was so limp and moist. I had never seen it in this pitiable state, imagining that it was always swollen, stiff and erect. But in my hand it was no longer slow in regaining the condition in which I knew it.

Lucette, who perceived what we were doing, was shocked.

'What you are doing with Laurette is outrageous,' she reproved him. 'Especially since you are her father.'

'You are partially right, Lucette,' he replied. 'But it is a secret that I wish to confide to you. It is to Laura's own interest that she keep her silence. Circumstances make it necessary that I tell you both.

'I had known her mother only fifteen days when I married her. The very first day after the wedding, I discovered her condition, but I considered it the wisest course to pretend not to notice it. In order that dates could not be put together, I took her to a distant province. After four months, Laura entered the world with all the vigour and health of a normal nine month infant. For six months more, I remained in that province, after which I brought the two back home. Now you recognize that this child who is so dear to me is not my own daughter in the strict sense of the word. Although she is not bound to me by flesh and blood, she is as dear to me as if she were.'

Then I immediately recalled the reply he had made to my mother's reproaches. The silence she maintained no longer appeared strange.

'But how could you have acted in such a way towards your wife?' Lucette wanted to know.

'Oh, I was never close to my wife,' my father nonchalantly answered. 'The Count de Norval, to whom Laura owes her entry into this life, is a likeable

61

nobleman, a fine figure of a man with a handsome face, possessing those qualities that interest women. I wasn't the least bit surprised to learn that my wife had succumbed to his attack. However, she was unable to marry him, for her parents did not find him wealthy enough for her. But if Laura is not my daughter by blood, the affection I have conceived for this adorable child renders her perhaps even more dear to me.

'Nevertheless, because of the mother's falsity I never approached her. I had an antipathy for her that I could not overcome. That is why I turned all my love to the innocent child.'

Lucette lavished on me hugs and kisses which told me that all her prejudices had been effaced. Warmly I returned her tokens of affection, even taking her enticing breasts and kissing and sucking the pink tips. My father stretched his hand to her and met mine, which he passed over Lucette's stomach and her thighs. Now my hand was guided over the fleece, the *mons Veneris*, and the crevice. I soon learned the names of all these portions of the female anatomy. Then I put my finger on the spot where I thought I would cause her pleasure. There I came across something rather hard and distended.

'Good, Laura!' my father complimented me. 'You are holding the most sensitive part. Move your hand without relinquishing the clitoris while I stick my finger in her little cunt.'

Lucette, her arm about me, caressing my buttocks, took my father's prick and introduced it between my thighs, but he did not put it in nor did he make the slightest movement. Soon my governess was at the peak of pleasure. Her kisses multiplied and her sighs became moans.

'Stop! That's enough!' she moaned. 'Faster! Put it in all the way, my dearest. My God, I am coming! This is the end.'

How these expressions of voluptuousness delighted me. I felt that her cunt was all damp. My father's finger came out, all covered with what she had discharged. I was beside myself with excitement. Taking Lucette's hand, I brought it to between my legs so that she would do to me what I had done for her, but my father, covering my mound with his hand, stopped her. He was too much of a libertine not to be sparing of his pleasures, and he moderated his desires, leaving me up in the air by recommending us to calm ourselves. We fell asleep, our arms interlaced, plunged into the sweetest intoxication. I had never spent such a delicious night.

When the rays of the morning sun brought us back to life. Lucette and I looked at each other. Then I noticed a note pinned to the chair. It was from Papa who wrote that he would be away all day, but he knew that Lucette would take good care of me. Excitedly, I reminded my companion that it was the servants' day off and we would be alone. We beamed at each other with radiant smiles.

I nestled closer to her for I loved to sniff the sharp odour that came from her svelte body. I nuzzled my nose between her breasts to breathe it in more deeply. It reminded me of carrots, and every time I smelled it, I quivered with excitement.

'I think I am too fat,' she remarked. 'Don't you think so?'

She lifted up her nightgown as if to prove her point. I wondered why she thought she was so fat. Her legs were lovely and well-rounded, and her buttocks dimpled and charming. There was not the trace of a bulge on her body. The magnificent breasts were so heavy that I wondered how they could jut out as they did. And I could not keep my eyes from the clump of luxuriant hair under her armpits. When she turned her back to me, I saw her derrière, two superb hemispheres that must have been fashioned in heaven.

'You are not too plump,' I affirmed again. 'On the contrary, it seems to me that you are just right.'

She gave me a pleased pout as she got out of bed and walked to the desk with the cheeks of her bottom swaying seductively from side to side. She returned to the warm bed with a large album of art reproductions, many of them of nude women and in colour.

'Look,' she said, pointing out one to me. 'She is far more slender than I.'

'Yes, but on the other hand, this woman by Rubens is far plumper than you.'

'That may be so, but I still should lose some weight. A massage does the trick, and you can help me if you wish.'

'I? . . . Massage you? I have never done that before. . . .'

'There's nothing difficult about it. It's just the sort of favour one does for a friend. And you are my friend, aren't you?'

I puffed up with pride at that. But I felt a certain uneasiness not unmingled with anticipation.

'And I have just the thing for a massage,' she added with a slight blush.

'What do you mean by that?' I asked her in some puzzlement. 'I always thought you massaged with the hands.'

'There are also appliances that are helpful in removing excess flesh. . . . I'll get mine.'

She went to her room and came back with a rubber glove covered with bumps. It reminded me of the skin of a toad. Lucette ran it up and down my arm. It gave me goose-pimples but the sensation was not unpleasant.

'How do you like it, Laura?' she asked with a glint in her eyes.

Then she applied it on her shoulders, her arms and above her breasts. I felt a twinge of envy.

'I hope I'll be able to use it correctly and not hurt you. I have never seen anything like that before. If I am clumsy, please forgive me.'

'There's no danger, but I'll have to lie down.'

Now she was on her stomach, lovelier than ever, particularly since her lush body was reflected in the wall mirror.

'Now start at the top of my back,' she ordered.

This promised to be fun. The skin quivered and turned pink where I touched it with my gloved hand. Lucette remained motionless, her head between her arms and her hair over her eyes. After vigorously treating the glorious buttocks, she suddenly turned over.

'And now the breasts, Laura.'

Nervously, I did as I was bid. The gorgeous globes shivered as much as my hand. Taking my hand, she made it descend to one of the rosy nipples.

'Look,' she said.

To my astonishment, I saw it dilate, swell, get hard and jut out. It became a crimson mountain peak. Then she made me put it on the other. As I rubbed the mound, there occurred, to my uneasiness, the same phenomenon.

'I'm in heaven,' Lucette blissfully sighed. 'That's the way nipples become when they are handled that way. Now the belly, Laura, and the hips. It is so wonderful when you do it, and I can't tell you how grateful I am.'

My eyes were glued to the hard breasts, the hollow navel, and the dark triangle whose hair extended almost all the way up to her waist. Mentally, I compared myself with her. I had only a pitiful little fleece there, while hers was a carpet, a beautiful luxurious Persian rug.

I revolved the glove on her stomach around her navel. I did not dare get too close to the triangle, for I was afraid that it might get tangled in the matted hair and hurt her. She was lasciviously wiggling her hips with her eyes shut. It was obvious that she was in an incipient ecstasy. Her toes contracted and sometimes her knee twitched when I got too close to the erogenous zone.

'Now between the thighs,' she murmured without opening her eyes. I observed that her nipples were straining more than ever.

Reassured that I was giving her pleasure, I redoubled my efforts as I rubbed the glove on the silky skin. But I could not keep my eyes from the luxuriant thicket. I wondered how what it was concealing would look like.

I was sure that mine would be put to shame in comparison.

The more I kept at it, the more pleasure it gave me. I was not a little disappointed when she told me to stop. Reading my feelings in my face, Lucette laughed.

'I can see that you are unwilling to give up, dearest Laura,' she said. 'But don't be disappointed, I need a bit of a breathing spell, for that puts my nerves on edge. Why, you are perspiring! Take off your night-gown. You'll be much more comfortable. I don't think you are bashful after last night.'

'A little,' I confessed, but I followed her suggestion.

'Completely nude, that's the way I want you,' she breathed. 'I adore nudity. I can never get enough of looking at myself naked in a mirror. I never feel alone when I can regard my reflection in the mirror. We were so excited last night that I did not notice what adorable little breasts you have. And what promise your delicate figure shows!'

The compliments gave me so much pleasure that I could not conceal my blushes. I wanted to bury my face in her arms. Hurling myself at her, I feverishly kissed her cheeks. She looked at me straight in the eyes, holding my gloved hands in hers.

'Continue,' she commanded.

Eagerly, too eagerly I resumed my task. She promptly rebuked me.

'Not so fast and not so hard,' she scolded. 'Just run it gently over my whole body. Do you understand?'

Now I did not press down so hard. Lucette closed her eyes in contentment.

'It's like a lover's caress,' she murmured.

In the mirror I could see the bed, the naked body of my new friend, and mine which was trembling and twitching. At the same time, I regarded my little, rounded, apple-like breasts with their tawny tips, and came to the conclusion that I was not too bad. Perhaps I was not as abundant as Lucette, but I was not her inferior. My charms were just on a smaller scale.

Now her mouth was agape and her breathing laboured. I twisted the glove on her stomach and breasts. Each time I touched a nipple, she gave a start, convulsively lifted a knee, and spread her legs. When I took the rubber glove away, she became motionless.

'Farther down, Laura,' she whispered as if I were neglecting her spread thighs. I massaged the inside of them. From the knees, the glove gradually ascended to the groin and the buttocks.

It was then that I noticed a curious movement of her pelvis. She kept lifting and dropping it in fits and starts. At the same time, she was rattling in her throat and trying to catch her breath.

Going up still farther, I put the glove on the hairs of her mound. Her jerky movements became more agitated and vehement. Suddenly, she grasped my hand and spread her legs as far apart as she could.

'There . . . there!' she panted. 'Don't take it away. Keep it where it is. How good it feels!'

I was a little afraid at the way she was flopping about. Her legs shot up in the air and then limply dropped. I watched her face. It was livid, contorted in a grimace that deformed her features. Horrified, I tried to take away the glove, but she held it firmly in position. I wondered what was wrong with her. After more convulsions, both her body and face relaxed. For several minutes she remained without life or movement.

When I took off the glove, wondering if I had hurt her with it, she opened her eyes and smiled sweetly at me.

'It was sheer bliss,' she said dreamily.

I was dumbfounded. How could she say a thing like that when I had seen how she was suffering?

'You don't understand, I see,' she told me. 'And I can't explain. It is something that you have to experience yourself. Do you want me to massage you in turn?'

'But won't it hurt?' I timidly asked. 'You were groaning and moaning so, and the words you said, I was really afraid.'

'Do you love me that much, Laura?'

'Yes, yes, I love you . . . more than anything.'

In such gambols we spent the day and night.

Three Times a Woman

When Princess Nelidowa went to bed for the first time with Alexey Sokolow she understood of a sudden what her marriage would cost her. She had known that His Highness, the Ex-Governor, her exalted Prince-husband, was wealthy and she would have social position and power. But there, lying next to her like an orang-utan was the ugly body of the man who was now by right and law her master, mentally and physically. He was bald but had plenty of woolly hair around the lower part of his head, growing into a long thick beard reaching to his chest which was covered with thick black hair. His chest was enormously broad, his arms short and muscular with broad short hands, and he had an enormous belly with a tissue of muscles all around the waist line. His skin was dark, his thighs almost brown. He had small piercing suspecting eyes and a big mouth with the lower lip especially thick and sensual. His prick was short and thick and his balls betrayed at a glance that they held plenty of ammunition and loved the shooting game.

During the long stupendous wedding with a thousand new faces congratulating her, everybody bowing deeply before the Prince, who was in a jovial mood, she had been thrilled. He had seemed handsome clad in a brilliant blue uniform studded with glittering medals and buttons of real gold and with a snow-white wig with a long pigtail, which had dangled frivolously over the gold collar of his costume. He had worn high patent leather boots and rings with dazzling stones. It was thus that Nelidowa, the bride, had first seen her new spouse. She had been startled to fright when the cannons bellowed on their arrival at the palace and was moved to tears when the Archbishop (think of it, a real Archbishop performing the ceremony, and in her home town, not even the lowest monk would listen to her confession) spoke the blessings for them. She had drunk it into herself, blinded with the splendour, and had made all kinds of good promises to herself. She had been in a trance, had kissed her new hand-maids and assured them heaven on earth when they undressed her late at night, and she had gone to her new husband (according to his orders quite nude) intending to thank and thank him, to tell him that she was going to be his chattel and his faithful wife. But when she lay next to him, when she observed how this Prince of the costly uniform had changed into an abhorrent brute, she had not been able to say a word.

Prince Alexey Sokolow did not expect a word from her. He had never thought of a woman as a human being but as his property. He owned many and kept dozens of serf girls always near his bedroom. He had them follow him on his voyages. He had had them since his father first ordered him to fuck a girl when he was sixteen years of age. He had never had an affair with a society girl, because she was somebody else's property. While he made many daring business ventures and acquired the estates of many men convicted for political or other reasons during his two score years as governor, women were something not to be taken illegally. If you liked a bitch, you could buy her; there was always a price which could be met.

During his trips to Western Europe, he had learned that there were harlots, whom one could buy for an hour or a day. He even brought to Russia with him some wenches who did a nice job in bed. It seemed money wasted, however, because his own slave girls could do as well and even better. They were harder, had no moods and were easily put in their places when they did not behave properly.

Alexey had no special love habits. He did not know about the refinements of copulation; he just wanted a good fuck. He wanted to put it in to his own satisfaction, regardless of the pleasure of his partner, and was satisfied when the arse moved up and down against him. That is, it had been so when he was younger and had not yet acquired his belly. Now he would not have been able to touch the spot with his machine had he laid himself on top of a girl. With his growing belly he had discovered a better position; the girl had to kneel straddle-legged over him and move up and down while he lay still, moving only the muscles of his enormous buttocks alternately. He also managed to give his shaft a to-and-fro movement without lifting his arse from the linen, because the muscles were well developed around his sex-organs.

He did not explain much of this to his bride. She really was stunning looking and he was well satisfied with this new acquirement to his bed assortment. He had not married her for love, and if she had not pleased him he would have fucked her once or twice (he liked to take maidenheads) and then probably forgotten her. But she was a good morsel and he was going to use her. He broke her in without further ado. He felt her over with his thick hands, he rudely forced his finger into her pussy, he pulled her on top of him, he spanked her bottom a bit, in short he first took possession of her with his hands.

Nelidowa tried to make it easy for herself by kissing him on the cheeks (with closed eyes) by snuggling against him (to her own disgust) and by not struggling when she felt his big finger enter her hole. Then with a jerk, holding her with his hands at the waistline, he sat her with his powerful arms on top of his testicles. Nelidowa knew well what it was all about; a married girl friend had told her, so she understood that Master Prick, now cornered between her Venus Hill and the steep wall of his belly, had to go into the cage and she knew that it would hurt her. But she was not only required to stand for it, she had to put it in herself; she had, with her own weight, to tear that little piece of skin which is precious only to virgins. She did not have the nerve. She stared with fixed eyes at the brute who was lying below her, a few hours ago still an utter stranger and now entitled to defile her.

'Put it in and sit on it and fuck,' yelled Alexey to her. Poor Nelidowa. She took that hard instrument, so broad but still not so long, in her nimble fingers. She moved it towards the entrance and nervously lowered her bottom. But things needed a more vigorous handling. Alexey was prepared for that. He did not like to induce a woman to do this or that; he did not like to fumble. He had taken more virgins than one since his belly had grown. He had expected even more resistance from his bride and the usual preparation had been made.

He struck a little gong on his night table. Three servant girls rushed in. Before Nelidowa knew it, two had got hold of her with an expert grip: one hand went underneath each knee, took hold of it and stretching the leg as far from the middle of the body as possible, the other hands grabbed her shoulder. She was lifted up a bit and lowered down carefully. Meanwhile the third girl took the tail of her master with one hand, opened up with apt fingers the unused cunt, and saw to it that both met in the right way. She then commanded: PUSH, and both women, holding the Princess, gave a satisfactory pressure to her shoulders. Satisfactory, because Master Prick was in and had pierced the little membrane.

Nelidowa howled, the Prince moved his bottom, the girls let go of her knees and took hold of her waist and shoulders and moved her up and down. It took about five minutes for the Prince to come.

The Princess received a washing and the master was likewise cleaned up from the blood. She had to lie down again alongside her master. 'You'll learn,' he said. 'And now we'll show you how the next part has to be done.' He bedded her head on his hairy chest, put her hand on his machine and told her to massage it tenderly. As she did so he groaned and snorted, his fat hand on her small bottom. It pleased him that her arse was small and her thighs straight and slim; when the girls were fleshy it was hard for him to bury his prick deep into their cunts.

After a while he was stiff again. The gong sounded a snappy order, and a serf-girl ready for work entered the room. She knew what to do. She mounted the master, so that her face was towards his feet and her back towards his belly. He put some more pillows under his head and managed to bend forward enough so that he could reach the behind of the girl, who was riding him with slow firm motions up and down. He lay perfectly still, his hand playing with her behind, and he found her arse hole and squeezed his finger in just as he came. After that he lay quietly and had himself washed with a wet towel.

He explained to his new wife that fuck number one was to be given with full front view; fuck number two reversed. He said that she was to come three times a week, that she was to learn her technique quickly and that she could now go back to her own bed-chamber, because he wanted to sleep. No good-night, no caresses, no good word for her. But also no bad word. He was instituting a routine which was kept from then on.

It was strictly kept because he liked her better than his slave girls and she soon learned how to squeeze out his prick properly with her pussy. Also it must be remembered that he paid more for her upkeep than for that of his other female retinue. Nelidowa did not mind the prick so much; she simply closed her eyes and managed to come and to get a thrill. What she could not stand was the play of his strong hand over her body before every jump, especially between the first and the second fucking, when he wanted to heat himself up again. At this time, he hurt her quite often. He fussed around with her breasts, pinched the nipples and laughed when she tried to avoid him. When he toyed with her love nest, he did not begin with any gentle play around the entrance, warm up the tickler and then intrude into the tube. No, he just pushed his finger rudely in as deep as he could, crooked it and rubbed it. It always gave her pain and a shock. But she did not complain and even gave him gentle words and told him how happy she was. It was the price demanded of her and she gave it.

The rest of their personal relations were also regulated by rules. They ate apart, except when they had guests. They went to all social affairs together and he liked to show her off and sent her for such occasions jewellery from the seemingly endless store of his iron chest. He spoke politely to her, in few words, and never told her about his own affairs. For example, she did not know that he had big estates in the South, until they travelled over them. He confided his affairs only to an old trusted man-servant and to very few of his friends. He was a man of few words, used to command, and he exercised his will with great determination.

Nelidowa had to find her life with her women friends. She chatted with her bed-maids and amused herself as she could with anything that was proper and becoming for the wife of a great Prince. He never beat her, as many husbands did their wives, and he never lost his temper. He had resorted to the lash only a few times in his life, sending the culprit to the stable master for the punishment. However, when he was seriously dissatisfied, he would have the guilty person stand while he smacked the face a few times.

He did this to his wife on occasions when her giddiness had aroused the mockery of other society people and he had heard of it. When he heard that she was beating her maids or had them beaten, he discussed it briefly with her. He said that she had the right to do so, but that if one of the servants should become seriously ill or die on account of the punishment, he would then inflict the same torture on her. 'They are my property,' he added, 'As well as you are.' That closed the incident because he remembered that his mother had whipped her maids also.

He had expected to have a child from the Princess;

78

he wanted an heir to cheat his relatives. She remained barren. He had a few virgins come from one of his estates, fucked them and held them under strict watch, so that they could not sleep with other men. Out of four girls, two became pregnant. Therefore it was Nelidowa, not he, who was at fault. But he decided not to take another wife. Not because he could not have got rid of her or because he loved her, but that it was not so important after all. She was there and she could remain there.

After the first year of her marriage, feeling secure now as a Princess and a powerful man's wife, Nelidowa was ripe to take a lover. He must be distinctly different from her husband, a bit exotic, maybe a Frenchman. As it turned out, he was a Pole. Gustavus Swanderson, he made known, was his name. He came from Warsaw, where his father had a string of disorderly houses. Gustavus, who then bore the name of Boris, managed, during a raid on his father's establishments, to get hold of some gold which the old man kept hidden. With this, he travelled to Sweden, changed his name, bought the patent of an officer and played the nice chap for the ladies. He was decidedly romantic, with a wealth of brown hair, elegant in his movements, enterprising, and not altogether a bad boy. His hobby was drawing and his satirical sketches of society people were quite the thing. He started to learn architecture, first just to play with it, but later became interested and took part in the erection of some military buildings and forts. When Peter the Great was already quite elderly, he came to Russia and offered his services as a builder. Peter, though not much impressed with him, sent him to Moscow where a big bridge was under construction and he began to be a slight success in his line.

When he met Nelidowa he was around thirty years of age, ten years her senior. He was different from the other men; his skin was white, he was not hairy, his hands were fine, almost feminine and tender. He kept himself clean and modish and his laughter was of a romantic sadness. Nelidowa selected him for herself at first sight. The man had very little choice as to whether he wanted her or not. He had to conquer her because she wanted him. Oh, she fixed it in a very romantic way. Poems fluttered through the air; secret words passed, only understood by the conspirators. Nelidowa played her part wonderfully, with tears and resistance and with faked fainting spells.

She won him and she was very satisfied. He was so tender, so full of caresses, so loving, so romantic and when, after long kissing and playing and toying, she finally felt his hot rod enter her hungry crevice, she nearly fainted with delight. Of course, when he built lovely castles in the air about elopement and how they would live in Paris as happy as doves, she listened like a happy but already grown up child to a smartly told fairy tale. While she avoided saying 'No', in her heart she never considered him more than a lover. Something necessary to a woman's life, but not to be mixed up with the reality of a Princess.

On the other hand, this reality bothered her three times a week when she walked nude, except for blue slippers, through different rooms to the bed of a big brute who offended her body and for whom she was nothing but an instrument for prick-massage. She could not pretend she had a head-ache or did not feel well, because if she did, her husband would send a servant with a brief message that he was not fucking her head but her cunt. As long as she did not have her monthly, she had to appear. No pity from that quarter and no excuse accepted.

Another incident occurred which proved to be annoying. Gustavus fell in love with her and the longer the liaison lasted the more enamoured he became. With this his jealousy developed, and while the brutal and elderly Prince in his strength entertained no slightest thought that his wife might be unfaithful, Gustavus, in his tender and weak constitution, was crazed with jealousy. She had once described to him in what way she had to fuck her husband and though this was still early in their affair, he was near to assassinating his rival. Lately he had pestered her to refuse to play the dutiful wife and in passionate words had threatened to take the life of the Prince and even hers. She told him she would do as he wished and, lying, said she did not go to her husband since at present he had a passion for one of the serf girls. Gustavus did not believe her fully and they had many scenes. She did not want to give up her lover. She could not stay away from her master. She had to think her way out.

Suddenly she was struck with an idea: didn't they tell her that Grushenka looked just like her, not only in figure but in face also? It was whispered that they were like twins, that nobody could really say who was who. If that was true then Grushenka could take her place in the bed-chamber of her spouse. This thought was so daring, so exciting, that she had to go to work right away. She commanded Grushenka to her presence and had herself and the girl clothed in dresses exactly similar and their hair done in the same way. She then had one of her maids ask other servants from the basement which of the two was the Princess. The servants looked uneasy, afraid to make a mistake. They tried to avoid a direct answer and finally pointed at random, missing the Princess as often as they chose her. That was fine! All that was now needed was for the Princess to teach Grushenka exactly how to behave with the master.

She dismissed all the servants including her handmaids, locked herself in her bedroom with Grushenka and made her kneel down and swear solemnly never to betray her. She confided her plan to the girl and rehearsed to the smallest detail the way the fucking parties took place. When Grushenka undressed, an obstacle appeared: Grushenka was clean shaven around the pussy. There was nothing to do but to wait until the hair had grown. So it was decided. During this time, for many an afternoon, Grushenka was told how she would have to behave during the coming fucking parties and Nelidowa, during this period, observed herself in all details when she was with her mate. She was sure of success. The bedroom of the Prince was lit by a single large candle which stood in a corner far from the bed and there was a small candle in front of the Ikon. This small illumination would not have permitted him to find out the difference between Nelidowa and Grushenka even if they had not been so much alike.

Another remark must be made concerning these confidential rehearsals between the young women. They began to like each other. The Princess had never thought of Grushenka before except as a low and silly serf girl. Now she wanted something from her. She ordered her, of course, to take her place. Grushenka could tell the master and the catastrophe arising from such a mishap would have been unthinkably awful! Therefore the Princess became kind to the girl, chatted with her and tried to discover her

character. She was captivated with Grushenka's
simple charm and faith. On the other hand,
Grushenka now learned that the Princess was
unhappy, uncertain of herself, that she had had a
hard youth, that she longed for kindness and that her
nervous and brutal behaviour did not arise from
coldness, but from unawareness. Grushenka became
a hand-maid of her mistress, was always around her,
was her confidante in her love matters and her companion during the long hours of the dragging days.
The whip was never applied to her, she was not
scolded, and she slept next to her mistress's room
and became something like a little sister.

When Grushenka's hair had grown, (they examined it daily) the day came when a male servant
announced that his Highness expected the visit of her
Highness. Grushenka put on the blue slippers and
both women walked through the several rooms to
the master's chamber. Grushenka entered while
Nelidowa, with beating heart, peeped through a crack
of the door. The Prince had come from a card game
where he had been drinking and felt tired and a little
lascivious. Grushenka held his stub in her hand,
worked it firmly, mounted the horse and worked his
machine into her tube. For quite a time he could not
come on account of the liquor he had drunk but she
came herself once or twice (she had not fucked for ever
so long) until he groaned and moved his arse and was
through. He was through for the night and sent her
away with a slap on the behind.

Nelidowa took Grushenka with her to her bed.
She was excited, joyously excited, while Grushenka
was very calm. She had done the whole job without
hestitation. She wanted to help her mistress. That
was her duty; for the rest, she was not concerned.

Nelidowa hugged and kissed the girl and aroused by the fucking she had seen, had two hand-maids come in to give herself and her friend (as she said now for the first time) a good sucking.

So it was that Grushenka became the master's wife as far as his bed was concerned. The first few times Nelidowa went with her to the door and peeped. After that she remained in the bed until Grushenka returned and a few weeks later was no longer concerned about the matter. When the servant came to announce that his master's prick was ready (that was the sense of the message) Nelidowa would say she'd come right away, and Grushenka who lay on the bed in the next room, got up, went to the Prince, fucked, washed her pussy and went back to sleep.

Until that time Nelidowa had satisfied the whims of her mate in spite of her repulsion. She now found her satisfaction under the pushing of Gustavus' considerate shaft while Grushenka had to look forward to the short but thick prick of her master. Grushenka had never known fine people, so the rudeness of the Prince did not shock her. On the contrary his brutal force and immense vitality captured her and made her forget the repulsion which his belly might have inspired. She loved his sceptre. She began not only to massage it, but to caress it, to kiss it and she soon began to suck him. He thought first that she wanted a gift from him, perhaps one of his estates or a will made out in her favour. But when no such demands came, he felt with pleasure what a passionate, refined and loving wife he had.

Grushenka had a much easier time with him than Nelidowa used to have. The Princess always used to aggressively try to stop him from taking hold of her body with his hands, but now the Prince was stiff before Grushenka was in bed and she sat on him before he could annoy her with his hands. Besides, she fucked with so much passion that she did not mind when he squeezed her nipples while his machine was in her pussy. During the intermission, he lauded her with teasing words about her newly found temperament but hardly touched her, waiting until she would take hold of his prick again. She sometimes lay between his legs, raising his big behind with a pillow, and licked his dark brown balls with intense ardour, the hard strong smell of his balls and the odour of his rim was a sensation to her nostrils. She quivered all over and got immensely excited and worked herself up by pressing her legs close together. She did not want to follow his orders to come up and mount him; she wanted to make him come with her lips, to drink the liquid, but he never let her.

Sometimes Nelidowa would watch this scene out of curiosity, jealous that the girl enjoyed it so much. Afterwards she would pinch her and scold her about something and then again she would kiss the girl's mouth, lick her lips and teeth, because she felt the contamination of the sex excitement which had got hold of Grushenka. Sometimes she would decide to go to her husband herself, but at the last moment she would change her mind, and go to her lover. If he were not in the neighbourhood, she would have one of her maids satisfy her caprice.

All went well except for some small incidents. For example, the master would tell Grushenka something he wanted done the next day and she, not familiar with the people concerned or with the facts, would have a hard time remembering exactly what he had said. Or the Princess would be asleep when she came from the master's bedroom and she would lie awake the whole night so as not to forget. At other times, Grushenka would have a rash or pimples on her face which Nelidowa did not have, and she would be much afraid of detection in spite of the subdued light in his bedchamber.

Nelidowa told her lover the huge joke she had played on her mate and smuggled him into her own bed room and prepared with care the comedy of watching the fucking party of her husband with Grushenka. When Gustavus arrived, she presented Grushenka to him and made him compare them to find out who was who. To her great satisfaction, he was not for a moment in doubt although they wore no clothes. The reason for his quick judgement was that Nelidowa alone spoke, while Grushenka kept silent with a smile on her lips. She wanted to please Gustavus of whom she had heard so much; she had a romantic affection for him through Nelidowa.

Grushenka liked Gustavus as soon as she laid eyes on him. He was so gracious in his movements, his bearing was elegant, his hands were white, fine and well taken care of, in great contrast to those of the Russian men. He was eager to point out differences between the two: a little mole underneath the shoulder blade, the different shape of the bust, the flavour of the hair. Of course 'his love' was more beautiful. Though this pleased her, Nelidowa had to show him that she was the mistress and Grushenka the slave. First she told him what a pig Grushenka was for liking the prick of the Prince and sucking him off, then she turned Grushenka around and around, exposing her in every fashion, Finally she pinched the girl and suggested that Grushenka prove her art by kissing his shaft, but Gustavus, ashamed of all this play, refused.

Just then a message came from the Prince, who expected the Princess. Grushenka moved her hand over her bust and belly as if she were stroking her skin, she lightly rubbed her pussy with her fingers and opened the lips a few times just to have everything ready. She then stepped into the little blue slippers and went towards the bedroom of the Prince-husband. Nelidowa and Gustavus followed. Tip-toeing quietly, they took posts at the crack of the door.

Grushenka, well aware of the watchers and annoyed by the humiliation to which Nelidowa had submitted her, did not follow the usual behaviour. The lovers at the door could see the Prince on a bed with light blue silk covers, resting on his back, his fingers playing a happy rhythm on the bed sheet, his lips sensually pursed; the picture of a man who knows that he will be taken care of shortly. The door through which the lovers peeped was toward the foot of the bed, and his monstrous hairy body and big belly were plainly visible.

Grushenka leaned over and took in her left hand the big balls, caressing them while reaching underneath them and playing with her finger in his rim. Meanwhile her right hand held his prick, which she massaged. The prick was half asleep but with good inclination to wake up. The gentle treatment soon made the machine stiff. Grushenka did not kiss it; she pointed maliciously with her tongue in its direction and smacked her lips, but she did not embrace the shaft with them.

Instead, she mounted. The lovers could clearly see how she held the prick with two fingers of her right hand, how she opened her cunt with the left hand, and how Master Priapus slowly poked his nose into her love-nest. Grushenka bent forward, and giving over her splendid breasts to his grasping hands, made a few firm and deep up and down movements.

Then of a sudden, she bent back. Opening her knees as wide as possible, getting a deep hold of his machine with her cunt, she leaned so far back that her elbows almost touched her own heels. Of course the fat master was unable to reach any part of her body in this position, and groaning with excitement, he swore at her to bend forward. He used all the curse words he knew and his short arms waved with helpless strokes through the air. It was a funny picture; the riding girl with a determination on her face to squeeze his prick out with her cunt, and the pinioned monster who had to submit to his excitement, though mad to reach her. It was so funny a picture that Nelidowa and Gustavus could not restrain their giggles. Until this had happened, they had stood close together, Nelidowa holding his prick while his fingers fondled her love nest. When Grushenka had engulfed the Prince's shaft, they had keenly felt their own sex excitement.

The Prince was startled. Who was at the door? He moved and was about to throw his fair rider off to investigate. Grushenka, sensing the danger, threw herself forward and pressing him into the cushions with her weight, began to love up his face and head with kisses and the caresses of her hands. This brought about his crisis. He came with all his force and was unable to do anything but squirt his sperm into her. Thus the lovers had time to escape. Of course, the second party when Grushenka was riding the other way around, could not be observed by them, but, as by that time Nelidowa was already squirming under the pressure of her beloved 'soldier' perhaps it did not matter much.

With Open Mouth

Lean cheeks hot, heart pounding, Avelino the singer heaved himself quietly up the last two centimetres of rock to look down on the naked unsuspecting woman below.

The noise of a dislodged stone as he settled himself in a niche was drowned by the washing of the surf close to the woman's prostrate body. He gazed at her with the frightened, formless anguish of his twenty-one sexless years and it was as if cold sea-water had suddenly swamped his loins.

Avelino had come upon the woman quite by accident three days ago. He had been trying to catch a lizard on the craggy, solitary isthmus when, reaching the summit, he had looked down the sharper face and seen the slim, brown body stretched out on a ledge near the water's edge. Since then he had crept every day to the same spot during the sweating heat of afternoon when others were working or taking a siesta. Each day he had watched the woman for the few hours she lay in the sun, body brown and gleaming from her sun lotion. Each day he had mas-turbated desperately until his passion was spent—and even then he was unable to draw his fascinated eyes away until she made movements to leave. Then he would slither away like a rock snake and dash for the grove of olive trees which cut off the jagged isthmus from the dusty coast road.

At other times during the day he had seen the

woman in the little town which had not long outgrown its village state. He had seen her, too, at the open air dance in the evening at which he sang with the nine-piece band which all the tourists liked so much because, they said, it was typically Spanish.

At first he had thought she was Swedish. The Swedish women had a reputation from some of the older members of the community for bathing in the nude. But later he had found she was English. She was always alone and she was beautiful. She sat alone, danced a lot, but always refused invitations to join another table. She appeared to be a rich woman who wanted soft music and to be left alone.

She always came to this spot alone—with a book, a bottle or two of wine, wearing a scanty bathing costume under a bright, striped beach jacket. She would swim expertly in the deep blue waters of the Mediterranean, climb gently back onto her ledge, careful to avoid the prickling sea urchins which clung to its underwater surface, and then strip off her two-piece before soaking herself in lotion to imbibe the sun.

Although she was much older than him, her body was the sort which would never grow fat, Avelino told himself. The bones were small, well formed, the skin tightly stretched on them.

She was lying on her front now, reading. Her buttocks jutted from her brown slimness below him like twin balloons, small but well inflated. They were just slightly paler than the rest of her back view.

Today while he watched she stiffened, cramped a little with her position and her bottom tensed, hollowing provocatively as if she were pressing herself against a lover. And then she rolled over onto her back.

Avelino withdrew his head until he judged she had made herself comfortable in her new position and then peered over the ridge again.

Now he could see her breasts, bulbous and glistening in the fierce yellow light of afternoon. The slimness of her body below her breasts, the supple broadening into the hips with their central muff of blonde hair, the long smooth thighs—all were revealed to him.

His eyes roved hotly, half-fearfully over the first unclothed woman he had ever seen, but it was already becoming not enough to watch. He did not know what more he could do. He felt icy fingers run through his belly at the thought of discovery—but it was no longer enough just to watch. He longed desperately for the unbelievable happening of contact.

Sometimes his mind floated off on a fierce fantasy in which he imagined himself in this lonely spot suddenly falling on the woman, pressing her nude rotundities under his weight and raping her with abandon. The horror of the thought made him sick and it was always a relief when he forced himself back to reality. At other times he thought of calling out to her—who knew, after all, what her reaction would be. Perhaps she would call him down, invite him to make love to her.

He wondered what he would do if she did. And his mind would wander off again through the detailed action. She must be thirty. She would take the lead. He had to admit to himself that, although he knew how it was done, he wouldn't know how to set about it.

For a long time he lay flat on the hot brown stone, aware of the white-flecked sea beyond and the occasional white sail far out, but never consciously taking his eyes from the woman's body.

His hopeless desire was a sharp, hot pain against the rocks at his loins. His head ached from frustration. His body was sticky from the heat under his clothes and the rock had become almost too hot for his hands.

Below the woman read, eyeless with the large sunglasses she wore, short, blonde hair sparkling— and gazing into the very pores of her skin, Avelino felt the thrill of an idea tremor through his veins.

It was not a very good idea on the face of it, but it would take him nearer the woman and reveal him to her.

Trembling with excitement so that he almost urinated in his thin gaberdine trousers, he slithered gently down the slope of the jut of the isthmus towards the mainland. On the flat neck of land over which the sea sometimes swept at high tide, making an island of the higher crag behind him, he walked quickly towards the western point of the isthmus.

In a boulder-shaded cove close to the shore, he hurriedly slipped out of his clothes, experiencing the sharp thrill of the forbidden as he did so. He made a neat pile of his shirt trousers and the light espadrilles which all the local folk wore to protect their feet, and then stood for a moment in the sun, breathing heavily.

The sun and the whisper of air on his body gave him a mixed feeling of freedom and evil. Particularly to the areas not usually exposed—his buttocks and his genitals—it seemed like softly caressing fingers.

He hesitated for a moment. His body was slim and hard, but it had been well tapered by the sea. He knew he would probably have had a woman by now if it had not been for the timidity which a strict upbringing had instilled in him. Perhaps, then, he would have got rid of this inturned, mind-wracking torture which filled his thoughts and prevented him any peace of mind.

By the time he dived cleanly into the sea, the sweat had already begun to glisten on his chest. He plunged deep and swam a few strokes towards the sea-bed before raising his hands towards the lighter region above.

His head broke he surface with his eyes stinging and all desire momentarily gone.

He had not been sure what he was going to do and now, for a moment, he considered swimming in the opposite direction, away from the woman, leaving the water after a few minutes and returning to the town. But he knew that with the evening, the long night of thought and solitude, she would flood back in him so that the next day he would be back with the same hopelessness, heightened by his failure to alter it.

So he began to swim with a strong crawl, out, through the light undulation of waves, to the open sea.

For the moment he was cut off from sight of the woman by a jutting promontory of rock, but in a few minutes when, he judged, he would be some hundred metres from the isthmus, he would be able to see the ledge on which she lay. He would then swim round the isthmus until he was parallel with the ledge. He had no thought except to see what reaction his presence would produce in the woman. He was not even sure he would allow her to see him.

For some time she did not see him as he swam in leisurely fashion opposite the ledge and then, from the corner of his eye, he was aware of her glancing in his direction. He continued to swim without looking at her, making no secret of his presence, as if he did not realise she was there. He saw her reach out for her beach jacket and slip it on.

It was in the hurried carelessness of the movement that she knocked her gaily coloured towel so that it fluttered down to the surf a few feet below, receded from the shore, was washed in again, receded once more and then, sodden with water, showed signs of sinking.

The woman tried vainly to reach it with her hands, lying flat along the ledge; then with the aid of the bottle of wine—to no avail. To plunge in after it meant she would have to strip off her beach jacket and don her swimming costume in his presence.

Avelino turned openly towards the isthmus now: to pretend he hadn't seen the flutter of movement would have been ridiculous. He made a quick, nervous decision and then went racing in towards the ledge.

The water here was deep and dark. She would be unable to see that he was naked unless he swam immediately under her.

The woman had seen him coming in towards her and had relaxed her vain efforts. She watched as he approached, with an expression of uncertainty. Her beach jacket reached only a few inches down her thighs.

By the time Avelino reached the spot some yards from the ledge at which the towel had disappeared, it was drifting down through the depths—a hazy shimmer of colour.

He dived without hesitation, realising in the instant that his naked buttocks must have momentarily met the woman's gaze.

With the towel in his hands he came to the surface.

He indicated he would throw it to the woman and she held out her hands with a smile. He threw and the heavy wet ball was caught deftly in her arms.

'Thank you very much,' she called out in Spanish, above the wash of the surf.

'It was nothing,' he called back, dark eyes lighting up in a nervous smile.

The woman spread the towel out on the rocks and he began to swim away, feeling the strangeness of the occurrence at that particular time.

Seeing that he was swimming off, out to sea, the woman cupped her hands around her mouth and shouted:

'Would you like a glass of wine?'

Avelino could hardly believe that what he had heard was true. His immediate reaction was to pretend he had not heard, but that would have been too embarrassing as she was looking straight at him.

He hesitated, mind searching frantically for a reason for refusal. And then he called out the truth.

'I have no swimming trunks.'

The woman laughed merrily and even from there he could see the evenness of her teeth. She didn't seem the slightest disturbed.

'It is much better swimming without them,' she called back. 'But I have another towel here that you can wrap round you. I won't look while you climb out.'

Avelino was astonished, in the first place by the fluency of her Spanish, in the second by the ease of her manner which made the boldness of her words—unacceptable from a Spanish girl—seem perfectly natural.

The ardour-dampening wash of the sea had dispelled much of his nervousness, even his desire and he called back:

'I don't want to disturb your reading.'

'Not at all,' the woman shouted. 'I'm tired of reading.'

'Very well. Where is the towel?'

The woman indicated the dry towel and placed it along the ledge at some distance from her.

With a spurt of energy, Avelino raced in to the ledge. Grasping it above his head, he glanced along at the woman. She was staring in the opposite direction, into the bay of the far side of which the white houses of the town shone in the sun. He hauled himself onto the ledge and wrapped the towel lightly around his waist. His nervousness suddenly returned.

'May I turn around?' the woman asked.

'Yes,' he said. And his voice sounded thick.

When she turned towards him and he found himself so close to the object of his surreptitious desire, Avelino felt an acute embarrassment. He could think of nothing to say. But the woman was prepared to do all the immediate talking.

'I'm afraid I would have lost the towel if it hadn't been for you,' she said as she poured the wine into a glass. 'I was too slow and I hate swimming underwater.'

Avelino smiled. He could think of no answer.

The woman seemed more beautiful at close quarters. She had a large, rounded forehead, a straight, thin nose and a firm, but not aggressive chin. Her possible age became more of a mystery to him. She was free from wrinkles and the whites of her eyes were almost luminously clear. Yet, somehow he had the feeling she was well over thirty.

'You swim almost as well as you sing,' the woman said, smiling as she handed him the glass.

Avelino stared at her in surprise.

'You recognise me?' he said. Never during the dances had the woman appeared to even glance in his direction.

'Of course,' she replied. 'How could I hear such a voice and not want to look at the owner.'

'Oh, no!' Avelino gave a little laugh of self-disparagement.

'Oh yes!' The woman laughed back at him. 'You have a beautiful voice. In England I think you would be a hit!'

Avelino felt highly flattered although he did not believe the woman. Perhaps she did like his voice, but the rest could not be true.

However, he began to find the woman was easy to talk to and his self-confidence slowly returned. She had another bottle of wine and they both drank luxuriously while they talked—or, rather, while she questioned him and he answered.

They sat almost side by side on the ledge and with the return of self-confidence, Avelino was aware of the return of desire.

Occasionally as they talked the woman's eyes gazed out over the sea at a distant ship on its way to Barcelona and then he would drop his eyes from her face to the brown, bulging skin of her upper breasts in the deep V of the beach jacket. She seemed to be not the slightest perturbed at the flimsiness of her covering, at the fact that the length of the jacket barely covered the junction of hips and thighs.

After a while, Avelino had forgotten how much wine he'd drunk—the wine at home was neither so strong nor so plentiful—and his face was hot with a more urgent heat than that from the sun. Under the towel which draped his slim hips his penis had risen into a stiff cudgel of flesh which bulged obviously against the covering, try as he would to conceal it.

'Do you often swim here?' the woman asked, eventually, turning to him with a lift of her thin, finely-drawn eyebrows.

'I never have before,' Avelino answered, trying to cross one leg over the other to hide the enormous mound at his loins.

'I'm glad you swam here today. How did you come to?'

Avelino looked into the hazel eyes, serious and holding him. Could it be that he imagined a flicker of invitation? She too had drunk a lot. He stared down at the lipstick on the opposite side of their one glass which he now held.

'Why did you swim here today?' the woman repeated softly, as if she knew the answer, wanted it confirmed.

'Because I knew you were here and I wanted to speak to you,' he blurted.

'You knew I was here—but how?' Her thoughts were inturned, racing back over the meaning of what he had said.

Made honest with the wine and almost uncaring, Avelino replied with the truth.

'I have watched you from the top of the rocks behind us for the last three days,' he admitted.

There was a moment's silence and then the woman's gentle little laugh cadenced softly amongst the rocks. She looked at him again and her eyes took in the bulge at his hips as if he had given her a signal.

'What a pity you watched from so far for so long,' she said as the laugh faded.

Avelino gulped back the dregs of wine in the glass and looked at her. It seemed there was no mistaking her tone, but he had no idea what to do. Now, in fact, he felt a little more frightened than he had before. It occurred to him suddenly that she was, perhaps, being sarcastic, but her next words dispelled the thought.

'Have you ever made love to a woman?'

'No,' he admitted, taken aback at the bluntness of the question.

'A virgin,' the woman whispered. 'How delightful. I thought you were rather shy.'

'Yes, I am shy,' Avelino heard himself saying. 'I wish I weren't.'

Again the woman's eyes lowered to his hips. She had understood the implication of his words.

'We all must learn,' she said softly.

It was as if in a dream that Avelino found himself kissing her. The motion must have come from him, but it was as if she had directed it. He had kissed girls before—at parties—but this was different. The woman was breathing hard and she pulled him back onto the ledge. He felt, with momentary surprise followed by pleasure, the silky, foreign pressure of her tongue in his mouth. He had heard of this. Her arms were around him, fingers digging sharply into the flesh of his shoulders, of his neck.

For some time they kissed, lips moving over each other's faces until he, too, was breathing as heavily, it seemed, as his uncle's donkey. She pulled him against her on the rock so that his penis under the towel was crushed against her hips. Her mouth opened and she gasped with quick little intakes of breath at the feel of his against hers. Under the towel he felt his penis throbbing as if it were undergoing a self-masturbation.

Her hand slipped down between them and pressed

against the mound. Softly she moved her fingers under the towel, slipping them up until with a sudden stroking caress they had contacted with the fleshy heat of his organ.

Avelino's hips recoiled automatically at the unbearable intimacy of the sensation. It took his breath away.

But the fingers followed, stroking, stroking until he could bear to let them stay. He recoiled again as they roamed over his testicles. He began to gasp and moan, unable to control himself any longer.

The fingers, so cool against his heat, were relentless. They drew themselves up and down his throbbing penis while the woman pressed her face at his, darting her tongue moistly into his mouth.

His hips writhed, his mouth opened wide, he was suddenly overcome by an unbearable sweet pain behind his genitals. The woman, as if she divined it, suddenly grasped his penis in her whole hand and squeezed it in a rhythmic motion which brought little cries from him. The pain grew so that he could no longer bear it, his head rolled, he had to escape— and then with a cry of sweet agony he had suddenly gained release and his sperm was shooting all over the towel, the woman's hand and his thighs.

She continued to squeeze and caress him until his passion had died and his organ deflated. She opened her beach jacket and nursed his head against her breasts while his breathing still choked in his throat. Lying against her, feeling too embarrassed to move or look at her, Avelino realised he had never had such a quick orgasm. He felt the more embarrassed, now, from a sense of failure. The woman had obviously wanted him, intended him to make love to her.

She kissed his head, pulling his face close to her so

that his lips brushed the smooth, glassy skin of her breasts. He felt depressed, but, as if she understood, she said softly:

'We have plenty of time.'

They lay still for a long time until the sun sank behind the cliff face behind them, although it continued to light up the sea beyond in a warm sparkle of azure. Even in the narrow ribbon of shade it was warm on the ledge. With the disappearance of the sun it seemed a little more secluded.

Pressing his lips against her breasts, moving them over her abundant nipples, surprised at the situation every time he allowed himself to picture it from outside, Avelino felt a fresh stirring at his loins. A slow breeze of excitement began in his hips like the deep rumblings of a volcano long before it erupts. He was astonished at his ability to recover so easily.

Between his legs he felt his penis rising again, felt it moving, apart from him, with an electric tingling as it grew and thickened. He kissed the cushioning breasts with greater passion and the woman responded, clasping his head against her flesh as if she would hold it there forever.

He kissed the nipple, sucking it, the way he thought a child would. She drew in her breath sharply and gave a little cry. She slithered down against him so that her breasts now pressed warmly against his chest and her lips sucked at his. He in turn forced his tongue through her lips and her mouth opened wide to receive him.

'Just a moment,' she whispered as he slithered his lips down her neck.

He released her and she reached around them gathering towel, a cushion and her bathing costume. She arranged the articles under and around them before clasping him around the neck once more.

As his passion rose afresh so that his whole body seemed fluid with fire, her hand wormed in through his towel again to caress his genitals. His penis rose yet more sharply at the contact of her fingers and he strained his buttocks together, crushing the weight of his hips towards her body.

His hands now moved over the glossy-textured skin of her breasts and, bolder, down over her ribs until he was gently massaging the soft flesh of her belly.

The woman's beach jacket had fallen wide open and she was naked and writhing her hips gently. With a deft movement, she untwisted the towel covering his loins so that it fell away and his pulsing, fiery-tipped penis shot into view.

Avelino was too overcome now with the chill of anticipation to feel embarrassed. He felt as if he were being led by the hand blindly down into an inferno.

With them both breathing as if they had swum for an hour, the woman caught one of his hands and moved it down over the triangle of blonde hair at the junction of her thighs. She moved it a little further still and then caught it between her thighs in a fleshy imprisonment. She clasped it with her thighs for a while, pressing, relaxing, rubbing, wriggling and then she let her thighs fall apart and kissed him fiercely.

Tentatively Avelino tickled the inside of her thighs with the tips of his fingers, exploring, creeping up a little. She pushed her lips down toward his hand, trying to precipitate his progress. But at the sudden sensation of moist, soft flesh Avelino stopped, a little afraid of his ignorance. He brushed the moistness for some time while the woman panted. It became more moist to his touch.

'Go on,' the woman encouraged him between gasps. 'That's right.'

Avelino wormed his finger up against the softness and it opened so that his finger was suddenly gulped into her body. She dug her tongue into his mouth, whimpering slightly and he moved his finger right into her.

He was trembling. His finger was right inside her. He could feel the soft contraction against his flesh. The moist channel in which he was pressing his finger and wriggling it around, opened out, seemed to grow larger and wetter as the minutes passed.

'Come on—now!' the woman whispered sharply.

She practically hauled him onto her so that he could feel the soft warmth of her flesh like a sensual mattress beneath him.

His penis was somewhere down between her open thighs. It seemed to be too low to enter but he could do nothing. He felt overcome by a paralysis. His whole body was trembling and his hands, grasping her shoulders, shook.

The woman drew up her thighs around his hips so that he could feel their soft, clasping pressure.

'Move up a little,' she whispered.

As he slithered achingly up her body, her hand came down under her thighs and met his penis in the shock of unexpected contact. She held it a moment, fondling it and then directed it at her open vagina.

Avelino, eyes closed, his penis seeming to sing like telegraph wires, felt himself drawn against the central chasm of her body.

'Now—push in,' she commanded softly.

He pushed and felt the soft warmth of vague substance around the tip of his organ. And then there was a pressure and then a hot breaking through as he entered fully. The entry was such agony that he felt he wanted to cry. His lips breathed the word 'wonderful!' and other wordless sounds.

The woman had gasped as he took possession of her and now, moaning, she pulled him higher still on her, pushing her sensual core down onto his stiff penetration.

She kissed him now, clasping his shoulders as in a vice, thrusting her tongue deep into his mouth as if she wanted him to swallow it completely. He felt her hips swivelling and undulating under him as his penis was squeezed in contraction, released slightly in expansion of her enclosing channel.

Avelino's head rolled on hers as he dug deeper and deeper into her. His penis was like a great fire burning with a fierce heat. It was agony and bliss, unbearable yet indispensable, a dark nightmare and yet beautifully unforgettable.

The woman pulled her thighs higher, level with his chest. She moved her hands down to his tensing buttocks and pushed them, exhorting him to move farther into her.

Avelino gave himself over to the wild ecstasy. Embarrassment could play no part in such a sensual abandonment and soon he was aware only of his penis, tight and bursting, in her body, of her hands squeezing his shoulders, his back, his buttocks, and her lips with the mad abandoned tongue in his mouth.

The woman grunted and groaned as she writhed nudely under him and it seemed so natural for him to breathe furiously:

'I love you, I love you, I love you,' over and again as his face crushed hers.

Avelino ground his organ into the coaxing passage

with greater and greater strength until the hair at his loins had met hers and there was no more length to go. Her hand came down again under her thighs and gently held his swaying testicles with a sensual shock which brought a fresh gasp from his open mouth.

With his knees spread, now, on either side of her buttocks, he wriggled his hips like a dancer, ramming into the receptive channel from shades of angle, experimenting in a blind way for greater penetration, greater pressure.

At one moment he became briefly aware of the sun on the sea, the shade on the rocks and the incredible fact of himself athwart this attractive woman whom he hardly knew, having intercourse with her.

Below him her head was moving from side to side, eyes were half closed, lips mouthing, shoulders swaying in her passion. Head, eyes, lips, shoulders all an incredible, beautiful dream—and he plunged his head down once more to her and lost himself in the abyss of carnality.

The woman's gasps began to grow more continuous and her hips began to jerk against him as if she had lost control of them. Her nails dug into the flesh of his shoulders so that it hurt him with a pain which added to the sweet agony of the union.

Her gasps became a long, soft whimper through which she implored him:

'Come on, come on, come on.'

Her further abandonment brought forth automatic echoes from Avelino. The feeling and sight of her lust-wracked body seemed to numb the whole of his body except for his loins. And there grew a great reservoir of sensation, gathering behind the sharp pain of his probing penis.

'Quickly, quickly,' the woman breathed. 'Together, together.'

She thrust her tongue again into his mouth and flickered it in and out, moving it along his lips.

From the sweating numbness of his body, Avelino, panting uncontrollably, felt all sensation pulled down to his penis. It was the only part of him that had feeling. His gasps developed into wounded, agonised 'Oh's as he thrust and thrust. He felt he could not get far enough into the woman with his one thick finger of flesh which could reach into her and make them one. Inside his loins he felt the growing of pain, growing, growing to bursting point. He cried out and the woman panted 'Now!' And then with a great shudder in his loins, the sperm was flowing with scalding warmth through his tube and spurting in needles of pain far up into the woman's belly.

As his flood swept raggedly into her, she strained her hips up at him, crying out at her fulfilment, while her lips tried to fasten on his, failed in her excitement, and her teeth dug into his neck.

His movements dwindled and dwindled while the woman's hips relaxed. Her thighs continued to clasp him and her hands to caress his neck until his final hip-jerk had passed and his body subsided exhaustedly onto hers.

They lay together for some time with her stroking his neck gently. He noticed that the sun had withdrawn farther out to sea and he felt a slight return of his previous embarrassment. He was not sure how to move off her, although he felt he must be heavy upon her. Inside him, apart from the embarrassment was a feeling of wonder and achievement at what had happened. But he could not bring himself to look at her.

'Look at me.'

It was as if she had read his thoughts.

'How does it feel to be no longer a virgin.'

Avelino stared at her searchingly for a moment. There was a warmth in her eyes which melted his embarrassment and in answer he kissed her gently on the cheek.

She laughed quietly, clasped him fiercely against her and then whispered:

'We'd better have a quick swim before we go.'

They swam naked out to the sun and afterwards he collected his clothes and they climbed the wall of hills which enclosed the town, to the little café with its open-air terrace overlooking the bay.

The Altar of Venus

One afternoon as I was lazily debating the advisability of commencing preparations for my return, my detective friend presented himself. We chatted a bit and then, putting on my hat and coat, I accompanied him downstairs, intending to have a parting drink with him before saying good-bye. We seated ourselves at a table in front of a little café, and ordered our favourite liquors. In the process of consuming these, my companion suddenly leaned toward me and whispered:

'Glance over your left shoulder in a moment at the girl sitting at the table just behind you. I'll tell you something about her after we get away from here.'

A moment later I glanced casually around. Sitting by herself sipping some coloured concoction through a straw was as neat a little Parisienne as I had seen during my stay in France. Apparently eighteen or nineteen years old, dressed in a very short skirt, her shapely legs clad in black silk hose, and wearing a blouse of white crepe-de-chine, so diaphanous that the pink, lace-edged brassiere shielding her exuberant bubbies was plainly visible, she formed a picture whose details registered themselves with lightning rapidity in one brief glance.

Not wishing to be caught staring I turned away, and a few minutes later looked around again, this time concentrating my gaze on her face. It was entirely at variance with the extreme coquetry of her apparel, and the careless elevation of her skirt, for her features were demure, modest, almost angelic in their pure beauty.

She was altogether too pretty not to awaken my instant admiration and after I had paid the account and we were out of earshot I exclaimed:

'The sweetest little darling I've seen since I've been here!'

My companion smiled cynically.

'Sweet is right! Entirely too sweet. She's a crook.'

'A crook?' I repeated, incredulously.

'Yes, a crook. And a very clever one.'

It seemed incredible and I could scarcely reconcile the facts as he related them with that demure sweet face and modest downcast eyes I had seen at the little sidewalk café.

'And she'd have cleaned you of every franc you possess,' he answered with a dry smile.

'I'm not so sure it wouldn't be worth it at that,' I added, as I recalled the multiple and diverse charms of the exquisite little houri which were visible to the eye, and mentally conjured up naked visions of others hidden beneath the silken trappings.

'Ha!' retorted my companion, 'That's the funny part of it. None of the birds she snares ever gets as much as a feel of it. She's really married to this fellow she works with, and completely infatuated with him. All the suckers get for their money is to see her half naked for a few moments before the husband shows up. He's always right on time.'

'How do they manage that?'

'Some system of signals probably. We'll get them sooner or later.'

After I retired that night I lay awake for some time thinking of the girl. There was something about her which had touched a responsive chord in my being, and it was not to be suppressed even by the undisputable charges of my detective friend. And the more I thought about her, the stronger became my desire. I even studied the possibility of making her acquaintance and endeavouring to win her affection, but the idea was discarded with the recollection of my friend's statement to the effect that she was deeply enamoured with her accomplice. Finally, just as I was dropping off to sleep, the gem of an idea came to me.

The next day I called on my friend and told him I had decided to remain in Paris a week or two longer.

'What's happened? Something new in skirts?' he asked, astutely.

'No . . . that is . . . well, I'll tell you . . . : that girl we saw yesterday . . .'

'What!' he broke in, 'A waste of time, son. You couldn't open her legs with five thousand francs. And it wouldn't be worth it, even if you could,' he added, laughing.

'Wait a minute, now, before you start laughing. I've got a plan. It may open her legs, as you so crudely put it, without costing a single franc!'

'What is this plan?' he asked, cynically.

'Before I explain it, I want a little information.'

'What do you want to know?'

'Do you know where she takes these Lotharios for their cleaning?'

'She takes them to the apartment she and her husband occupy. They move right after each operation. We know their present location.'

'Do you know whether there are any other people involved, that is, have they any confederates who participate in any way?'

112

'No; they work by themselves. They don't need any help the way they handle it.'

'You said yesterday they probably have some system of signals that enables the man to know the exact moment to come in. Do you think he is already in the building, or does he come in from outside?'

'I can't answer that but one of the men who talked to us after deciding that he had been 'framed' said that the fellow stepped into the room with an overcoat on and a travelling bag in his hand, as though he had just returned from a journey.'

'Do you know where she could be found, in case I wanted to get her attention as a prospective victim?'

'At any given moment, no, but she frequents cafés, in the neighbourhood we were in yesterday. But why waste your time and risk your money on a wild goose chase? Aren't there enough pretty girls on the streets of Paris without wasting time on this particular little crook?'

'I'm not interested in street chippies. See if you can't find out whether the husband secretes himself on the premises during the preliminaries or whether he comes in from outside. The practicability of the plan I have in mind depends mostly on this one detail. After you find out about it I'll explain everything.

'All right, I'll try, you're just wasting your time, son. Don't do anything foolish.'

'I'll not make any move without consulting you first. If you think it imprudent I'll drop it. I'd have to have your co-operation anyway.'

'Well, I'll be in to see you tomorrow evening, and let you know if I've been able to dig up anything.'

I was waiting impatiently in the lobby the following evening when he arrived, and as we seated ourselves in a secluded corner, I handed him a cigar, lit one myself, and waited expectantly.

'I've got the information you wanted, son. The man comes in from the street. They either have their operations nicely timed, or else a signal of some kind is passed from the window, which, by the way, fronts . on the street. Their rooms are on the third floor.'

'Fine!' I exclaimed, 'Exactly what I was hoping! One more question and I'll tell you my scheme. Could you, on some pretext, arrest that chap and have him detained temporarily?'

'I could get an order to pick him up for investigation . . . but what good would it do?' he replied, doubtfully. 'We have no kind of case against him, and he would be out in a short while.'

'Okay! Now I'll tell you what I have in mind. I propose to attract her attention with a display of money. If she rises to the bait, and does me the honour to accept me as a prospective victim, I'll play into her hands. Now here is where you come in. When the appointment is made you'll be on the job and follow us at a discreet distance. When we enter the building you'll wait outside, and when hubby shows up, nab him and remove him quietly from the scene. And I'll guarantee that if I'm assured of an hour or two alone with this tricky Lorelei, safe from the intrusion of wandering husbands, I'll have better success than my predecessors had. What about it? Will you help me?'

'Your idea is good in theory, but it won't work in practice!'

'Why won't it work?'

'Because she's too clever. When her man fails to show up she'll know something has happened, and find a way to get rid of you.'

'She won't dare make any racket and I won't be so easy to shake. Are you willing to help me give it a try?'

'Of course! I'll help you! Make a date with her, if you can, and keep me posted. It won't cost anything to try, though it will probably knock our chances of landing the girls by frightening them off.

'What's the difference,' I rejoined, 'your infernal bastille is full enough already.'

Before he left that evening we perfected the details of the plot.

All the next day, I loitered around the café where we had seen her previously, carrying with me a flamboyant roll of money, small notes on the inside, a few more pretentious ones on the outside. But my vigil was in vain. In the evening my friend called me by phone, and I was obliged to report an unsuccessful day.

'It's the neighbourhood she frequents,' he said encouragingly, 'If you keep your eyes open you'll spot her.'

It was not until mid-afternoon of the fourth day that my patience was rewarded, when suddenly, out of nowhere apparently, appeared the object of my search. She seated herself indolently at a table in front of a small café, and gave an order to the attendant.

With beating heart and studied nonchalance I followed her, accommodating myself at a nearby table. With but a casual glance in her direction I ordered a bottle of vin rouge, leaned back in my chair, and pretended to be watching the passers-by. When I had finished the wine, I summoned the waiter and asked for a second bottle. And at the same time I brought forth the 'flash' roll from my pocket, peeled off one of the larger bills, and tendered it in payment. When he returned, I carelessly flipped a generous tip on the table, trusting that the damsel was observing my affluence and lavishness. A few moments later I glanced as though by accident in her direction. Our eyes met. She returned my gaze for a few seconds, and then demurely lowered her vision. I straightened up, twisted my chair about slightly, and continued to eye her from time to time, endeavouring to indicate with my glances the admiration she had inspired.

For some minutes this little farce was kept up. Finally she smiled at me—and there was an invitation in the smile.

I arose and approaching her table, begged her in my best French to permit me to join her. She consented modestly and was soon laughing delightedly at my efforts to pay her expressive compliments in French.

When we separated that afternoon, an appointment had been arranged for another meeting the following day.

For nearly a week our mid-afternoon meetings continued, and during this interval our friendship progressed rapidly. I missed no opportunities to convey an impression of prosperity and affluence, making many allusions to imaginary possessions, and business interests in England, and sighed regretfully over the fact that our acquaintance would be of short duration because of the urgency of my early return to London. And night by night, I reported the developments of the day to my companion in the conspiracy.

The sixth day she confided pensively that our visits were soon to terminate as she had just received a telegram from her husband announcing his return the following Saturday, and I knew that the moment had arrived to speak my little piece. With all the passionate ardour I could summon, I exclaimed:

'Mon cherie, I just can't give you up without something to remember you by! You know I'm returning to England next week, and if your husband is going to be here, I will probably have to leave without seeing you. Darling, don't think me bold, but couldn't we go somewhere and have a day or two together, all by ourselves? Some nice quiet place, where we can be alone, and spend everything of the time just loving each other?'

The little hypocrite wiped an imaginary tear from her eye and assured me soulfully that she had never, never done such a thing before, and that I must think she was a light woman to have even suggested any such thing, that if it weren't for the deep affection I had inspired in her heart, she would be greatly offended, and so on.

'I know it sounds bold, darling, but I'm just crazy about you, and my only hope is that you'll be generous!' I pleaded.

'Well,' she finally agreed, 'I believe my husband would kill me if he ever found out but . . . I'll tell you what we can do. I'll take you to my apartment and we can spend a few hours together. It wouldn't be safe for me to go to a hotel because somebody might see me and tell my husband. You can meet me here Thursday afternoon.

That night I saw my friend, and advised him that the date for the trimming of the sucker had been definitely set and he promised to make all necessary arrangements to take care of his end of the programme.

The anxiously-awaited hour arrived, and

117

punctually, in accordance with her promise, she was there waiting for me. And across the street idling before a shop window was my detective friend. She and I got into a taxi, and though I did not look behind I knew he was not very far in the background.

After a winding drive we drew up before a tall edifice, and as we got out, another taxi passed us slowly and came to a stop near the next corner.

We entered the building and stepped into an automatic lift. At the touch of a button the car moved silently upward and a few moments later she was conducting me down a lengthy corridor, before the last door of which she stopped, lifted a key in the lock, and we were inside.

Evidently there was no intention to delay things, for she lost no time in getting down to business. Seating herself on my lap, she pressed her lips to mine, favouring me with a voluptuous tongue caress which aroused every primordial instinct in my body, in fact so ravishingly intoxicating was the caress that for a moment I forgot, in the swirl of my emotions that it was simply calculated to render me as an easy victim to a blackmailing scheme.

Her next move was to withdraw one of her breasts from its silken shield. Tilting it upward with her hand she pressed the nipple between my lips. To the accompaniment of expressive sighs and voluptuous shivers on her part I sucked the protuberant little tit and played my tongue over the rosy circle which surrounded it.

The movement was emotional and one of my hands, which had been resting on the bare flesh of her leg, just above the hose, began an upward exploration under the semi-transparent garment. But before it got very far, she detained me, suggesting that we retire to the bedroom where I could remove my clothing and be more comfortable.

Carrying the decanter of liqueur with her she conducted me to the privacy of the sleeping quarters of the apartment.

Placing my faith in the efficacy of my detective friend's co-operation, I slipped off my clothing, and at her invitation lay down on the bed. No sooner had I done this than she stepped to the window, and closed the Venetian shutters.

'Ah,' I thought, 'the signal for hubby.'

She returned to the side of the bed and slowly unfastened the diaphanous garment which, when removed, revealed a seductive picture. But it was not entirely a nude picture. For in addition to the silk brassière whose form-sustaining pockets fitted her pretty breasts as though moulded over them, and her hose and slippers, she had on another article of apparel of old construction which fitted like a glove about her hips and thighs. It was something like the abbreviated tights feminine exhibitional dancers use which, though effective in concealing the most intimate parts of the body, leave all else exposed. Enough of this girl's body was visible to reveal a physical perfection worthy of sincere admiration and, crook or no crook, she presented as pretty a spectacle as ever delighted a masculine eye or excited the envy of feminine one.

Alas, she was doomed to wait somewhat longer than she imagined at that moment, for down on the street below, a travel-stained gentleman, in a dusty ulster, a small valise in his hand, returning unexpectedly from a long journey, walked right into the arms of a detective who was lounging in the doorway, and was quickly whisked into a waiting cab. He raved, swore, threatened, and pleaded in turn, but to no avail. He was not even permitted to use the telephone in the police station, despite his last, despairing plea.

Sufficient time had now elapsed to assure me that the gentleman's detention had been realized without a hitch, and I felt free to make a few moves of my own. My only preoccupation was that she might possibly raise a clamour which would be prejudicial to my plans. But in this moment, as though the heavens themselves were in sympathy with me, or actuated by her own reference to rain, the room darkened—and preceded by a sharp gust of wind a torrential deluge began to fall. It clattered and thundered against the sides of the building and the Venetian shutters over the windows and I knew that as long as it lasted any unusual noise in the room would be effectively cloaked from other occupants of the building.

Applying my mouth to the nipple of one of her breasts to distract her attention, I reached down and began to search for the buttons which would release the tight garment that up to the present had obstructed both my visions and my fingers. But I could not find them nor did I discover just where or how this singular garment was fastened. I tried to slip my hand up under it but it was skin tight and resisted my effort.

As she made no motion to assist me and comprehending that she had no intention of doing so, I decided to remove it myself without wasting any more time in search of mysteriously concealed hooks or fastenings. Inserting my fingers under the waist band, I got a firm hold, and gave a quick, stout jerk. The garment ripped straight down the front.

The results were electrical. In a second's time she

was converted into a scratching, snarling, clawing little wildcat. It was all I could do to prevent her from doing me some actual physical harm before I got her clamped down in a manner which rendered her helpless.

'Cochon!' she gasped, her face livid with rage. 'You've torn my panties!'

'I couldn't get them off any other way, sweetness!'

'Let me up!' she hissed.

'What do you want to get up for? Aren't we going to do something first?'

'I've changed my mind! Let me up instantly! I am afraid my husband is coming!'

'But you told me he wasn't coming until Saturday!'

'I have a presentment he's coming to-day! He may be here any minute!'

'Well, if you're afraid he may come, let's hurry up and finish before he gets here!'

Securing her two wrists firmly with one hand, I reached down with the other and pulled away the remnants of the torn panties. So closely had she kept me occupied during the brief struggle that I had not even had a glimpse of what the torn garment revealed—but now I glanced downward, and received a surprise.

Her cunt was as devoid of hair as that of a baby. I placed a hand on it, and found that it had been cleanly and neatly shaved within recent hours.

The discovery was interesting for I knew that when Parisian girls keep this particular portion of their anatomy shaved off it means that they are submitting their bodies to a certain caress which hair rather tends to interfere with.

In plain words, somebody is sucking them.

The contact of my hand galvanized her into fresh action and I had all I could do for several minutes to subdue her again. Finally, heaving and panting, half suffocated, she lay still. And a moment later, somewhat to my surprise, the tension of her muscles relaxed, and the angry expression disappeared from her face.

'You're hurting my arms,' she murmured plaintively.

Cautiously, alert for some new move, I relaxed my grip slightly.

She snuggled up to me and at the same time extended her hand downward. Her fingers closed about my cock and clasped it firmly. Still suspicious of this sudden change in tactics, but seduced by the contact of her soft hand, I adjusted myself to a more comfortable position by her side and awaited developments. The hand on my cock began to move back and forth, and the manipulation set a series of pleasant little thrills to darting through my body. Instinctively I hugged her closer. The sensation was so agreeable, that for a moment I forgot her unexpected change in comportment and abandoned myself to the caress. Soon the pleasurable sensations intensified and her hand began to move more swiftly. And, in a flash, I understood what she was up to.

The little fox was attempting to jack me off, hoping to get rid of me in this fashion.

Adroitly, I slipped one of my knees between hers, and then, before she had time to realize what I was doing I had her legs apart and was on top of her, with the head of my cock right against her cunt.

'Oh!' she exclaimed, when she felt it penetrating her, 'Wait! Wait! Don't do it to me that way! I'm

122

afraid of getting a baby! Take it out! Take it out! I'll suck it instead!' ·

The offer was tempting, but remembering her elusiveness, I thought better not to surrender the ground already won. I gave a shove, and the result of the shove was that I found my cock sheathed in positively the tightest little cunt, not presumably virgin, of its entire career.

'Oh!' she gasped, 'My husband will kill you for this!'

Curses, threats, epithets and maledictions poured from her lips in a steady torrent. Indifferent alike to threats and revilements, I worked my cock in and out. The tight constriction was delicious, and the obscene epithets with which she continued to shower me, instead of dampening my ardour, seemed to stimulate it. It was a unique experience. When the exquisite sensations reached the maximum of their intensity I stopped moving and let the tension relax. When the equilibrium was restored I began again, pushing my cock in and drawing it out with slow measured movements, calculated to prolong the pleasure as long as possible.

Meanwhile, the flow of curses and revilements continued without interruption. But now I began to note something incongruous. She was lifting her bottom slightly to meet my thrusts! And between her revilements and the movement of my cock as it slid in and out of the tight, little hole, was a curious synchronism—a rhythmic relation. It brought to my mind the recollection of a funny story I had once heard, about a little boy caught in the act of masturbating himself by a maid servant who reprimanded him with a lugubrious warning to the effect that he would die if he did that. To which the boy, too far along with the business in hand to stop, replied:

'I don't care if I . . . do . . . die . . . do . . . die . . . do . . . die . . . do-die do-die do-die-do-die!'

While my cock was going in, she held her breath. And while it was coming out she gasped some epithet. But at the same time her bottom was coming up to meet each thrust.

I smiled down into her face. She looked at me angrily in the eye for a moment, and then suddenly her expression changed. She lay still for a few minutes and then, with a tremulous little 'O-o-o-h!' began to raise and lower her hips with greater energy. I increased the rapidity of my own movements and at the same time released her hands which, until now, I had pinned down tightly with my own. Her arms came up and folded about my neck.

I had conquered the little vixen.

A moment later, heralded by several passionate exclamations, orgasm overtook her, and as I perceived it, I let go also.

When the final tremors of our mutual orgastic exaltation had died away, she sank limply back on the bed, one white forearm doubled across her face. The little red lips which but a short time before were hurling maledictions at me, were quiet now. In silence, I slowly disengaged myself and rising from the bed, began to put on my clothing. I was almost dressed before she stirred, then sitting up suddenly, she glanced downward, to where some starchy fluid was trickling slowly down between her thighs onto the white linen of the bed. She sprang to her feet exclaiming:

'Oh! You've probably given me a baby!'

Precipitately, she rushed into the bathroom from whence the sound of splashing water spoke eloquently of her precautions to avoid unwanted progeny.

I had completed my dressing when she came back into the room with a towel stuck between her legs. The spectacle she presented as she stood there eyeing me in a puzzled, undecided way, her cheeks flushed and her short black curls in disorder about her face was extremely enticing and for a moment I almost regretted having put on my clothes. Suddenly, however, I noticed tears glistening on her eyelashes. A wave of compassion swept over me, and my complacency at having bested her changed to pity. She had tried to trick me and had failed. But she was a woman. More than that—a young and beautiful one, naked and crying. What combination imaginable could be more effective to move a masculine heart?

I had intended to leave quickly for I had been in the place longer than I expected and knew my detective friend would be uneasy, not knowing just what might have transpired. But I was stirred by her melancholy demeanour. I had outwitted her, and could afford to be generous. Seating myself in a chair I said in kindly tones: 'Come here, little one. I want to talk to you a minute before I go.'

Hesitatingly she approached the chair in which I was sitting. I put an arm about her naked waist and, taking one of her hands in mine, said:

'You're far too sweet a girl to be mixed up in such games as this. The police know all about it and they're just waiting to surprise you. Get out of it, my dear, before they have a chance. Tell your husband to find some way to make a living without exposing you to such danger.'

'Are you a policeman?' she gasped in a frightened whisper.

'No, darling, I'm not a policeman. But I have a friend who is, and he told me all about it. I knew right from the start.'

To my consternation she began to weep in earnest. The tears streaked down her cheeks and fell on my hand. Touched and embarrassed, I drew her down on my lap and tried to console her.

'Now don't cry little one. There's no great harm done. There's still time to fix things up.'

'Is my husband in jail?' she asked, tremulously.

'Don't worry about him. He'll be back in the morning. Maybe I can fix it so he'll be back tonight.'

'Oh, will you, surely?'

'I will if I can, but if I do, you must promise me you won't let him put you in such a situation as this again.'

'I promise! I promise!' she exclaimed heartfeltly and then, as an afterthought struck her, she asked timidly:

'Will he know what you . . . what . . . I mean, we did?'

'Not unless you tell him, my dear. He has no way of knowing just what happened. You can tell him you sent me away when he didn't come. Heaven knows,' I added, smiling, 'you certainly tried hard enough!'

'Oh! you're a good man! I'm sorry I tried to fool you!'—and again she burst into tears. 'The others (sob) weren't (sob) like you; they were just (sob) fresh old men!'

'I expected maybe they had it coming to them all right, but they will make trouble for you sooner or later, sweet,' and as the tears continued to flow, I took my handkerchief and endeavoured to dry her cheeks, soothing her with what reassurances I could.

Suddenly she threw her arms about my neck and began to kiss me.

'You're a good man,' she repeated, and then, lowering her eyes, she whispered: 'If you want me to, I'll do it with you again before you go!'

Surprised and pleased, I glanced at my watch. It was getting later and every minute my stay was prolonged would increase my friend's anxiety. He might even, if I failed to appear soon, show up at the apartment. At the same time, the virginal aspect of that nude, shaven little cleft awakened powerful temptations. I placed the palm of my hand over it tentatively. Little electric-like shivers chased themselves up and down my spine at the touch, and my cock stiffened out in anticipation.

'Come on if you want to. One more won't make any difference now, anyway.'

'What do you know about psychic stimulation?' I asked, my thoughts reverting to Irma and her theories.

'Psychic stimulation?' she repeated, wonderingly, 'What do you mean by psychic stimulation?'

'Oh, nothing much,' I replied. 'Darling, I'm British but I like France and I like some of the French customs. I have little time left, but if you're really willing, I'd like to do it to you with my tongue.'

'All right!' she answered tensely, 'I'd rather have it that way. I'm terribly afraid of getting a baby!' and she slipped off my knees.

Placing herself on the bed she put a pillow under her hips, separated her legs and in less time than it takes to tell, my face was down between her thighs, and my lips united with another pair of lips, which ran up and down, instead of crosswise. Two soft little hands clasped my cheeks as my tongue penetrated and explored the secret depths. And when its activities were transferred to the tiny little protuberance in the upper extremity of the naked incision, she writhed and moaned with ecstasy, and the little hands gripped my cheeks convulsively.

'Oh!' she gasped, 'you're making me come again!'

The warm flesh against my mouth began to exude moisture. Her body stiffened out, maintaining its rigidity for a moment and then relaxed.

I got up and with the towel she had cast aside, wiped off my lips.

'Before I go, tell me your name, darling. Your right name, I mean!'

She flushed at the recollection of the false name previously given me, and replied:

'Georgina.'

'Georgina,' I said, 'if your number wasn't already drawn it would be easy to fall for you in a big way.' And my words were sincere.

'It looks like I already have fallen for you,' she responded pensively.

'Thank you, sweet. I'll go now and see about your husband.'

A feeling of sadness, almost of regret, that I would never see her again enveloped me as I walked rapidly down the street.

'Sentimental fool!' I said to myself, endeavouring to shake off the gloomy sentiments which had invaded my thoughts. I had got what I went after, but in my heart I knew I was taking something away with me which I had not calculated on, and that the memory of a little figure, with its disordered curls and wet cheeks against my face, its breasts, firm and white, pressed to my heart while I looked down over her shoulder at the softly rounded curve of a naked bottom and the lissom swell of daintily sculptured legs, glistening through the black sheen of her hose, would haunt me throughout the years to come.

Fifteen minutes later I was at a telephone, and when the call was connected, the uneasy voice of my detective friend inquired:

'What in the world happened? I was about to take a man and go out there. Thought maybe that little witch had stuck a knife in your ribs. She stalled you off, didn't she?'

'No, she didn't stall me off. I'll tell you later.'

'Well . . . I'll be . . . did you really . . . ?'

'Yes, yes; I'll tell you all about it when I see you. But that fellow . . . where is he?'

'Detained for investigation.'

'Could you get him out tonight, if you wanted to?'

'Tonight! Why . . . I could, I expect, but what's the rush?'

'Get him out, if you want to do me a favour. It's important to me. I've given my word, and I want to make it good. I'll get a cab and be down soon. Try and have him loose by the time I get there.'

And I hung up the receiver.

The Devil's Advocate

She draws her chair around the corner of your desk. It is very important to her that you get a good view of her excellent legs, and she says 'Mister Garnett . . .' Her red hair spreads around her head like a halo, and her voice is that of an angel. 'I'm in terrible trouble, and you're the only person who can get me out of it.' She allows two big tears to well up in those innocent green eyes. 'You see, I know this man—Abie the Goat they call him—and right now he and some of his friends are in jail on a counterfeiting rap—charge, and they're afraid the district attorney is going to throw the book at them. They told me to get the best criminal lawyer in town to get them off. Of course I came straight to you.

'Of course,' you echo softly.

'For an ordinary lawyer, it would be a real tough case. But for you, it'll be a breeze. I just know you can get them off without half trying.'

She draws her skirt a bit higher and crosses her legs, showing a generous portion of white meat. The fan which you have set in action against the mid-afternoon heat ruffles the frills on her blouse, drawing your attention to them. She leans forward encouragingly, and her breasts strain maturely against the black gossamer fabric of her shirtwaist, so cool and soft against the crisp white tailored suit. You have to give her credit, she has a quick eye for the direction of your gaze, and she's anxious to be as obliging as she can. You look far into her blouse through the transparent material. The two melons on display are really ripe. These well-kept molls have what it takes and know how to dress it up.

Slowly, deliberately, you light a cigarette. You don't offer angel-face one. If she wants a cigarette, she can smoke her own. Garnett's Law: 'Never do anything for anybody unless you're sure that the profit derived from your generosity will far exceed the expenditure.'

You lean back in your chair and assume a business-like expression. 'Of course,' you say, 'I'll have to speak to your pals before I can agree to defend them. Then, if I decide to take the case, I'll want a ten thousand dollar retainer plus two hundred a day and expenses for every day I spend in court. And, no matter what I decide to do, I'll want another hundred for today's conference, and for my visit with your boyfriend.'

The tears are back, for real this time. Her lower lip quivers and her voice trembles as she says: 'He's not my boyfriend, and I haven't got that kind of dough. Not now. Once you get Abie off, I can pay you whatever you want. But now . . . a hundred bills is all I've got in the world.'

You study her face for a minute, watching the silence grating on her nerves. Then you say, 'If he's not your boyfriend, just what is your relationship to Abie the Goat?'

'Relationship?' she echoes, like she's never heard the word before. 'Why there is no relationship between me and Abie. He's just somebody I know, like an acquaintance. You don't think that I'd get involved with anybody like a counterfeiter, do you?'

What you are thinking about her right now would

melt even this little ice cube's composure. But you're in a kindly mood, so you don't say anything; you just smile.

'Please, Mr Garnett, you must believe me. My friends are all very high class types. I don't ordinarily have anything to do with people such as Abie the Goat. I certainly wouldn't have even spoken to him if I had known what kind of person he was. But I must get him off. I just must. It's a matter of life and death!' Her eyes widen as she realises she's said too much.

You give her another minute of silence and then you ask, keeping your voice very low, 'Whose life . . . or death?'

'Mine.' Her own voice is scarcely audible above the whirring of the fan. It's her turn at the silence bit. She waits for more than a minute before she says: 'All right, I'll tell you the whole thing. You see, I met Abie through my room-mate. Of course, like I said before, I didn't know he was mixed up in the counterfeiting business, honest I didn't. Anyway, I went out with him a couple of times, just for drinks and laughs, that's all. This was about a month ago. The first time I saw him, I mean. Then, after the couple of times we went out together, he stopped calling. Well, I didn't think anything of it, except maybe he didn't think too much more of me than I did of him. He wasn't my type, you see.'

Her glance makes it very clear that you are her type. How flattering.

'Anyway,' she goes on, 'I'd actually forgotten all about him until yesterday, when this man came to see me. A man I'd never seen before. He said he was a friend of Abie the Goat's, and that Abie and some other guys were in jail on this counterfeiting rap.'

By now her high-class pretensions have fallen by the wayside, and you notice with inner amusement how easily she has slipped into a vernacular she claims to know nothing about. She is saying: 'He told me that Abie said to get him a lawyer, the best there is. If I didn't the man said, I'd be killed. So you see, Mr Garnett, my life is at stake. And you're the only person who can save it.' She gazes at you appealingly, and the skirt slips a little higher. 'I know what a mess I've got into. I should've been more careful about going out with a man I didn't know anything about. I've been a very foolish girl. You know, if my daddy were alive today, he'd probably spank me for my foolishness, big as I am?'

'So you think you ought to be spanked?' You take a final drag from your cigarette and glance along the line from her knee to her hip, the full line of her nicely rounded thigh. Her skirt is drawn tight along the upper part of it; it looks as though a hand applied there would cause a fine, resounding smack.

'Don't you?' she asks you coyly. She watches you grinding out your cigarette in the heavy glass ashtray, and a little smile comes to her lips. That smile would play hell with a jury . . . an all-male jury, of course.

'So you want me to be the big, understanding, gently reproving daddy, do you? You wouldn't by any chance be trying to arrange for my services on the promise of how warm that little fanny of yours can get, would you?'

You reach out suddenly and pinch her thigh. She doesn't move her leg, but she makes her eyes bigger. You can see her calculating whether to register coy surprise or lascivious promise. Her purse drops to the floor and she reaches to pick it up, stretching her leg out towards you. You feel the silk clad muscles under your hand, and you run the hand under her skirt. 'Come here and sit on my lap.'

She's certainly prompt. Her buttocks spread comfortably on your thighs, and she puts one arm around your neck, pressing her breasts against your chest. Your hand fits around one of her buttocks and squeezes. She's pleasantly soft.

Next, you feel along her hip and down her thigh to the knee. You raise her skirt and look at the milky prettiness of her legs, the laciness of her high-cut panties and the swelling temptation which they mask. You open her blouse and remove one of her breasts from the brassiere. You fondle it for a moment, then tuck it back into its cradle.

'I'm going to spank you just the way your daddy would,' you tell her. You remove her gently from your lap, and brush the papers from the desk into the top drawer. 'Come on, lift your skirt.'

You look at her standing there, placidly holding her skirt up, awaiting your pleasure. She isn't a bit frightened. When they put her together, they left out fright and put in a double portion of shrewd whorishness.

You make her turn around so that you can see your target. And quite a target it is. Just the way you like them. Two full, white globes. A beautifully matched set. This is going to be even more fun than you'd thought.

You lock the door. Then you flip on the intercom and tell Jackson that you don't want to be disturbed. You lean casually against the desk and watch her standing there, her skirt still up around her hips. You tell her to take her panties part-way down. You figure she'd take them off and hang them out the window if you asked her to. But there's no necessity for that. And you're a reasonable man.

She complies with your request, and you tell her to bend over the desk. She places her head on her purse and grasps the edges of the desk with her hands, so that her buttocks rise until they're well within your reach. You fondle them in turn, then slap them briskly with your whole palm.

'Ooooooh!'

'Not coyness, but shock. You didn't hurt her, but you did surprise the hell out of her. You point out to her the impracticality of yelling in an attorney's office, and right away she's apologetic. She promises to be quiet. She won't make the slightest sound, she says. She knows that she deserves a spanking, she says. You resume.

The lace panties flutter. Her heels fly up. She reacts very nicely to the spanking. You give it to her mildly, not really hurting her. But the slaps do sting a bit—you can tell from the bright red splotches that are appearing on her white, satiny skin.

You spank her for a long time because, you tell her, she has been a very bad girl this time. Fun for the feebleminded, you think. And then you notice that your penis is rapidly hardening. Funny that it should be sexually exciting to paddle a girl's bottom. But you like the idea of having a girl whom you've known less than twenty minutes so much under your power that you can slap her bare bottom.

She has stopped yelling, just as she said she would. But she sucks her breath in hard each time your hand makes contact with her flesh. She doesn't particularly care for spanking, but she's far too old a hand at high-class whoring to complain, expecially since she's extremely anxious to please you.

You don't disappoint the lady. You unbutton your trousers and take out what's inside. The large, up-thrust instrument looks a little ridiculous against your well-creased trousers and fitted jacket.

She looks at it and at you. You tell her to lie down again. She does, and you come up behind her, slapping your rigid tool gently against her buttocks. She seems to like the feel of it, for she twists her head back and gives you a nice, lewd wink. What a sweet little tart she is.

You look at the delightful cavern between her legs and insert a finger in it. She appears to like that, too. She wriggles and clutches the edges of the desk wildly. Well, this is a day of new experiences. You've heated up a pro.

You rub the tip of your organ between her buttocks, then slide it gently between her legs. Now she really wants it. She shoves her buttocks back towards you, reaching for it with gaping lips. You slide the tip of the organ between them and it disappears practically before you know what's happening. Well, what do you know? An educated vagina. Verily, there's nothing like professional work . . . all too rare these days.

She lets out her breath in a lascivious gasp. Suddenly she giggles. 'Daddy would never have done anything like this to me.'

You're not so sure about that, but you don't see any reason to insult the memory of the dead, so you keep your lip buttoned and concentrate on what you're doing. You don't really have to concentrate, though; just relax and enjoy it. She's doing enough work for both of you. She's rotating those buttocks as though they were made of rubber, giving it to you wide open. She isn't holding back a thing. You're in her as far as anybody has ever been, and if you go much further you'll probably come out her throat.

'If you want me to do anything else,' she gasps, 'Just tell me, and I'll do it. Do you want to see me again tonight? Or any other time? You can have me like this, or give it to me any way you like.'

She means it literally—Any way. Snap it up, chum, it's a bona fide offer. Spank her, make love to her, wipe your feet on her if you want to. Her life is on the line and she'll pay to the best of her ability in the only coin she's got. And the best of her ability is damn good.

You draw her buttocks against you, and you feel yourself going even farther inside her than you'd thought you could. You hold her hips with one hand and reach around with the other to tickle her. She's really giving you her all now. She rolls and groans. It might be an act, but if so, it's an excellent one. Rotate your weapon inside its lovely, warm, wet sheath, and watch the fan blow the hair across the back of her neck.

Suddenly everything gets hazy and dark. You stop noticing things. In . . . in . . . IN!! That did it! The warmth wells up inside you. This time you're going to explode for sure. Your fluid floods her . . . it's all over.

You drop into a chair. Somehow you don't feel much like standing—or doing anything else, for that matter. She looks at you as though asking permission to let her skirt drop. You nod.

The telephone rings.

Perfect timing.

You motion her to get on her knees and kiss your almost-limp organ. Then you pick up the receiver.

'This is Clara Reeves,' a clear voice says.

You can see her in your mind's eye, and you amuse yourself imagining the expression on her face if she could see you now, with a petite redhead delicately washing your parts with her little pink tongue.

'I just got a call from a woman,' the voice continues. 'She says the ring belongs to a friend of hers. She wants me to meet her for tea at the Clive Hotel. I said I'd be there at four.'

'Fine. A woman, eh? Well, try to make friends with her. And under no circumstances give her the ring until you've found out something about her—and her friend. Get her to tell you where she lives, then check it in a phone book.'

The girl on the floor is running her tongue along your shaft, holding it like an asparagus stalk in her fingers and nibbling at the tip. She puts her mouth full on it and kisses it, smiling up at you. We aim to please, the smile says.

'Don't worry,' the voice on the phone assures you. 'I'm not simply going to hand the ring over. And I'll see you tonight to tell you what happens, if—if I come back alive.'

You smile.

She says: 'Will you come to the house again—tonight—about ten?'

The redhead is taking it in her mouth, pressing her rouged lips on the bare flesh. Her lipstick is marking your organ. That's fun.

She squeezes you between the legs and tickles you with one well-manicured finger. You slide forward in the seat and motion for her to pull your trousers down.

Now she runs her finger down the groove between your buttocks. You slide forward even more, letting her slip her forefinger into the hole. Wondering how much longer you'll be able to control your voice, you say into the phone; 'Yes, I'll come up to the house. And don't worry. You'll come back alive. Just be careful.'

She tells you she will be, and you tell her that you've got to run. She hangs up and you do likewise.

The redhead is still kneeling at your feet, dragging her mouth up on your organ and pressing it down with an expert side-to-side movement of her head. You let your mind go, and your body becomes one mass of sensation.

She goes faster and faster, and your hips begin to jerk spasmodically. She squeezes and presses your buttocks, and her tongue flicks around the tip of your shaft in rapid circles. 'GOD . . .'

You open your eyes. She is leisurely cleaning you off with her tongue.

You say: 'You might as well get up now.'

'You don't want to do anything more?'

'No. We've done everything we're going to do, toots. Now fix yourself up so you can make a handsome exit.'

She stands and puts on her panties. She straightens out her skirt and adjusts the ruffles on her blouse. She takes a gold make-up kit and a mirror from her purse, and works small miracles with them. She pins back her hair into an identical facsimile of the coiffure she had when she came in. 'I feel so much better about everything now.' she says casually. 'I feel just the way I used to when I'd been naughty and had something on my conscience for a long time, and then daddy gave me a good spanking and I felt all . . . well, forgiven and everything.' Just the right note. You have to give her credit.

'How soon do you expect to need another spanking?' you ask.

'As soon as you think I need one,' she says.

'So it's a permanent arrangement? I just go on spanking you and punishing you in whatever other ways I see fit for as long as I see fit. Is that it?'

'It can be that kind of an arrangement if that's what you want.'

'No. I think you've been punished enough.'

You see the surprise in her eyes. She hadn't thought it would be that easy. She's almost afraid to ask, but she knows she must: 'And Abie the Goat? You'll see him? You'll take the case?'

'Don't worry your pretty red head about it. I'll take care of it.'

She pecks you on the cheek and turns to go.

'Haven't you forgotten something?' you ask.

'What?'

'The hundred bucks I told you it would cost you for the conferences with you and Abie the Goat.'

She blanches. She had thought she had you hooked. 'But I told you, a hundred dollars is all the money I have. I can't just give you all of it.'

'All right, make it fifty, then. After all, you have shown me how really sorry you are that you got involved in all this. But I want it now. Cash.'

By this time she's recovered her poise. She doesn't bat an eyelash. Opening her purse, she takes out a roll of tens and counts off five of them. As she hands them to you, she even manages a smile. She's a realist, this girl. She knows that a fifty buck fee for a conference with the best criminal lawyer around is quite a bargain. As she starts to leave the office you goose her and she emits a coy, girlish giggle that any virgin would be proud to call her own.

'Goodbye . . . daddy,' she says and walks undulatingly out of your life.

You flip the intercom switch and tell Jackson you want to see him in your office. When he comes in you tell him to call the Tombs and get a line on a forgery pick-up. Alias Abie the Goat. 'Then,' you tell him, 'call Judge Harwin's resident and get his son on the phone. Tell the kid I want him here nine o'clock tomorrow morning. I've got a case for him.'

You're very pleased with yourself. In one fell swoop, you get a broad out of your hair and you repay the judge's favour. Very clever. You always like to throw the cases you won't touch to struggling young lawyers, especially ones like the judge's son, who don't need the money but can use the court experience. And young Harwin won't have to worry about damaging his rep when he loses the case, 'cause he hasn't been around long enough to build up a rep to lose.

All in all, a very satisfactory solution. You smile as you imagine the expression on the hooker's face when she looks for you in court and sees Harwin Jr. instead. Too bad. But it's her own fault. She's certainly been around long enough to know that you shouldn't play the game if you haven't got the chips. Abie the Goat! How could the great Garnett ever defend a goon with a monicker like Abie the Goat?

A Night in a Moorish Harem

'Anna, take the scarf,' interrupted the Italian, 'and tell the Captain something about Circassia.'

The lady thus addressed was about nineteen years of age and she was very tall and slender. Her limbs were finely tapered; so was her round waist, which I could have spanned with my two hands. Her nicely cut breasts were as erect as if they had been carved from alabaster, which her skin resembled in whiteness. The hair on her small head was of the palest blonde, but that at her loins was fiery red, which I had read was a sign of uncontrollable wantonness.

If so, this lady's face gave no indication of it. Her large blue eyes looked at you with the innocence of childhood, and the delicate roseate hue of her cheeks varied at every changing emotion. She stretched herself between my thighs, where she leaned with her elbow on the cushion, supporting her graceful head with her hand. Her bosom rested on my loins and my shaft was imprisoned by her snowy breasts from between which its red crest peeped out while she looked me in the face and told her lascivious story.

'The powerful old chief to whom my mother was married had no children of his own. I was her only child by a former marriage and her fondness was all centred on me. Our religion, which was the Greek, forbade a plurality of wives. The old chief was not likely to have a direct heir, and, as he was now seventy, her great object was to have him confer on me the succession of principality; this last he consented to do if she would countenance his amours with other women.

She consented to do so and the strange compact was formed. I was present as witness, but unknown to either of them, I had been in the habit, for a long time, of frequenting a little alcove in their bedroom where a few books were kept. It was separated by a curtain from the rest of the room and communicated also with my chamber by a sliding panel. This secret panel, which I had accidentally discovered, was a kind often met in such old castles as we inhabited. It was known to me alone, or, if the old chief knew it, he never thought of it.

I had there witnessed all the secrets of the marriage chamber, and of course my passions were rapidly developed. My mother was still plump and handsome; she enjoyed keenly the marriage embrace, but always had to work very hard in order to finish the tardy rapture of the old chief. On the occasion of the compact I heard her tell him she could give him all he wanted. He could only reply that a man liked a variety.

'Very well,' said she, 'make out the deed for Anna's succession and I will not only countenance but assist in your amours. We can in that way at least secure secrecy and avoid scandal, for no one will suspect a wife of conniving at her husband's amours.' The old chief then confided to her that the present object of his desire was Leuline; the handsome wife of the steward of the castle.

The next evening I was at my post early. My

mother had already managed with Leuline. She was a large and voluptuous looking woman with dark hair and blue eyes; her bosoms were not much developed, but her thighs were immense. She got into bed with my mother and pretended to be asleep when the old chief came in.

He undressed and got into bed with them and mounted Leuline, who lay with her head on my mother's arm, close to her bosom. An expression of pleasure stole over Leuline's face, which became more ineffable at every thrust. At last their mingled sighs and the stillness that followed gave proof that the embrace had been mutually satisfactory.

('You can imagine,' said Anna, smiling at the other girls, 'how I longed for the embrace of a man.')

Plans for future meetings and jokes at the expense of Leuline's husband filled up the time, together with explorations of Leuline's charms, till the shaft of the old chief grew again stiff. He plunged it into Leuline's great loins, and she enjoyed it so highly that she finished and left him in the lurch.

I could hardly restrain myself, I so longed for the thrusts that were now wasted on Leuline. My mother must have felt the same way, for she asked the old chief to let her finish him. He had more than once sucked her fine bosoms during this onset. He now transferred his crimson crest dripping with Leuline's moisture.

The energy with which my mother received him made me fairly wriggle my loins in sympathy. She wound her arms around him and played up her loins to meet his descending thrusts, then their frames were convulsed for a few moments with the culminary rapture and they subsided into perfect repose.

I had often before felt wanton emotion at my post

of observation; I now left the alcove in a frenzy of lust. I wanted a man, and that immediately, I was about to seek one of the sentinels at his post and confer my virginity on the first rude soldier I met on the cover of the ramparts when I remembered Tessidor, a young priest, who was attached to the chapel of the castle. He was a delicate looking youth of about seventeen, with a countenance which indicated the purity of his character. I went to his room and timidly knocked on the door.

To my timid knock the answer was delayed; when at last he said 'come in,' I saw that he had employed the interval by slipping on a nightgown, for he had been just about to retire. He looked astonished, and well he might when he saw me.

'I have come to make a confession and ask your counsel,' said I.

'Had we better not go to the chapel?' he asked.

'It is better here,' I said, 'for the subject is a worldly one, though of much importance to me. I love a young man who is indifferent to my preference, nay, he is even insensible to my love. I would have my parents hint to him that his addresses would be accepted; but I shall have to marry a soldier and he is not a soldier. What shall I do?'

'Strive to forget him, my lady,' was the reply. I stood a moment with my look cast on the ground and my cheeks burning. 'Cruel man,' I said, 'it is you who have my heart.'

My head dropped forward, I seemed about to fall, but I put up my mouth for the kiss which he bent over to impress upon it. Regrets were then mingled with kisses, while I allowed my wrapper to part open and expose my bosoms. He ventured to timidly kiss them; his kisses became more and more ardent. I had got him at last where a man has no conscience. He stretched himself on the bed beside me, took me in his arms: our lips were glued together.

As much by my contrivance as his own, but he did not know it, my wrapper and dressing gown opened, and a skirt and chemise was all that separated a stiff little object from my thighs. Fired by lust as I was, I had shame enough left to leave the removal of these slight little objects to himself. I could hardly wait upon his timidity. I must have been the first woman he had ever entered, for he was very awkward in guiding his crest to the lips that yearned to close upon it. It was a little thing, but very stiff.

At last it penetrated me a little way and I felt the touch of his crest against my maidenhead like an electric shock; it set all my nerves tingling with pleasure, and expectant of the coming connection. I could no longer even feign modesty. I involuntarily wrapped my arms around him and he gave the fateful thrust.

His little crest pierced through my maidenhead with a cutting pain which I felt no more than a bulling heifer would have felt the stroke of a switch. The pain was drowned in overwhelming pleasure. The thrill swept over every fibre in my frame, not only at the first thrust, but three times successively, and at each plunge I gave a sigh of rapture. Then my tense muscles relaxed and I received with pleasure at least a dozen more thrusts.

Something was still wanting. It was the gush of sperm that Tessidor at last poured into my heated sheath like balm. He sank heavily upon me for a few minutes with his face buried in my neck. I was enjoying a voluptuous languor, when I felt his little shrunken crest floating out of my sheath with the mingled blood and sperm.

Remorse had already seized him. He raised himself on his elbow and gazed pitifully into my face. I was past blushing so I covered my face with my hands. 'I have ruined you,' he said, 'wretch that I am, heaven forgive me!' He got up from the bed without even giving me another kiss and knelt before his crucifix. 'Will you join me in asking heaven for mercy on my sin?' he added.

I made some excuse and fled from the room. The next morning I heard that he had gone to join a convent in the mountains. By this time I had come to the conclusion that I had let him off too quickly. I had not had enough. Perhaps a warm bath would help to soothe me.

There was a large bath half the size of a room and deep enough when full to cover my breasts; it had a door into my room, also into my mother's who was busy at this time in the morning with her servants. It was the old chief's time to take a bath and he always had the warm water; I determined to share it with him. I had heretofore doubted whether the old chief would want to touch his wife's daughter, but my success with the young priest gave me courage.

I took off all my clothes in my room and peeped through the door. He was floating on his back playing with his shaft, which dangled limber in the water. I had most always seen it stiff, and I promised myself the pleasure of getting it in that position, which I preferred. Pretty soon he came to the side towards me, where he could not be seen by me; now was the time for me to come in as if I had not known he was there.

I opened my door suddenly and ran and jumped into the water. I swam across the bath, turned around and became the picture of astonishment at seeing him. I first covered my face with my hands, then covered my bosom with one hand and my loins with the other. I did not scream; that might bring my mother.

Then I turned my back on him. The side of the bath where I stood was perpendicular. He stood by the sloping side where we got out—of course I had to stay. 'It's all right, Anna,' he said, 'we will have a nice bath together.'

I started to dodge past him, but of course he caught me. 'I shall scream,' said I, but of course I did not scream. I was fast in his arms, his stiffening shaft crushing against my buttocks, and each of his hands squeezed one of my bosoms. My apprehensions of reluctance on his part were all departed, so I kept up more show of resistance. I struggled to get away, but only struggled harder to get around in front of him. This brought my back to the sloping side of the bathtub, against which he pressed me.

Half standing and half lying my head was still above water. The wantonness of the situation and the warmth of the water made the bath seem like a voluptuous sea. Of course I had put both arms around him to keep from sinking; his hands were thus both at liberty. He needed them both to work his half-stiffened shaft into me. Leuline and my mother only the night before had taken the starch out of it; nothing but the excitement of such a kind of rape would have stiffened it at all.

Half limber as it was, it completely filled me, paining me a little at first, but gradually feeling better and better, pervading all through me with the most lascivious sensation. The warm water churned in and out of my sheath at every thrust with a feeling like gushing sperm. All the water in the bath seemed to be of the male gender, and all of it embracing me and administering to my lust.

For fully five minutes I abandoned myself to the delicious dissolving feeling, not as thrilling as the young priest's had caused the night before, but more prolonged. Even after it had subsided and died away, the plunges of the old chief were still pleasant. Finally his shaft became for a moment rigid deep within me, he gave a throb or two which deprived him of his strength and he no longer supported me.

I scrambled from his arms up the side of the bath and, regaining my own room, shut the door and sank exhausted on the bed. We never pursued the intrigue, as the terror of my mother was too much before our eyes. Besides I was in a few days after engaged in an amour with Rudolf, the handsome young captain of the guards, while the old chief had been supplied with a fresh bedfellow by my mother. This time it was a young maid, who timidly blushed, in the place of Leuline, for I still amused myself occasionally peeping through the alcove.

A short time afterward the old chief was slain in battle and the sagacity of my mother was rewarded, for I succeeded peaceably to the principality, but my mother swayed the real power. I was willing she should do so, provided she did not interfere with my amours. It was by her advice that I did not marry. 'A virgin chieftain will be popular with the people, and you can control men,' she would say, 'far better unmarried.'

In fact, Rudolf, captain of the guards, was my abject slave, and so were Cassim and Selim, two of the bravest young chiefs in the army. I admitted them all to my bed in turn, Rudolf the most frequently, for he was powerfully built and had genitals correspondingly large. When I wished to be tickled deeply, the tall and slender Selim received the secret summons to my chamber. Cassim was short and stout—it was agreeable sometimes to be stretched without being deeply penetrated. Each of these suspected that the other also enjoyed my favour, but they were not certain of it.

One evening I invited them all to my secret apartments. The sideboard had been replenished, the servants had been dismissed for the evening and the doors locked. I was dressed in a purple velvet bodice with a petticoat of red silk. I had on my richest lace and jewellery and the crown of the principality was on my brow. The handsome young officers glittered in their splendid uniforms; suspense and curiosity were mingled in their countenances.

I waited until several toasts had been drunk in my honour and my wanton eyes devoured the fine proportions of the young men, and I thus addressed them: 'Should not a Circassian princess have as many privileges as a Turkish pasha?'

'Certainly,' they all replied.

'Should she not be entitled to a harem as well as he?' They hesitated but answered, 'Yes.'

'You then, shall be my harem,' said I, rising. 'You Cassim, should be lord of the lips.' The polite young officer set the example of devotion by coming to my side and kissing the lips that I had committed to his charge.

'You, Selim, are the lord of the bosom.' He came up on the other side of me and kissed the bosom which peeped out about the lace front of my bodice.

'You, Rudolf, shall be the lord of the thighs.' He knelt before me, and raising my skirts, planted a kiss on the hairy mouth they concealed.

Then I felt his tongue penetrate the lips beneath; it caused a flush of desire to mantle through my frame. 'Let us divest ourselves of this clothing which makes mortals of us and become like the ancient gods,' I said.

My example, together with the champagne, now broke down all reserve. We stripped entirely naked and amused ourselves by imitating the attitude usually given by art to the most celebrated heathen divinities. It was not enough for me to compare the forms of the young men by observation. I freely caressed and handled their genitals with my hands until they lost all restraint and gathered so closely about me that I was squeezed in their joint embrace.

I flung my arms around Cassim and bid him lie down on his back with me on top of him; his loins were elevated higher than his head by the piles on which he lay. I worked backward while he guided his shaft completely into me.

My buttocks presented a fair mark for Selim, who mounted me behind and slowly worked his shaft into the same orifice that Cassim had already entered. It was the tightest kind of a fit. The first entrance had stirred my desire to a flame and made me welcome the second with great greediness. Cassim's position was such that he could hardly stir, but Selim plunged his long and slender shaft into me again with thrusts that required all his strength. My sheath was stretched to its utmost tension by the two shafts, but all its distended nerves quivered with lust.

Rudolf now knelt close in front of me, with his knees on either side of my head. I lay for a moment with my flushed cheeks on his genitals, then I grasped his shaft in my hand and played rapidly up and down it.

Cassim, with his arms wrapped around my waist, was sucking my bosoms. Selim squeezed my thighs in his grasp at every thrust he gave. I felt my crisis coming, overwhelming in three-fold intensity. In very wild abandonment I sucked Rudolf's crest in my mouth, then I thrilled and melted with a groan which resounded through all the room. All three of the young men followed me to the realms of bliss where I soared.

My sheath was overflowed with the double tribute which jetted and spurted and gushed into it. My mouth was filled with Rudolf's sperm. Both pairs of my lips were dripping. My whole frame seemed saturated with the fecund moisture. When the mingled sighs of the young men, which echoed to my prolonged groans of rapture, had died away, I sank into a semi-conscious state from which I did not rise that evening.

It was a deep, dreamy, voluptuous repose which an occasional smarting sensation in my strained sheath did not disturb. The wine and profuse organs had done their work. The young men put me to bed and quietly dispersed. It was the only time I had my harem. The next day our troops lost a battle, the castle was taken by the enemy, and I was on my way to the slave market.'

Anna finished her story. My shaft still peeped out from between her bosoms, but it was now stiff with desire. The fat Italian had aroused it to vitality, though she had failed to exact any tribute from it. My stones had again filled while I listened to the innocent Circassian's passionate tale.

Still holding her between my thighs I turned so as

to bring her on her back beneath me. Then, changing and adjusting my thighs between hers, I parted the fiery red hair that concealed lips equally fiery and commenced the onset. The delicious heat and moisture set the blood dancing in my veins. My crest lingered a moment at the lips, then glided past them into the clinging folds of her sheath. When I was completely entered, it gave a convulsive contraction around my shaft and Anna melted—indeed the ladies were all ripe to the melting point, while I had to meet their fresh successive ardour.

Anna became passive, but she still seemed to enjoy the deep and rapid thrusts which for several moments I continued to thrust into her white loins. At every thrust I became more and more furious. I buried my hilt again and again in the vain attempt to touch her womb. I felt that if my crest could only reach so far up in her long slender person, I could consummate the exquisite connection. She seemed to divine my wish; she opened her thighs and drawing her knees upward, wrapped her long, slender legs around my waist with a strength I had not thought her capable of.

Fixing my look on her sweet face I gave another plunge. She was so fairly exposed to my thrust that I rammed her womb clear up her belly. The sperm gushed from my crest in consecutive jets and I gave a sigh of perfect satisfaction. I was completely exhausted; my nerveless frame stretched itself at full length upon her and I sank into a voluptuous languor that gradually turned into sleep.

The Pleasures of Lolotte

Translated from the French by
Frank Pomeranz

At last, the midnight hour was about to strike. The same preparations were completed as the night before. The ladder was set up, the garden reconnoitred and then a quick and light-footed ascent to our window. But then there appeared one visitor, a second—and then a third!

'Good Lord,' Félicité exclaimed in an anxious tone of voice, 'three men! What is the meaning of this?'

'Only,' our angel of last night said, 'that apart from bringing somebody for you know who, I also brought along for you a charming and reliable friend, who is my equal in all respects, because unfortunately I, myself, cannot stay.'

Félicité was not the kind of girl to take this swap for an insult and she did not raise the slightest objection.

Our obliging Mercury had done one thing which seemed rather odd. Before getting his friends to climb up the ladder in front of him, he had made them blindfold themselves and demanded that they say and do nothing in our apartment without his permission. The entry of two sightless men could have been a trifle embarrassing but it was not in the slightest dangerous and the two of them managed marvellously.

'You no doubt understand the reason for the precaution I have taken with these two gentlemen,' our friend said. 'If the arrangement I deemed suitable pleases you, they will stay; if not, I shall take them away with me, because these are the conditions on which I brought them, and I have their word for it that they will bow to each and every one of your commands. All they know is that we are in a community of women: they do not know your names, your ages or what you look like. In short, I promised them nothing except that I would bring them here; the rest is up to you. However,' he said with a conspiratorial wink, 'I did drop a hint about your tendency to the vapours, skinniness and drooping breasts. In a word, I have prepared them for what they would find.'

At this point, the two others shook their heads, as if to say, 'Never mind, we'll risk it.'

But Félicité, who had a considerable, and often original, sense of humour, wanted to enter into the spirit of the game and add to it. So she went out quietly and returned noisily and said in the cracked voice of an old woman,

'Very well, my chaste sisters, I could not sleep and saw and heard everything that passed here. I shall not agree to your beautiful tryst here unless I get a go first. If ordinary nuns of forty to fifty can allow themselves to entertain gallants in the sheepfold of Our Lord, then a Mother Superior scarcely above sixty can also conceive the notion of getting paid for keeping the secret. Come, my chicks, it's with me first of all that you'll have to settle accounts.'

While this was going on, it was amusing to see one of our 'blind men' nudging the other and hear him say under his breath, 'Let's get out of here.' But it was too late for that. The master of ceremonies was already outside and on the ladder, wishing them good luck and promising to come and fetch them later. At this point we each restored his eyesight to one of our visitors.

Their surprise at our appearance was beyond description. They were prepared for elderly nuns: instead they saw two worldly and enchanting creatures. What a ravishing dramatic coup!

'Heavens,' exclaimed the one who had counselled retreat and to whom Félicité had restored his eyesight.

'What a divine child,' his friend said with equal enthusiasm on seeing me.

They vied with each other to heap praises on their friend.

'What a man the Maltese Knight is! The king of friends!'

We were hugged, kissed and practically devoured.

'What supreme artistry on his part!', one of them said.

'What skill in multiplying our pleasure a hundred-fold', the other replied.

The gentlemen seemed to be perfectly at home as regards the etiquette of nocturnal trysts in the nunnery. Each set to work quickly undressing the girl facing him. To be sure, they performed this task less rapidly than the knight had done but, to make up for that, employed greater delicacy. The one into whose hands I had been delivered handled me like a precious and fragile jewel. Félicité, though patently my social inferior, was not treated any less respectfully for all that.

The bed was not at all suitable for a double performance. Félicité did not fail to remember that the night before it was rather uncomfortable for three—for four it would be impossible.

'We could give up the place of honour to these children,' she said to her beau. 'On a good mattress, we can pass the time just as well on the floor; what do you think, my dear stranger whom I hope to get to know much better very soon?'

'With you, my dear,' he said gallantly, 'I'd prefer a soldier's plank bunk to a Prince-Bishop's four-poster stuffed with eiderdown.'

'Well said,' she replied, shaking him vigorously by the hand. 'A true lover does not inspect his surroundings too closely. I can see we are suited to each other and shall have no difficulty in becoming the best of friends.'

While they were talking like this, my penetrator-to-be took off my skirts and slip; in a word I was naked—and kissed from head to foot—by the time what we were left to lie on was ready to receive us.

I could not yet guess how the night would develop. Luckily, the pretty boy who fell to me was ravishingly made, slender, full of grace and beardless; he had chestnut hair, a sweet expression and a tender smile so that, dressed as a woman, he would hold out promise of sexual bliss to any red-blooded man. In spite of all that, however, this gallant would turn out to be a monster as far as I was concerned if what he had to offer me was a prick as ludicrously gigantic as his friend, the cunt-cleaver's. Such thoughts were running through my head; but my fears were only slight and my hopes unlimited. Yes, everything seemed to augur that I would at last be deflowered— and very pleasantly, at that.

Félicité's companion was handsome, tall, young and fair-haired with a military air, a proud but not rough look, built like a model with rather more flesh on him than my partner. His manners were not as studied as the Maltese Knight's, nor did he have his attractive impudence. All the same, he was no less ardent or knowledgeable than he. The tribute he paid to the many charms of his lady was sincere and detailed. In a word, neither of us could have been served, or serviced, better. You are anxious, gentle reader, to see us in their arms? Believe us, we are no less impatient to get on with things.

'My handsome young friend,' Félicité said to my partner, 'possibly you don't know that you are going to encounter a maidenhead? It is only rarely one comes across such things all ready to be plucked. In the ordinary course of events, they are a bit shy; they have to be hunted with cunning and need to be wheedled: they defend themselves craftily and when, at last, the huntsman has bagged one, he can congratulate himself on a good day's chase. But this one here is different; it is tame and comes out of its own accord to face the hunter. Whatever its qualities, though, make the best of them. But you're to make no babies, that's all we ask of you.'

'A good man,' the boy replied in an accent which, though slight, revealed he was not French, 'and a gallant one does not need to be told such things. As for the maidenhead, what do I care about it? At such a lovely age and with so many charms, what need has anyone to be a virgin to arouse the most ardent desires?'

'All the same she is one and you'll have to act accordingly. . . . We are very delicately made. . . . Just have a look.'

With impetuous folly she parted my thighs and displayed my little cunt to full advantage. The pretty boy kissed it as soon as he saw it.

'Touch it,' she said, 'try and put your finger up.'
He tried but scarcely made any progress.

'Go on. You'll certainly have your work cut out
for you—but do it kindly and gently.'

She said all that bent over the bed. My pretty
sparring partner, who was kneeling between my
legs, set to work as soon as this long preamble was
over. At the same time, his bigger friend, tormented
by his own desires, occupied himself with the poster-
ior charms of the maid, who was so exclusively preoccupied with me that she scarcely seemed to be
aware of the lips, the fingers and finally the prick that
were paying her homage. The last-named, encoun-
tering no obstacle, tried to establish itself doggy-
fashion but little shoves of the buttocks each time
dislodged him, as if by accident. Félicité was prima-
rily concerned with what was happening to me. My
own little fucksman had just revealed a real
deflowerer's prick, roundish, longish and slender.

'Marvellous,' the mistress of ceremonies
exclaimed, 'just what the doctor ordered. . . . Oh,
my little mistress, what a lot of good that one is going
to do you.'

She immediately took her mouth to it, inundated
it with spit and placed it against my burning quim,
craving to be pleasured. She herself positioned and
guided it, without for a moment giving up complete
control of it. It entered me, not without difficulty, to
be sure, but successfully and without causing me too
much pain. I had already taken in about two-thirds
of it and the sweet actions of the shaft had been going
on for about a minute when Félicité thought she
could detect the symptoms of an imminent ejacu-
lation. Pitilessly, she separated us—so very much in
time that the little rascal was scarcely outside before

he poured forth his life-giving balm in profuse quantities, with which, but for Félicité and in spite of his promise, I would have been flooded internally, whether because of the novice fornicator's inexperience, his selfishness or his clumsiness.

Not that I was grateful for all the care that Félicité had bestowed on me.

'Ah, Félicité,' I said to her sadly, 'this was a poor service you rendered me.'

'No doubt you'd have preferred me to have let him put you in the club! You should be infinitely grateful to me. Remember this, Mademoiselle. Never, ever, on any pretext let a man come inside you during the first fuck. After that, . . . well, there might still be some danger, but very much less, with seventy-five per cent of men and with the rest none at all.'

While giving me this useful homily, she watched us and very amusingly pushed away with thrusts of her haunches her impatient fair-haired suitor, to whom she seemed to be paying no attention but who could not lodge himself as much as an inch up her cunt without being devaginated again. When he appeared to get impatient with these struggles and at last appeared to be about to secure a firm bridgehead, she said—

'Please wait a moment. I like to be all there when such nice things are being done to me. Whatever you do, don't over-excite yourself because, should you come, I warn you that won't count.'

The teasing tone of her challenge flattered the skirmisher and he withdrew. This enabled us to see a charming prick, well fleshed out, vermilion in colour, full of grace and pulsating proudly in his hand. Still, what a difference there was between it and that of the Knight of Malta. All the same, Félicité did not seem to disdain what was intended for her.

'There, there, my plaything,' she said, patting it amiably. 'In a moment you'll have someone to talk to.' She then turned to us. 'Now I'll leave you; be sure you do nothing unwise.' She smiled at her impatient fucksman. 'Now I'm all yours.'

At the same time, she threw herself on the mattress and supported herself only by the heels and the nape of her neck, so that her body formed an arch with her cunt standing prominently on guard. She seized the shaft threatening her with one hand and threw out this boastful challenge to it:

'Just now you occupied it by treachery; this time it braves you face to face. Let us now see which of the two will sustain the assault better.'

The proud engine had already disappeared; two shakes of the hips and it was implanted to the very roots. Their lively movements, their kisses, their loving words, in a word their utter bliss, added to our own delight. I passionately desired my Adonis and he me; I took him in my arms and I was re-entered . . . I imitated Félicité in everything without leaving out the slightest detail; I kissed, I bit, I moaned, I jigged up and down. . . . This time I experienced the incomparable delight of being well and truly fucked—and *fucked completely*. Félicité might have worried about it but I wanted to be and my adorable little fucksman, himself, in spite of his alleged principles, did nothing to stop himself gushing all he had into me.

What an epoch in my life! What magic voluptuousness! What mysterious gift of the Gods! You are indescribable. The fortunate creature that knows best how to savour you will forever be deprived of words to express your heavenly delights.

I warned you, gentle reader, that I am the very devil for randy pleasures but the rest of this story will prove that I have an honest heart. I pride myself on a few good qualities: I know the way of the world and nobody is better at saving appearances when I want to. However, lest anything connected with fucking should surprise you as far as I am concerned, I repeat that on this point I am possibly the most determined creature that this century has produced. The seed of this passion, this vice, this crime (if it pleases your prejudices to describe my nymphomania thus) has been with me since birth. I had scarcely begun to be conscious of my identity when I became uncontrollable in my desires. And once I had had my first orgasm, I became equally abandoned in my flights of licentious fantasy.

I challenge any sentimental beauty, madly in love, who has for long resisted and finally succumbed to the blandishments of her beloved—I challenge her to show that she got more enjoyment from doing so than I got from my charming young man's second accolade. All the same—be indulgent to me, gentle reader, and cast no stones at me for the wickedness I am about to confess to you—all the same, I say, I had scarcely emerged from his arms when I felt a pang of envy of Félicité, who I thought had done even better than I.

Since I had been idle, I delighted in watching the other couple. The fair young man was marvellous at his work: four times, almost without a break, he had proved his ardour to the happy maid and now he was preparing for the fifth. . . .

But, horror of horrors, disaster of disasters! Our

door opened. Not the communicating door which, that morning, had enabled me to see Mother engaged in such surprising activities—we had taken good care to remove the key to that; it was the main door to our rooms from the corridor that ran through the entire sleeping quarters of the convent and one that, as is customary in such establishments, had no bolts. The devil must have handed my mother a second key; the only one we knew about was in the possession of the Mother Superior. In short, it was my mother who came in. Her appearance was like a bolt from the blue to us.

Félicité and I were—it will be recalled—stark naked and our hair was dishevelled; the gentlemen were just as tousled as we and had on nothing but their vests and silk pants, which clung to their skin, garments that were, in any case, useless because Félicité, lying on the mattress hard by the door, had just for the fifth time implanted in herself the object the name of which I am tired of ceaselessly repeating. It was this configuration that first met my curious mother's eyes.

As for me, I was on the point of behaving just as scandalously because, after a few moments of rest, my little fucksman had become proudly upstanding once more. So, as I could not at the moment put into practice the idea of a swap which had tempted me. I was going to use instead what I had in my hand.

Félicité's beau preserved complete self-control and evidently did not think it appropriate to devaginate; he merely asked drily.

'Who on earth is that woman?'

'Good heavens,' I exclaimed. 'It's Mother.'

At this point, they did separate.

I hurried to draw the curtains to conceal, if still

possible, my nudity, that of my young man and the unequivocal activities in which we had been surprised, from a mother's eyes. Mother—whether on account of violent emotion, fear or pretence—suddenly appeared speechless and sapped of all strength. She fell into the nearest chair and seemed to faint. Straight away, nature overcame my shame and horror and, naked as I was, I rushed up to her to offer my assistance. Félicité quickly put on a shift. As for me, two equally important concerns made me forget the incongruous situation in which I found myself: one was to revive Mother and the other to prevent her going back to her room, getting dressed and then raising the alarm. Quite soon Mother came to or pretended to; as soon as she did, she fought off my arms which were hugging her. She pushed me away and leant back in her chair, her face buried in tightly crossed hands, apparently heart-broken. Our young men had already dressed and as they could now take my place in guarding the door and stopping my mother leaving the room, I was able to put my clothes on in turn. But whatever would be the outcome of this bizarre scene?

In the first place, what was the meaning of my mother's immobility and her hesitation at a time when one would have expected her to explode with angry reproaches? Let us try and analyse her first reactions and investigate whether her conduct could be considered natural.

There must have been a lot of noise coming from our room and she must have heard it; we were at fault in not being more careful, the men as well as ourselves, and behaving as if we were the only people in the world. But what could Mother have imagined? It had to be some act of wrong-doing. So why turn up?

Was it to prevent some kind of disorder? She must surely have known it was too late for that. Did she want to take the participants of whatever was going on to task? If that were the case, it should not have been she who came, or at least not by herself; it would have been more suitable and more certain to have called the Mother Superior and for the two of them to have faced us together. Perhaps she feared a scandal and my being disgraced? That could be.

But here was another way of looking at things. My mother was the same woman who had got herself so excited that morning. Was it not likely that, exhilarated at the thought of some libidinous scene, she was quite drawn to the idea of surprising us in the act, though planning to make a great fuss, if need be, for form's sake? She probably did not expect us to be involved in proper love affairs, each one of us with a man; she probably expected no more than some lesbian skirmish. It was probably the extreme lengths to which we had gone that shocked her.

If we were embarrassed by the situation and if my mother was, the gentlemen were no less so. Nothing would be easier for them to depart as they had come but reaching the garden was not enough. To get out of the convent, they needed the knight; only he could guide them to a certain secret place, of which I shall have more to say later, through which they had come in. They did not have much to fear on their own account—but what troubles would we be exposed to after their departure? For her part, my mother was waiting for them to withdraw—that was the only explanation for her present silence. Yet they refused to budge. This stalemate had lasted almost a quarter of an hour when at last the Knight put in his eagerly awaited appearance.

'Well, my children,' he said as soon as his head appeared at the window, 'how are you? How did things work out?'

Four long faces, sad looks and a mournful silence immediately apprised him of the fact that something untoward had happened. He stepped through the casement window and saw a fifth person.

'What is the meaning of this?' he said, addressing Félicité's fair young man. The latter made some reply in a foreign tongue. When informed of the situation, the knight collected his thoughts for a moment.

'What a business,' he said emerging from his brief reverie. He then went straight up to my mother who—probably resigned to whatever this strange night might bring—had not made the slightest movement when a sixth person joined us, nor even as much as glanced at him.

The bold Knight then fell at her feet; she had nothing on but her night-dress and a carelessly arranged shawl—but no matter! He shamelessly pressed against her, embraced her thighs and said,

'Oh, worthy lady. How culpably we have acted towards you!'

The crowning offence she thought she detected in this sham act of contrition made her furious. She turned the eyes of a Gorgon on the speaker . . . their eyes met . . . they stared.

What a dramatic turn of events, how unexpected and how striking! Some trouble, the result of some violent emotion, agitated my mother; satisfaction, taking the form of roguishness, could be read in every one of the lascivious knight's features. In the twinkling of an eye, the two had changed roles.

'I can't believe my eyes. It's you, Séraphine!'

That was my mother's Christian name. 'What miracle brings you here?'

Instead of answering, my mother again hid her chagrined face; she seemed desperately unhappy.

'Vouchsafe me another look, so that I can be certain of having seen again the dearest and most regretted of my lady friends and that this piece of good fortune is no mere dream.'

As she stubbornly refused to budge, the Knight had all the time in the world to assure us by gestures that he was on such good terms with the ruler of our destinies that he would be able to arrange everything to our advantage.

'Do please look upon me,' he said in the most dramatic tone of voice. 'Can you have failed to recognise or, worse still, can you repudiate the old friend who. . . .'

My mother, without replying, pushed him away, as if wanting to brush him aside.

'Ungrateful creature! After all the favours! . . .'

Here the poor woman, fearing with good reason a flow of reminiscences, sat up sharply, covered his mouth with one hand and said in a voice full of pride and anger which, for the moment, made her interesting, 'Fill the measure to overflowing, you traitor! Spare no effort to dishonour us!'

That was saying a good deal and could not now be unsaid.

'Indeed,' the seasoned Knight answered, getting to his feet but still holding my mother in his arms. 'This is no case for guarded words; in your hands they would become dangerous weapons. Yes, my friends, yes, ladies, whatever excesses you may have permitted yourselves together, take note that Madame has done worse than that and that I can tell you all about it. Can she have forgotten all our many assignations'—at this point he looked at her—'or that notorious street? . . . Or the woman at whose house. . . .'

In chorus we asked him to spare my mother who seemed about to pluck out her eyes and her beautiful hair of which she was so proud.

The Knight skilfully resisted all our efforts.

'Let her then come to her senses; let her do herself justice and above all promise to pardon us all.'

'Pardon you, you monster, for my own dishonour and that of my daughter! To forgive your infamous pimping? I can see very well that it is you who arranged everything. Forgive the insolent gutter-snipe who has perverted an innocent creature too lightly entrusted to her perfidious care? No, no, you rogues. You shall all hang.'

Neither remorse nor fear was contained in the violent tirade with which Félicité reacted.

'Just listen to Madame's fine speeches! Anybody would think she was as pure as the driven snow and that we are not worthy to kiss the dust off her feet. Tell us, your ladyship, this morning when with a dirty book in your hands you were doing you-know-what with such gusto, what would you have done if one of these gentlemen had happened to be there, I ask you? And what would you have put in the place we saw you so clearly stroking with your finger?'

My mother was stunned at these words.

'Oh,' the cruel maid went on to even wilder reaches of impudence, 'don't these words provoke depths of pity! She may be a whore like all of us but the wolves must devour each other all the same. I detest this kind of hypocritical claptrap.'

I severely bade the disrespectful servant hold her

tongue and everybody supported me. My mother was dumbfounded and turned to stone.

As for the Knight, who had just one aim, he seized upon what he felt would lead him to his goal by making the following plea.

'Beautiful Mother,' he said tenderly, 'it is up to you to help yourself and I am here beside you. No, I shall never allow you to fast like this when the food I know you crave is there for the asking. I had no idea you were in this dreary place. What name do you go under here? But let that pass; the only thing that matters is that we are reunited; I am, as ever, at your command, I swear it. As heaven is my witness, but for the most extraordinary adventures, which took me away from these parts for such a long time, I should never ever have ceased to be indefatigably at your service.'

These jaunty gallantries were accompanied by gestures which my mother had great trouble in preventing from flowing over into extreme insolence.

If her bosom was skilfully protected, her cunt was in danger of being occupied. She struggled to free herself but every movement revealed another sample of her mature charms. In spite of her thirty-six years, she was still most attractive. Fair like myself, and—like me—without the insipidity with which that type of beauty is often reproached, she was plump without being flabby, with two dazzlingly white breasts, which were closer to being a pair of little rogues than old reprobates[1], with a smooth belly, a well-rounded *bum*, she greatly benefited, and did not suffer from all that the knight laid bare. He himself had caught

[1] It was Voltaire who once said to a lady who displayed her once beautiful bosom: 'little rogues have become old reprobates.'

fire and displayed quite a different order of courage than he might have done if it were not—for reasons of policy—a question of making my mother commit an act of folly which would stop her exposing our own. It was this that made him brave the blows, the scratches and the bites with which Mother sought to defend herself.

I shall not, gentle reader, spin out this description of a scene that was more amusing than sexually stimulating. My mother was lifted up from her chair by the hips and thighs, lightly carried through the room and deposited across the middle of the bed, the same bed that I had been so deliciously fucked on. It was now Mummy's turn and this demon of a Knight got down to work on her.

To tell the truth, we saw him start in a somewhat questionable condition, similar to that of tired horses which do not recover their strength until they have gone a few paces. His tired prick had scarcely touched the edges of her cunt when it entered it, sheathed itself to the hilt and got going at a respectable pace. It must be confessed that morality would have required this penetration to be effected with more difficulty in view of the courageous resistance my mother had put up to begin with; still, it was a case of rape and my mother, by now doing nothing positive to help him could be said to be protesting against the violence that a villain was doing her.

As soon as the Knight had achieved his principal aim, he thought about us.

'Oh, my children,' he said to his comrades, 'it is high mass I am celebrating here. To make it more solemn, I need a deacon and subdeacon. So each of you must seize one of these delightful young rogues. . . . That's it, bravo! I expect one on the right of me and the other on the left, and I invite you to follow my example.'

I found myself within reach of Félicité's fair young man.

'She's yours, Count,' the Knight said in a tone of command.

So, without actually doing anything about it, I came to change horses (or should it be riders?) in mid-stream.

'Go on, Your Highness,' he now said, in a tone that was less familiar, to the younger man who did not disobey the order and pushed the very willing Félicité into the vacant space on the bed. So we were both thrown down, very closely flanking my defiant and still scowling mother, who was on the point of taking this new arrangement and our close proximity as a fresh affront. But what woman can get really angry when she is engaged with a prick eight or nine inches long stuffed into her by a most charming young man and when two other people offended against in the same way as herself take it all with a laugh?

All the same, I dreaded the moment when my new penetrator would implant his enormous joy-stick in me but I armed myself with courage. It was as hard as iron and as hot as a fire-brand. No matter, the handsome, fair young man fondled me, adjusted my position, kissed me and half opened me up; he thrust, I counter-thrust and performed at least half the work; my little cunt fulfilled all my own hopes, withstood the assault, allowed itself to be penetrated and finally lodged within itself all the young man had. Thanks be to Venus, all went well. We now proceeded to fuck in great style; I was still stimulated by the proximity of my mother, who—quickly overcome by pleasure—had forgotten she was being raped, at first moved her body with a reluctant expression, to be replaced by a more complaisant one until she could no longer be bothered to keep up appearances, raised her buttocks, jigged up and down and made the bedstead, which before us had hardly been used to such goings-on, not squeak but groan. . . . If my mother could behave like this under my very eyes and beside me, I had the right to let my hair down, too. So I at once wriggled lustily under my fair attacker, which made him laugh, and I was mischievous enough to say to him, before the solemn moment which brings with it the supreme voluptuous crisis,

'Don't be surprised. I may be young but spirited souls do not wait upon the years to show their mettle.'

My mother, without for a moment desisting from her own interesting preoccupations, still had the presence of mind to punish me for my boldness by slapping me with the back of her hand under my thigh. The while, Félicité was not idle with her charming greenhorn: she tossed him about with variations and, mistress of her art that she was, gave him a memorable lesson. There we were then, three inflamed *cunts* under three masterful *cocks*, jigging our *arses* up and down, sobbing with delight and giving the impression of waves on the sea raised by a gale. As the three athletes were a little fatigued—the Knight had not spent the night without giving evidence of his manly prowess elsewhere—the scene lasted a long time to the great satisfaction of all concerned. Nobody was shy; nobody needed to be asked and everything went off swimmingly: mother, daughter, lady's maid, knight, count and the little prince all came simultaneously.

That was the finale of our lovely fuck in concert.

When it was over, we could not help smiling at one another and the Knight did not have to ask us to embrace with the greatest tenderness. We swore peace and secrecy and it was agreed that reconciliation with my mother should be celebrated with a luncheon in the country, proposed by the Knight, who undertook to make all the necessary preparations for it that very day. My mother, it should be said, was quite free as far as the convent was concerned because of her court action and was able to go where and when she pleased and take us with her. We were to meet at the pleasure gardens at the end of a royal promenade not far from the town. We were promised that the carriage would be at our door on the stroke of noon.

Finally, the gentlemen withdrew; nothing untoward happened to them on the way out of the convent. My mother, on returning to her room, expressed the wish that I follow her to give her some explanations. Félicité remained behind by herself in the place I might from now on call our brothel and was able to rest her wearied charms at her ease.

The Diary of Mata Hari

I had to visit a well-known captain of industry in our town to pay off a gambling debt with my body. The debt my husband had incurred was so enormous—over 3000 guilders—that there was not the slightest chance he could ever pay this amount in cold cash. This particular visit I had to make was to have far-reaching significance, and it altered my life completely.

Only my husband's threat that a scandal would bring about my beloved father's utter ruin made me obey his command to visit van Boom and—'to put myself at his disposal.'

'Our stout-hearted Mister van Boom likes you very much, so much that I am convinced this rich filthy pig has deliberately driven me into a position where he can demand almost anything from me, especially the pleasure of my beautiful wife's company. Well, he can have that . . . it's a hell of a lot easier for me than to try and scrape up 3000 guilders. He wouldn't find them on me, even if he put me on my head and tried to shake me!' These cynical words were the 'instructions' which told me the exact situation in which I found myself.

'And this time I fully expect from you complete cooperation. After all, it's a debt of honour and I have to pay it. If you feel like it you can put on a few airs and politely refuse a little bit . . . many men love it that way; it makes them think that they really conquer the broad.'

I went to van Boom. Bitter experience had taught me that it was useless to cry and every word spent on pleading would be a waste.

Pieter van Boom was an elegant man of around 39 years and extremely attractive physically. If my task had not been such a horrible one, and if my mind had not been continually occupied with my bitter fate, meeting such a man could have been very pleasant. But I was not even in the mood to contemplate whether such a man—if met under different circumstances—could be capable of attracting me . . .

Van Boom's reception was very polite and friendly and he ignored my confusion and shame completely. He acted as if I had come to him voluntarily and as if we were old friends. I knew, of course, about his reputation with women. Most of the ladies in town fought for his attentions, and I was sure that he expected me to fall for him, that my modesty and propriety would melt away before his charms. My reputation was spotless and the people in our city often said that 'the fascinating beauty of Captain MacLeod's wife is surpassed only by her exemplary virtue.' They were completely unaware of the terrible indignities I had to undergo at the hands of my husband's gambling buddies to whom I was fettered body and soul. Of course, the initiates knew, but they took good care that these practices remained a deep secret. After all, they were the beneficiaries.

'Madame, it is my pleasure. I hope that you will allow me to have the honour of your company. And I want you to know that I have been your secret admirer for a very long time, and that your visit gives me the greatest satisfaction.'

I tried to remain very calm, though I could not help but retort immediately if he knew *why* I had come to see him, and if he was aware of the fact that I only made this visit to his home upon direct orders from my husband. Moreover, that my call was connected with a certain debt of 3000 guilders . . .

'But, Madame, how could you think such a thing! Admittedly I have desired to meet you here in my home, just the two of us between these discreet four walls, but it would deeply hurt me if I had to believe that you construe my admiration as lack of respect and that you view my desire to be more to you than just a stranger, as an importunity!'

'I understood that you wanted . . . that you . . . I mean, my husband's gambling debt . . .' the words stuck in my throat. Did I have to beg all over again?'

'Oh, yes, certainly, there is a certain debt. But, please believe me, I only used that as an excuse to meet you. You are the most beautiful woman I have ever seen and I beg you to believe me that I will not abuse this opportunity to talk to you. I would not force you to do anything. Yes, it is true I desire you with all my heart. I am enchanted by your beauty and your figure. Your type, that dark hair, the charming exotic individuality of your silken skin, your beautiful eyes, your beguiling lips, your gorgeous arms— no, no, please allow me to admire you . . . don't try to hide yourself—I want you to understand, most beautiful of all women, that all this drives me out of my mind! But I would not want to frighten you. I want to earn your friendship, your love—may God grant it—on my own terms; I want you to like me because of my admiration for you, because of my complete devotion.'

Never before had a man talked to me in this way. I did not know what was happening to me. This charming man, used to conquering every woman he met . . . did he really mean that? Or was it merely an excuse to avoid any settlement other than payment in cash?

But when he handed me a receipt for the full amount my husband owed him, with the words: 'My dear lady, I believe this is what you were looking for . . .' and started to help me with my coat, I knew he had spoken the truth. A hitherto unknown feeling took possession of me. I felt sorry and at the same time compelled to thank this man as affectionately as the circumstances would allow, to show him my heartfelt gratitude for his generosity.

I asked him if I could be permitted to stay awhile. His eyes lit up and the happiness they betrayed told me that my request had fulfilled his highest hopes. When I left his home several hours later, his desires had become reality and I—ah, I finally knew what it meant to be in love . . .

I was giddy and intoxicated, I floated and cried softly out of sheer happiness. I was walking on clouds. This man had caressed me, kissed me and finally possessed me, and I felt as if I had finally become a woman when he encircled me in his arms. It was as if only his kisses, only his glowing embraces had made me a complete woman. I forgot the misery of my marriage, the many men whose vilifications I had suffered because my husband told me to, and for the first time in my life I was truly happy, cheerful and exuberant . . . in short, I was crazed with love. This man had awakened me, had shown me what love is; he also showed me that love without physical pleasure is a monstrosity.

His embraces melted away everything which is

doubtful, improper and smutty; his kisses were so divine that they ennobled everything which is dirty, filthy and animalistic with other men.

But how had it come to this?

We were drinking tea and talking as if we had been old friends. I felt at ease and I was very happy that this entire sordid affair had somehow transformed itself into a fairytale. I realized that Pieter had been very generous, but in those days I was still not experienced enough to fully understand the will power it must have cost him to let this sure prey escape from him.

I allowed him to kiss my hand. He caressed it softly and I was pleasantly surprised with the emotions this touch released in me. After a few small glasses of liquor I felt lightheaded and happy. The clock on the mantelpiece played a soft melody with its chimes and—even today I still don't understand how I summoned up the courage—I got up and tried some light dance steps.

Pieter applauded enthusiastically and beseeched me to continue. When I laughingly refused, he, too, got up, took me in his arms and started to whirl around the room with me. We danced till I became quite dizzy . . .

That was when Pieter kissed me on the mouth.

It was a soft, infinitely sweet kiss. The first one . . .

How they turned into so many, I cannot clearly remember. Anyhow, Pieter's sensitive fingers, his hypnotic caresses, his incredibly soft and sweet touches, robbed me completely of my senses.

Suddenly we found ourselves down upon the sofa which was standing in a corner of the room. Our lips were pressed together and did not separate. We had only eyes for each other, and the rest of the world ceased to exist. It felt like a dream when Pieter's hands, softly and carefully, removed one piece of clothing after the other. I remember only that the more my cool skin was exposed, the hotter became his kisses . . . They covered me like an exquisite stole; they enveloped me like a summer shower; I felt their soft yet persisting pressure all over my body, like soft refreshing drops on my burning skin.

I felt them everywhere. They lingered at certain places and it seemed as if they were eternally impressed upon other spots. They deluged my entire body so that it seemed as if they were at all places at the same time. Now they would rain down upon my breasts, then they trickled into my armpits, another time they would sweep along my hips or they would drip into the especially soft flesh on the inside of my thighs . . .

Pieter's hands had long since finished undressing me and they were now feverishly busy elsewhere. They caressed me without interruption, so incredibly soft and hesitant that at first I believed I was again with my dear Henriette . . . they fondled my shoulders, hugged my back, caressed my breasts— whenever his lips were tasting another part of my body—and fluttered their way into my thighs. They wormed themselves under my body, raising me almost unnoticeably, and arched around my buttocks. Once they had reached these full, meaty globes they became more energetic; they clutched around the well-rounded forms and started to knead, push, pull and squeeze till I overflowed with delicious rapture . . .

I cannot recall how I suddenly came to feel Pieter's nude body. I had not noticed that he had undressed. He must have done this with a magician's agility because his fondling hands did not stop caressing my body for a single moment. But suddenly two strong male legs, cool and hard as marble, encircled my body, loosened again and slowly pried in between my 'marvellously long dancer's legs,' as Pieter later always referred to them. His hard-muscled, nude torso pressed against my soft, defenceless bosom.

But how good it felt! This strange male body, it smelled strong and spicy and new—so completely different from that of my husband with whom I had slept for so long. And it was exciting! Was this man that much different? How was it that no other man had ever excited me so much? Could it be that Pieter was exceptionally handsome, or was it the particular smell of his body which almost drove me out of my mind?

Could it be the strength of his arms? Oh, how I came to feel that strength which somehow never hurt me. I had never experienced anything like it in my entire life . . .

And again his mouth pressed itself upon my lips. Very softly at first, I hardly noticed its insistent pressure; slowly, however, a hot tongue slipped out and I could not resist, allowing it to penetrate between my lips, explore my mouth and coax my tongue. I soon understood that this play was an invitation, a challenge to reciprocate, to send out my own tongue and return the visit. I was obedient. The effect this had upon Pieter was stupendous. His amorous caresses tripled and his kisses almost turned into love bites. He sucked my lips and my tongue as if he wanted to devour them.

His body trembled. He rested upon me and I could feel the delicious heaviness of him. For a short moment he rested as if to gather his strength but soon he started to rub his body against mine; at first slowly, almost hesitantly, yet so intensely that it almost frightened me; after a short while I had become used to it.

Something else diverted my attention. I could clearly feel his incredibly hard member. It was stuck between our rubbing bodies, resembling a short heavy club which somehow had become lodged in that spot where I could feel it most clearly.

But—it could either be that Pieter had changed his position slightly, or maybe I had without thinking spread my thighs a little wider—suddenly this club was no longer pressed between our stomachs but had settled itself right between my legs, pushing against that secret little spot with a feather-light touch . . .

Pieter's breathing intensified and his voice was almost rough when he asked me, 'Do you love me at least a little bit, sweet lady—would you please make me very, very happy?'

I had no choice—I answered, 'Yes, I love you—do with me whatever you will—I belong to you . . . take me . . completely . . . utterly . . .'

'Darling, you make me feel so ashamed . . . I . . . I . . . aah!—I am so terribly happy right now . . . later . . . later I will tell you—what's—on—my—mind . . . how terribly much I love you!' During these words, which sounded so infinitely sweet to me, his hot, virile and pulsating member shoved slowly and carefully, yet surely and without stopping, between my widely spread thighs and pressed against the entrance of my sacred spot. A short, hardly noticeable hesitation, more like a slow probing and tasting, and the sweet pole penetrated calmly and securely deep into my lap. It succeeded without any difficulty—the way had been well prepared, the excitement of the situation, Pieter's skilful caresses, his manly tenderness had put me in that mood which knows of only one release. My very being had to be drowned in the juices of his love. My healthy body and loving disposition had done their duty well . . .

Pieter's hands had slid under my back and forcibly taken hold of my buttocks, keeping them in his tight grip. He carried me in his strong hands while the arrow of his love forced itself deeply into my grotto. And when he slowly pulled back with carefully measured jolts which, though they did not devastate me, made me shudder to the utmost depths of my soul, I slowly came to realize what ecstasy is. His beautiful tool penetrated me, a true messenger of Cupid, light as a feather, continually courting, completely irresistible . . . And whenever it pulled out impishly my entire being shivered longingly for its return. I was afraid it would depart forever instead of preparing for another jump which would take possession of my hotly glowing hole.

The regularity of these delicious humps have been burned into my memory and will remain there forever. There was something unbelievably confident, terribly powerful in the calm and regular artistry, the almost majestic behaviour of this truly royal sceptre; one might say, Pieter fucked me regally. I sighed and groaned; I had never experienced anything like it. I felt myself floating as if in a dream; I wanted to sing with pleasure, cry with desire.

I was very proud that I could give Pieter pleasure; there was no doubt I was doing just that because he groaned as lustfully as I did; he stammered loving little nothings and even his groaning and grumbling, though it seemed inarticulate, reminded me of a big love-sick bear and convinced me that he was in the grip of the same delirious mood as I was. Every time his powerful, swollen instrument (I had the distinct impression that it had grown even bigger and more stiff once it was firmly implanted within my belly) sank deeply into my lovingly clenching cleft, Pieter moaned voluptuously and I could not resist softly pushing toward him with my swaying hips . . .

However, my actions did have unexpected results. As soon as Pieter found out that his movements caused my body to sway in a similar rhythm, he speeded up his tempo which, in the beginning had been majestic and had remained imposing even though I now noticed an increase in enthusiasm. Now, however, every push became more impressive, livelier and, all of a sudden—I was, at first, completely taken by surprise—I had to endure an incredibly quick succession of hammerlike blows which raced like wildfire against my loins. Pieter romped in wild frenzy against my body; he was sweating, every muscle in his body was tense, his powerful arms had pushed my thighs wide open, spreading them more than they had ever been before.

Even though these powerful jolts followed each other in rapid succession, every single one of them released delicious shivers throughout my entire body. It was the peak of undreamed-of delights. It was impossible that anything could exist on this earth more majestic than being loved the way Pieter loved me . . .

Pieter's eyes twinkled above me like the stars and their heavenly shine told me that he had to be as happy as I was. The words he murmured, interrupted by his heavy sighs, were hardly distinguishable from his grunts and groans that were caused by his lustful rutting, but they proved to me the truth of my assumption.

'Oh my darling, my pet—could you stand it that I torture you to death with my token of love . . . that I perish in your lap . . . oh, please . . . allow me . . . to—die—in—your—arms . . . !'

His tender words were not belied by the brutal jolts that ran through my body and pierced me like so many fiery stakes. He could have whipped me, stepped on me—I would have considered it to be my greatest delight. To this man I felt truly married—he was really the Lord and Master of my body, because he possessed my soul . . .

'Darling . . . my only true love . . . you really love me . . . could you truly, really . . . love—me?' His powerful marble-hard body jolted against mine without interruption. 'You allow me so much . . . you give me . . . you are showing me . . . what true delight really is . . . aren't you afraid, that I . . . could . . . never . . . do . . . without . . . you . . . ever again?'

'No, my dearest Pieter . . . you are now my only true love, and I want to be yours forever and ever . . . I am at your beck and call . . . whenever . . . you . . . want . . . me . . . I'll . . . throw myself . . . into—your—arms . . . !'

'Oh, darling . . . divine one . . . so much happiness makes me dizzy . . . Be careful . . . you could kill me . . .' With these words, Pieter doubled his already incredible efforts, and—though it seemed impossible—speeded up his tempo.

'Do you notice how you set me on fire . . . how my forces double . . . oh, my darling . . . I can't stand it much longer . . . I can't . . . much . . . longer . . . darling, I . . . have . . . to . . . now . . . *aaah* . . . now . . . I'm coming . . . *aaah* . . . !'

I could feel how his powerful thing bucked deep inside my body, how it swelled even more powerfully and suddenly I was pierced by a hot pulsing jet, so strong that I feared for a moment I had been set on fire. But at the same time I, too, had reached the ultimate point and I came . . .

A few more jolts vibrated the quickly dwindling arrow of my lover—then it was over; we sank back into the soft pillows that covered the sofa.

Later, when we had gathered our breath, our lips found each other again. Our kisses were stronger and more pure than before since there were no excited nerves or weakening senses that could distract our attention. It seemed as if we consisted only of mouths seeking each other and tasting the honey from each other's lips.

Our arms were resting, completely relaxed around each other's shoulders. When my hands stole slowly down Pieter's body I saw his member, small and peaceful between the finely curled hairs. It had changed so much—was this the same mighty club with which Pieter had shown me his undying love?

It seemed as if we wanted to kiss eternally to make up for all the time we had not been together. Our tongues penetrated deeply into our eagerly opened mouths. They met and kissed and played around as our lips had been doing for a long time. They petted each other, playfully avoided each other; our teeth played along and we bit lightly and enticingly. Pieter looked so handsome when he laughed happily! I tickled him to make him laugh louder. His teeth were regular, beautiful and white as snow. He enjoyed himself tremendously and played along with me. After a little while we romped around like a couple of excited school kids. This went on till I became especially wanton and swung my body on top of his, pressing his arms against his torso with my full thighs. Now I 'punished' the helpless man to my heart's content.

I bent myself over him so that I could tousle his hair, but he seized this opportunity to quickly grasp one of the red berries that crowned my breasts with his lips. I pushed my full bosom into his face to teach him a lesson but I enjoyed this manoeuvre so much—especially since he cried 'uncle' and begged me not to pierce him wrathfully with my pointed breasts—that I repeated this game alternately with the hardening nipple of one breast and then the other. Finally I wound up literally boxing his ears with my taut, full globes, yes . . . I truly whipped him with those large elastic balls that were heavy and ripe as they should be when they belong to a full-grown enticing woman . . . Finally I pressed my bosom with all my force into his face, forcing him to breathe the heavy mixture of perfume, my perspiration and the peculiar odour of our sexes . . .

At first this game seemed to have a peculiar narcotic effect on Pieter, but after he had suffered these sweet tortures for a while, breathing heavily and panting with excitement, he suddenly sat upright and lifted me off his muscular body.

'Do you really think that I could stand much more of this, you little brown devil, you sweetest of all dark Satans—you drive me out of my mind . . . I'd lose it if I allowed you for one more moment . . . even the tiniest fraction of another minute . . . look . . . look what you have done . . . with your breast, with that sweetest of all bosoms which is going to get

me into an insane asylum one of these days . . . !'
And he pointed in playful wrath at his virile member.

Good heavens, the way that thing towered up into
the air! How stiff and straight it stood. I was positively fascinated. I could not help myself—I had to
stretch out my hands, irrepressibly attracted by this
magic wand, this towering sceptre; I had to touch it
to convince myself that this hardness was no illusion,
that this stiffness was real.

When my hands—how small they seemed next to
this enormous pole—encircled Pieter's regally presented member, a light shudder went through his
body and at the same moment he took me into his
arms.

'I can't take it when you touch me there—come
on, please, come on . . . I can't play this game any
longer . . . I am much too excited—let me enter you
quickly, I am expiring . . . *oooh* . . . how sweet is
that body of yours . . . your bosom . . . your thighs
. . . your divine derriere—everything . . . everything belongs to me . . . tell me . . . everything . . .
Am I right . . . ! Everything . . . ?'

I rested upon his chest. One arm encircled me
firmly as if he were afraid that I would flee from him;
with his free hand he tried (behind my back) to push
his stiff and unruly member into my crevice. I helped
him as well as I could: I wriggled my lower body,
blindly searching for the club that was about to
pierce me.

Finally, Pieter succeeded in putting his big boy—
after he had been fingering around unsuccessfully for
some time—into my body. I must admit that I
helped a little bit with my hands. My fear that Pieter
could have slipped out, or even worse, missed his
goal altogether, was too great. And shame? I did

not feel any . . . Pieter and I had become too intimate . . .

But now my lover started to ram into me anew. And I had the impression, right after the first few jolts, that he penetrated deeper into me than ever before. It felt as if his member was about to come out through my throat. He screwed me as if he were a maniac. Every other man would have scared me to death because his thrusts were rather brutal—but I knew that this vigour and power was his token of love for me and the almost animal rutting was proof that I, or rather the charms of my body, whipped his flesh into a frenzy. It was pure ardour . . . the stallion in this man had taken full possession of him.

The animal within me was also awakened by his powerful jolts . . . they would have awakened the dead. Though at many moments the almost bursting member of my lover tore my tender orifice nearly to pieces, rubbed it raw and split my cleft to its utmost capacity, the tickling it caused was delightful and blissful beyond description. And the feeling of utter happiness that now took possession of me made me forget everything else; my entire being had become subject to this pleasure and only one single thought filled my grateful mind: I was being screwed with the fierce passion of which only a truly, idealistically honest man in love is capable. But this delicious thought did not prevent me from screaming wantonly and airing my passionate desires with rutting groans. First it was only a sigh, then a stammered exclamation and finally my inhibitions exploded and I hollered rather than spoke, 'You . . . aaaaah, how fantastic . . . what marvellous jolts . . . please, don't slow down . . . no . . . a little faster . . . faster . . . more, more, more . . . so . . . yes . . . oooh, how

fantastic . . . ! It feels so good . . . oh, please, darling, screw me as hard as you can . . . it feels so good
. . . your prick is so sweet . . . *aaah . . . aaaaaah*
. . . you . . . you . . . let me die in your embrace . . .
no, I want to enjoy you to the fullest . . . do you hear
me . . . ? Often . . . always . . . always . . . you
must screw me like this . . . *aaah . . . ooooh* . . .
now—I—finally——know—what—a—good—fuck
—means . . .'

I did not realize, nor did I care, that my words
overstepped the boundaries of good taste; I only
knew one thing: Pieter screwed me as I am sure no
woman has ever been laid before and even though I
could barely take it to be possessed in such a mania-
cal way, I was obsessed with the tremendous desire
that his power would increase and that his possession
of me would only become stronger. The thought that
the inhuman force of these powerful thrusts would
slow down, or even worse, might stop altogether,
was more unbearable than the incredible punishment I underwent . . .

My wild utterings caused Pieter to become more
ardent than ever, and his jolts became more and
more powerful with every filthy word I uttered. A
peculiar gnashing of his teeth and the shuddering
along his flanks proved to me that it made him
extremely passionate. And despite his previous
polite language, Pieter was also capable of using a
similar vocabulary and no longer hesitated in doing
so.

'Oh, darling . . . do you really think that I can
fuck you the way you deserve . . . ? Oh, I wish I had
a cock that would be worthy of a cunt like yours . . .
twice as heavy and much longer . . . aaah, isn't that
what you really want . . . ? Hah . . . you need a dong,

a fat big cock, as heavy as an arm . . . that's what you
want! . . . You're right . . . one man is not enough
for you . . . but I want to pin you down and make
you . . . it is so heavenly . . . pretty soon I have to
. . . please . . . please . . . push back a little harder
. . . aaaah, how sweet . . . what a fantastic piece of
ass . . . oooh, those buns . . . so firm . . . those
sweet, sweet . . . buns . . . *aaah* . . . you . . . darling
. . . my darling . . . *aaah* . . . *aaaahh*, you
—on-ly—one . . .'

All barriers were down. We were a man and a
woman. Two hungry sexes. Nothing else. That's
how we saw each other. Filled with boundless desire
and giving in to it without shame, knowing full
well that this complete surrender to our voluptuous
desires, this sovereign disdain for all civilized
bounds, could only increase our enjoyment.

I revelled in the foulest expressions I could think
of without really knowing where I had acquired
them. A common prostitute would not have the
courage to use such language, but to us it became a
precious ingredient, the pepper which spiced a
sumptuous meal and tickled our palates, increasing
our desire for more and stronger stimulations . . .

'You . . . fuck . . . fuck me . . . ha . . . fuck me
. . . with all your strength . . . harder, quicker . . .
don't be so soft . . . come on, I want to feel your big
prick . . . I want that dong of yours to tear me apart
. . . *aaah*, now you're doing it . . . you fuck like a
bull . . . you know how to give it to me . . . My
husband is a stupid dog . . . he can't do it . . . like
you . . . Give it to me . . . Oh, you don't know . . .
how I hate . . . that bastard . . . aaah, darling . . .
sweetheart . . . fuck me . . . please, I beg you . . .
fuck me . . . fuck me hard . . . don't ever leave me

. . . don't spare me . . . you, take me . . . be mean
. . . do something . . . come on, fuck me really hard
. . . push it deeper . . . what's the matter with you
. . . are you getting tired . . . ? Come on, come on
. . . fuck me harder . . . stick it in deeper, hump as
hard as you can . . . yes, yes, that's it . . . quicker
. . . stronger . . . don't stop . . . *aaaah* . . . deep
. . . deeper . . . I want to feel you, deeper . . . Taste
you? Oh, lover, come, please . . . come . . . I am
coming too . . . at the same time . . . *aaah* . . . I . . .
am . . . coming . . . right . . . now . . . now!
aaaáah! . . . *Aaaaah* . . . *aaah* . . . *ooh!*'

A final convulsive bucking of my thrashing body
and then I collapsed. Everything seemed to spin
around me. My legs trampled around, foam formed
upon my lips, my throat was suddenly parched and I
felt as if I were about to choke. I barely had the power
to ask for a glass of water . . . then a heavy fog settled
upon me as if I had been nailed down to the pillows . . .

Pieter, the man with whom I have been in love
purely and totally, was the only true love in my entire
life. I have never had any regrets and his being there
was the only ray of light in my otherwise dark marriage. I was truly grateful to my husband for bringing
Pieter and me together; even though his intentions
had been foul, the result was the most wonderful
thing that ever happened to me.

If I could have foreseen what I was going to have to
endure in the East Indies, I would never have followed my husband when he was transferred to that
mysterious land. His conduct was no longer toler-
ated by his superiors and he was given the choice of
accepting either a dishonourable discharge or a garri-
son position in a particularly dangerous and

unhealthy district in the Colonies. As I said, if I had known then what I know now, I would have committed suicide.

And, of course, I did not know either that I was going to lose my darling Pieter . . .

When we were in the process of softening the blow of our parting with an especially tender rendezvous, Pieter told me, 'I will follow you and meet you in a certain city; I have to put my affairs in Holland in order and then I will go after you.' Three months later Pieter was no longer among the living; he fell off his horse and died before help could arrive.

With his death, I lost everything that had given me the courage to endure my life, especially my marriage to MacLeod. Pieter was the most perfect lover a woman could wish for and it was he who gave me the idea to become a performing *artiste*.

At first he asked me to walk up and down the room either nude, or—since I knew how excited this made him—with my skirts raised high up to my thighs . . . And I was glad to perform this little revue for him.

'Your dancer's legs haunt me night and day,' he often told me and he did not rest before he had got my permission to have them pictured by a great Parisian artist who, at great cost to him, had come to our town for that purpose. 'I need their portrait,' he said, 'I always want to have your legs right in front of me.' He finally had many portraits done of my legs, one of them life-size; he wanted my legs in different poses. One portrait in particular stands out in my mind. The top of the picture was formed by my petticoat and silken chemise, held up by my hands; the fine lace of my panties peeked out from under the hems of my skirts. And then, my legs . . . in beautiful, black, crocheted stockings which stretched tautly around my full calves, slim ankles and ripe thighs, so taut that one could almost hear the silk rustle with any imagined movement of this beautiful painting. The position I had to take up embarrassed me greatly, especially in front of the painter who was doing his preparatory sketches. After all, this man was a complete stranger to me. The posture was rather inviting, to say the least; I stood like a wild dancer who is just about to throw one leg up high during the can-can. Most exciting were my thighs, partly nude and clearly visible in their white nakedness between the tops of the black hose and the hem of the skirt—Pieter could never get enough of looking at that particular spot in the painting. Sometimes I was truly jealous of that painting and I tried everything in my power to distract his attention. I would stand invitingly in front of it, lift my skirts and then . . . Then whatever I wanted would happen . . . the living flesh would triumph . . .

Oh, happy days!

Secret Talents

You remember, my friend, how I told you I believed I was born to love? Well, I am more convinced of it than ever. Think back for a moment: Even before I left home I met a woman who opened my eyes to the joys of sex. True, it was an unnatural love to be sure, but what of that? I have never suffered from it; I acquired something of an education through it all, and though it was the wrong kind of an education— as some will try to make you believe—it had its advantages in that it was to provide me with the talents necessary in the years to follow. Such talents, I firmly believe, are necessary to a career such as mine.

I believe I have already mentioned that I was desirous in wishing to retain my virginity until I came to age; if I didn't I am mentioning it now. Even before I left Vienna I had been taken with the desire to have a lover, but I held off; even passing my eighteenth birthday, that age when it is quite proper and fitting for a maiden to be regally and royally fucked.

Even when making the journey into Frankfurt I was overtaken with these thoughts. I believe I had arrived at the age when it would be good for me to accept the love of a man, and as I reflected on my past life I was suddenly overcome with the desire for a man!

Yes, that was it. I was in love without a lover—a

most amazing state of affairs. It, however, never occurred to me that I was to have one so soon.

The day following my arrival in Frankfurt my manager had provided me with a housekeeper. It happened, however, that I wasn't to keep her; she for years had held the position of wardrobe-mistress in the various productions and was quite well versed in things both upon and off stage.

She was a motherly old soul and I was quite taken back when, that very day, she said: 'I do not wish to presume, my dear, but when do you expect to be joined by your lover?'

The question coming from her amazed me. At first I was inclined to resent this bold remark, but I thought better of it—and I have always thanked myself that I hadn't been harsh with her.

'My lover?' I asked, showing surprise at the audacity of her question.

For a long moment she stared at me, then: 'You have a lover, have you not?'

'No,' I answered, 'I have no lover. Why do you ask?'

'I hope you will forgive me for mentioning it,' she began, 'but don't you think it quite necessary—to your voice, I mean?'

Then it suddenly occurred to me that I had heard something or other about this, and I wondered if I could be mistaken in this woman's true meaning? Here I was a total stranger in a strange city with few if any friends. In the late past I had never been without a girl upon whom I could lavish my caresses, and I suddenly felt rather alone. Also, I wondered if it were possible that this elderly woman had designs on me? Feeling somewhat frisky at the moment I decided to put her to the test; she wouldn't be so bad;

and an old tongue was better than nothing.

Laughing, I said 'I am sorry, my dear, but I have no male love; mine, in the past, has been lady lovers,' and I stretched languidly, at the time allowing one bare leg to jut out between the folds of my gown, the only article of clothing I was wearing at that moment.

She shook her head. 'You are a very foolish girl,' she said. 'It is all very nice to have a sympathetic girl friend, but if you won't think me over bold I would say that you are abusing yourself in not taking a real lover—you understand, do you not?'

There was a merry twinkle in her eyes as she said this.

Becoming more daring, I said: 'You mean I should take one who will caress me in the manner I like to be caressed?'

She nodded. 'You will find it necessary in the developing of your throat muscles. Please do not think I am presuming too much,' she went on. 'Indeed, I am quite serious. You must do this, or sooner or later you will lose your voice,' and turning, she left me alone with my thoughts. You may rest assured my thoughts were conflicting.

The rest of the day I spent between reclining on a beautiful little flower-decked porch and fussing about a well-appointed kitchen.

To give you some idea of how the thought gripped me, let me tell you of how I ate my dinner that night. I had dismissed my housekeeper and had set the table for two places. I fancied I was entertaining my lover, and to make the picture complete I wore but a thin dressing-gown and mules, being careful that the gown was open down the front. It was foolish, of course, but I was having a grand time of it. Later, when 'we' finished our dinner, I fancied he carried me to a broad divan, in the living-room, and here he kissed and kissed and kissed me. Oh, I don't know what I thought!

I found myself eager for a man! I pictured him as a strong man; one qualified to administer real, brutal love—

Then, the following day, a strange thing occurred. It was as though my prayers were being answered. A carriage stopped at my door. From it alighted my aged manager, and with him was one of the handsomest men I had ever seen! From behind the curtains I gazed at him; I had no eyes for my manager; and he was handsome; black, silky hair—Ah! he was an Apollo!

They entered. To my surprise—and joy—this man was to play the part of Romeo, in the play in which I was to star.

Never shall I forget the expression that came over his handsome face when he was introduced. For almost a full minute, perhaps, I stood staring into his eyes, and it was he who broke the spell.

'Really,' he cried, his voice low, 'I had no idea I was to play next to an angel!' We all three laughed at this, and after a brief visit my manager left us. He had many duties to attend to, he said, and bowed himself out, leaving me to speculate on the outcome of it all.

Even in those first few moments I couldn't help but wonder how wonderful it must be to be fucked by a man such as this one! And even then I promised myself the pleasure of having this man in my arms! Yes! He would be my lover!

Even then I was speculating on how best to lure him to my bed.

In the theatre one sees nudity on every hand, and I

realized it would take more than mere nudity to bring about a union between us.

I might add here that I *was* dressed somewhat scantily; my only garment, besides a short silken under-vest, was a kimono of pale silk, and low bedroom slippers on my bare feet, and I took advantage of this scant apparel to bring about a better understanding between us. 'I must beg your forgiveness for allowing myself to be caught so,' I began, motioning to my dress.

'Pray forget it,' he said. 'I quite understand. It *is* rather warm and I am delighted that you are considerate enough of your own comfort to dress accordingly.'

'But,' I insisted, a wave of almost uncontrollable lust sweeping over me, 'I am almost naked!' I laughed to show I wasn't frightened.

'Pray! It is no matter,' he said smiling his sweetest. 'Again let me say I think your dress is quite satisfactory. However, since my visit here was but to meet you, may I withdraw?' He kissed my finger tips and withdrew before I could say a word to stay him.

I was vexed with myself. Why had I said such a foolish thing!

I spent a dreadful night. My thoughts were filled with nothing but that wonderful man. There was one consoling thought, however. That was, that on the morrow he would call again, and I promised myself that I would never be so silly again. In reality I had meant to call attention to my scant dress hoping in that way to attract him to my arms, but he was a gentleman, and took my remark as a desire on my part that he withdraw. I cursed myself for a fool!

If he had but known the easy conquest I would have been I am sure he would have stayed with me,

and instead of kissing my fingertips, he would have
had something far more substantial than fingers to
kiss. After he departed I slipped out of my gown and
under-vest and donned my nightgown. Standing
before my glass and viewing my image, I patted my
hairy mount, saying aloud: 'Very, very soon, my
dear, you shall have something far more thrilling to
caress than a mere tongue-tip.'

The following day was a long one for me, though
he came shortly after lunch. Taking advantage of his
suggestion that I dress for comfort rather than for
convention, I was wearing an outfit not unlike that of
the previous day; the only difference being that my
gown was of black georgette, and I wore black silk
stockings.

My idea of the black gown was to accentuate the
whiteness of my body and limbs. Somewhat daring,
don't you think, my friend?

But I can tell you I was desperate; I had been
pricked with Cupid's dart—it remained but to be
pricked with my lover's!

This time he complimented me on my thoughtful-
ness in dress.

'Do you realize that you are very beautiful?' he
asked, 'And that I'm afraid I shall never be able to
withstand your nearness?'

I thrilled as his eyes swept over me, for while my
gown covered, it did not in the least hide the outline
of my body and legs! 'Nonsense,' I laughed, 'You
have seen any number of handsome women, and you
seemed to have survived.'

We seated ourselves upon the divan. There we
went over the lines of the play. You are familiar with
the play 'Romeo and Juliet' so I won't tire you with
the story. Enough to say that the balcony scene is

unusually thrilling. Romeo, as you know, is supposed to climb the balcony, and here he is to meet his mistress, Juliet, and Juliet is supposed to have just got out of bed and is wearing but a nightgown.

If you will recall, I told you earlier in this story, that the whole of Europe had gone mad over exotic scenes both in and out of the theatre, and I had been given to understand from the start that this particular scene in our coming production was to be enacted in a somewhat unusual setting. Instead of wearing a nightgown, I was supposed to wear a white georgette dressing-gown, and as we sat there scanning our lines, he came to this particular situation. 'You are being called upon to assume a most unusual role,' he said without raising his eyes from the page.

'Yes' I said. I also kept my eyes riveted to the paper.

'Yes,' he said. 'I hope, however, that you will have no objection to wearing the scant attire this scene calls for.'

'Why should I?' I asked, trying to answer nonchalantly. 'After all it's all in the play, and the play's the thing, isn't it?'

'I'm afraid it won't be all play on my part,' he said.

'Indeed? And why not?'

'Because,' he answered, 'carrying such a beautiful lady, and having one so beautiful as yourself quite nude might prove too thrilling—I might drop you, you know.'

I laughed at this. I knew we were treading on dangerous ground, but I didn't care: I was more than ever determined to win this handsome man to my arms! 'Don't tell me,' I said, laughing, 'that I will be

210

the first naked woman you have held in your arms!'

This time it was he who laughed, then: 'I would rather not talk of that. However, if I have ever done anything like this, the lady was far less beautiful than yourself.'

'That is very beautifully said. I hope, however, that you will not be so overcome that you *will* drop me—That, I'm afraid, would be too dreadful for words!'

'Rest assured I shall not,' he said.

How we ever passed through this day without a demonstration from him I shall never be able to tell, for God knows, I did everything possible to impress him. On three distinct occasions I recrossed my legs, each time giving him a full view of my naked thighs to the very tops, and each time slowly drawing the folds of my scant gown over my knees.

Yet, nothing happened.

The following day it was the same thing, and the day after that.

By this time we had familiarized ourselves to the extent that we were ready to go over our lines together. That is, we were far enough advanced to practise our parts.

That day I had dressed very carefully. I was careful to the extent of ridding myself of everything except the lacey dressing-gown and slippers, and the gown being a buttonless affair, I was looking forward to practising the balcony scene, though I was careful to hold my gown together until that thrilling scene was to be enacted.

But again nothing happened. True, we went over everything again and again—but for some unknown reason he didn't think it necessary to practise the balcony scene.

Finally I came to the conclusion that if I were to get anywhere with this man I must make the advances myself. Going about practically naked seemed to make no impression on him whatsoever.

True, he never failed to compliment me on my attire, but compliments did little to quell the burning within my aching cunt!

It might be mentioned here that I had managed to get a very good maid, and my housekeeper was relieved of the burden of caring for my home. This maid, however, was the worst kind of a greenhorn; I doubt very much if she knew there was more than one use for her pussy; I had given her hints enough, but she simply looked at me when I would flit about in complete nakedness.

And, so, without even the comfort of a likeable maid, I found myself getting desperate. Something had to be done. I said: 'Why not arrange to have dinner with me tomorrow night! There is no reason why you shouldn't, is there?'

He hesitated a moment, then: 'Why—I would be delighted! No, there is no reason why I shouldn't.'

This was my first real step in paving the way to love! Real love! Already I pictured myself lying naked in his arms! Already I felt his lips kissing and caressing me from head to foot—

'You are married?' I asked, hardly knowing what I was saying.

'Whatever gave you that impression?' he asked.

I shrugged my shoulders. 'I don't know,' I said, 'I should hate to be the cause of trouble between you and your wife—I am glad, however, that you have none! I shall be expecting you—early!'

I'll never forget the strange light in his eyes as he kissed my fingertips at parting!

Believe it or not, my friend, I took an opiate that night before I could go to sleep. I didn't want to sleep; I took it for the simple reason that I might hurry the hours until I was to see him again.

The next day everything was hustle and bustle. I am the world's worst cook, but I managed, with the help of my maid, in preparing a delightfully cooked dinner. This done, I dismissed my maid, telling her I would not need her again that night; that she was free to visit her relatives if she chose.

From the icebox I produced several bottles of champagne and the choicest wines, placing them in a convenient place at table.

Then I took a bath. It lacked little time before he would arrive and I wanted to be at my best that night! This night! That's right! It was this night! My wedding night! This was the night I was to surrender my maidenhead! The night I was to be ravished in every pore!

Dried, after a highly perfumed bath, I arranged my hair. Then I began speculating as to what I should wear. It must be something unusual; of this I was sure. Already I had appeared before him in next to nothing! What, then, could I wear?

Finally, I chose a flimsy black dressing-gown. It was a daring thing, but I didn't care, I was desperate! Beneath this I wore a short chiffon undervest. Standing before my glass I viewed the result of this and even I blushed. If this didn't turn the trick for me, then I would give up all idea of ever winning him to my arms.

The gown came to about midway between my hips and knees, and since it was cut away daringly at the top, it was necessary to wear the frail under-garment or my breasts would have strutted bodily out of the gown. And while I was gazing at my reflection in the mirror, the bell rang! My hour was approaching! Snatching up a pin, I stuck it into my gown, to hold the thing together. Slipping my bare feet into low mules, I hurried to the door!

I noted he looked at me strangely. Entering and kissing my hand, he said: 'Your maid—she isn't here?' He couldn't seem to understand why I should have attended door for him.

'My maid,' I said, 'has been called away on account of sickness, but fear not, my friend, I have a splendid dinner for you!'

I wondered how I could be so calm in the face of those thoughts.

I saw him gaze at me, and I knew he was thrilled at what he saw, for this time the gown concealed nothing; even the hair about my aching cunt was fairly well revealed.

'I shall have to be your serving maid tonight,' I said as I flitted about him. The dinner, as you can guess, was a huge success, and long before it was finished we were both chatting away at a great rate. We consumed much wine; we both seemed to possess unusual thirsts.

'Let the table go,' I said as we went toward the living room. 'My maid shall attend to it tomorrow; besides, we might feel like eating something later!'

I must have made a rather startling picture as I sat there beside him upon the divan, my gown open down the front revealing both my legs naked to almost the tops. Ah, don't think I hadn't worked out a fitting campaign. I was desperate, and I was daring. Of course one could hardly expect a lover to make improper advances while seated at table, but at table I had added to my already daring plan!

I had brought a bottle of champagne into the living

room, and by way of starting the daring plan I had in mind, I said: 'Now let us drink to the success of our dinner, and our friendship!'

Even when saying it I could hardly control my voice. Knowing that in another minute or two I would have him in my arms was enough to thrill any one, wasn't it, my friend?

Very graciously he filled two glasses, and handing me one, we repeated the toast, and as I sat there holding the glass I realized that the moment had arrived! My well-thought-out plan was about to materialize! Leaning against him, I said: 'We should seal our friendship with a kiss—isn't that the proper way?'

I saw his eyes glance quickly at the windows! Then he slipped one arm about my waist and kissed me, and as his lips met mine, I deliberately spilled the contents of my glass across my thighs, at the same time giving a startled 'Oh!'

Quick to note this, he drew his handkerchief and attempted to dry me. 'It's nothing,' I said, 'I shall go and change it!'

With heart beating wildly, for now I was going to do the most daring thing of all! Quickly I slipped both garments from my shoulders, kicked the mules from my feet! Then I gave a piercing scream and threw myself down across the bed, in what was supposed to be a beautiful faint!

In an instant he was at my side! Seeing the apparent faint, he grabbed up a bottle of salts and pressed it beneath my nose. My eyes fluttered open. He placed his arms about me and kissed my lips again and again, then: 'Whatever happened? Why did you cry out?'

I smiled. 'I saw a mouse,' I answered, 'and I—I guess I fainted.'

Remember, my dear, I am an actress, but it took every bit of my skill to act timid then, for I was stark naked and I was in the arms of the man I loved! I made a feeble effort to arise, but he held me down. 'Please, dear,' he said, holding all the tighter.

'But, darling,' I cried, laughing faintly and trying to blush, 'I'm stark naked! What must you think of me!'

'I think you are the most beautiful woman I have ever seen,' he said, kissing me again and again, 'and I want to hold you in my arms, just like this, forever and ever!'

What could I do? While saying this, one of his hands had crept down to the hairs on my lower belly! I made not the slightest move to stop him; and as his hand slid further down, my thighs fell loosely apart and his searching fingers quite took possession of my cunt!

'I love you! I love you!' he cried.

My arms slid about his neck. 'And I love you, too,' I answered, and kissing his lips, I added: 'I have loved ever since I first saw you, and though I am still a virgin, I want you to make me a woman!'

Our lips met in a clinging, soul-stirring kiss!

Raising his lips from mine, he whispered: 'Will you be mine? Now! Here! Right here on your bed! I shall never be safe to myself until I have had you—body and soul!'

'You already have my soul, my darling, you have but to take my body—it is yours to do with as you like!'

'Then lie still and let me seal our love with a kiss!'

With a bound he was down on his knees and pressing burning kisses squarely on my cunt! The wine, my mad desire for him, the thrill of it all drove me almost mad! Grasping his head between my hands, I held it there and went off! No longer did I attempt to hold back! His arms were about me! His hands clutched my naked body and his greedy mouth sucked and tongued my cunt in a frenzy of delight!

Again I went off, and this time I almost fainted dead away, so intense was the shock! And while I lay there, my thighs still parted to his eager gaze, he quickly stripped off his clothes, a moment later springing, naked, into my waiting arms!

With a dexterous motion he placed the head of his monster of a cock to the flushed lips of my cunt and pressed it in where, thanks to the many tongues and my own fingers, he soon passed the barrier!

If I ever experienced a pain as a result of this, I know not; I know only that I was penetrated to his balls, and from the way he drove it into me, I thought he was trying to get them in too!

At last I was being fucked! Too late now to turn back, I bucked upward against him with all my might! Mad with lust for each other, we were like two animals! Holding it far into me, he went off, and almost instantly he began again! Our lips joined, our tongues darting in and out of each other's mouths, we fucked like mad! All the pent-up passion of years' standing was now let loose! How many times I went off I can't remember! How many times he filled my cunt with his prolific spend, I do not know!

I know only that I was supremely happy. I had never been so happy in my life! For a long time neither of us moved; just lay there soaking in bliss. Then he gazed into my eyes. 'Do you think this is acting on my part,' he asked, 'or do you believe now that I love you?'

'Of course you love me, Paul, darling. But let's reverse the question; don't you think I am the one to ask that question now that I have given you the one thing a girl has to give?'

I am not going into the details of all the things we said to each other that night. Many of them are too sacred to repeat, even to you, my friend. Enough to say that we swore eternal love for each other, and I believe he really meant it; I know I did.

But if I refuse to tell you of the things we said, I won't refuse to tell you of the things we did—You have a perfect right to that after the thrilling letter you wrote me, you naughty boy!

After relieving me of his weight he went to the bathroom, returning with a basin of warm water and towels. Bathing and drying me between my thighs, he bent and kissed my cunt in one long, clinging kiss.

Then he lay down beside me, took me in his strong arms and kissed me. Then it was that we talked. But talk did little to satisfy me: I had heard from both Vera and our prima donna of the joys of toying with and kissing the male organ. One of my hands stole down to it and my fingers clasped themselves about it; it was but half stiff, but I loved it. I squeezed and pressed it. It grew larger. I continued to caress it, and it grew and grew. Soon, however, it had swelled to full erection and I could no longer span it with my fingers. I thrilled with the thoughts that at last I had taken such a monster; I wasn't very well informed regarding the sizes of men's cocks, but I knew enough to know that this one was of an unusual size. Would you like to learn something about it, my dear? Yes? Then listen: It was, by actual measurement, just nine inches long from base to tip. Oh, it was a beauty, I can tell you. It was fully two inches thick and set in a bed of thick, crisp hairs. His balls filled both my hands, and they, too, were thick with hair. Wasn't it a beauty, darling? And is there any wonder that I fell so desperately in love with it?

During the short time I had been toying with it, one of his hands was busy with me. From hip to titties his soft hand caressed, and then, no longer able to stand it, he said: 'Oh, darling, I love you so! Please let me fuck you again!' And he made as though to roll me on my back, but I would have none of it.

'Wait, dear,' I cried. 'Wait until I have proved my love for you, too! Let me kiss your lovely cock! Then you can have me whenever you choose!'

I scrambled out of his arms and slid down upon the bed. God! How handsome it looked then! Standing straight up in the air, its ruby head almost bursting with inward blood pressure!

Stooping, I kissed the purple and pink head! Staring at it and working my hand up and down its length, I became fascinated! I loved it! Dropping again, I kissed it once more! But I wasn't satisfied; I wanted more of it! Rising to his elbow he stared down at me, hardly believing what his own eyes saw being enacted before them! I kissed it again; this time with open lips, and I heard him give a little gasp as I quite swallowed the head! Still I wasn't satisfied! I felt something was lacking! With a downward lunge I plunged it far into my mouth, and then I sucked it with all my might! He was trembling; he tried to draw it from between my lips, but I wouldn't have it! I was out to show him that I too could love; that I was no half-baked mistress! I wrapped my arms about him, held him in a tight embrace, and seeing that I wasn't to be done out of it, he clutched my head in his hands and holding it far back into my throat he delivered the contents of his massive balls deep into my mouth! Nor did I give up my position till the last drop had been given me, all of which I eagerly swallowed!

Then, and only then, did I allow it to slip from my lips, and coming up over him, I kissed his lips again and again! 'There,' I cried, 'I, too, have shown my love for you, darling! And now you can fuck me to your heart's content!' And as though to prove my word, I straddled him and placed the still hard head to my cunt and gave a downward lunge against it, taking it in to his balls!

You may rest assured, my friend, that I left nothing lacking in my love for him that night. When he tired of the sport, I sucked him back to erection, and three times I sucked and swallowed the sperm from his lovely crest.

What more is there to tell? How, further, may I convey to you the wonderful things we did that night? Why try when you know all too well what happens between persons who dearly love each other?

Enough to say that, after a most thrilling night, we slept only to renew our pleasing occupation the following morning. Then Paul left me, promising to return as soon as he had attended to his affairs.

My maid found me still in bed when she returned after her night off, and I guess I scandalized her puritan mind by the way I saw her staring at me, for I made not the slightest effort to hide my nudity from her gaze.

Of course, every girl suffers more or less after a night such as I had had, and I was no exception. I was happy in the fact that I had lost my useless maidenhead, however, and for the first time in my life I realized what it meant to be without one's love. I remembered, then, that I had allowed him to leave without his breakfast, and I promised myself that the breakfast should be served always after this.

Lying there against my pillow, thinking of all the delightful things that had happened to me the previous night and that morning, I became frightened. I recalled how Vera had told me of her few nights of love, and how she became pregnant as a result of it. And then I brightened. Why worry about it? Besides, it was worth it! What I had done I did for love, and if I was with child, it would be a baby of love.

I dismissed it from my mind; the damage—if any—was already done, and I had almost a full month to go before I would know anything about it!

Then I got to wondering about my maid. I wondered if she had discovered that I had entertained a man all night, and that he had slept with me? My thoughts were interrupted by her entering my room. In her hand she held the bloody towel, that same towel with which Paul had removed the traces of my maidenhead, a maidenhead gone forever. She seemed frightened, but I explained it away by telling her that I had had a slight accident.

After breakfast I played the piano. I wasn't very much of a musician; I played but for my own amusement. I sang. I tried out a piece I had been having some trouble with and found that I had not the slightest difficulty in reaching the unusually high notes.

This caused me to wonder if my ability to reach these notes wasn't due in some way to my recent experience with Paul? I recalled what my temporary housekeeper had told me about having a lover whose cock I could suck! Could this be a result of that? Could it have possibly been a reaction so soon! I promised myself that I would ask Paul about it as soon as he returned!

If this was true, then I would acquire one of the most famed voices on earth, because I loved it! I adored it! I had thought that kissing a girl's cunt until she spilled her love-dew into my mouth was the height of delight, but it was as nothing compared to sucking my lover's cock!

My thoughts lent wings to my feet! I flitted about the house with an abandon which quite startled my maid! In my eagerness to do something even more startling, I threw off my gown and ran all over the place in complete nakedness.

I saw her eyes following me, and I knew she was shocked beyond words. 'Very well,' I thought. 'If you are so easily shocked, then as soon as Paul returns I shall give you something to be shocked about!' I laughed inwardly as I pictured the expression on her face when she would see the costume I wore then!

Wishing to be ready when he did arrive, and hardly wanting to be disappointed in the fun I was going to have, I brought out the tiny under-vest I had previously worn. As I have already said, it was the briefest thing I had ever seen; cut low enough at the top to almost expose both my breasts, and so short that it came just to my hips in length, and so transparent as to amount to exactly nothing as far as concealment went, it was a naughty garment, indeed. Still, it lacked something. Can you imagine anyone wishing to appear in anything else than that, my dear, and still wearing something?

That was my thought, strange as it seems. I wanted to be as near naked when he arrived as it was possible to be! And above all, I wanted to shock this silly girl as she had never been shocked before!

Any minute now he was due to arrive; he had promised to have noon-day meal with me, and it lacked but a few minutes to noon. A plan of daring entered my mind! Why not make it a real naked reception! Why go about it half-way! Why, indeed?

Picking up a pair of shears, I cut the tiny garment up the front, making a gown of it, the tiny ribbons over my shoulders alone holding it from falling from me.

Watching from my bedroom window, I saw him coming up the gravel walk! Calling to my maid to admit him, I took a final look in my glass! I heard him enter! Drawing the top of the thing well back from my titties, I quickly stepped into the room and went to Paul, my arms raised to greet him!

Even Paul gasped at the daringness I displayed, but I quickly whispered into his ear my intention in shocking my silly maid, and he, great actor that he was, quickly took the hint! 'You darling,' he cried, holding me off at arm's length and gazing at me. 'You are a million times more beautiful than I thought! You're adorable!'

And drawing me close and slipping his arms about me beneath the garment, he hugged me close, kissing and tonguing my mouth with all the zest he could muster. And all the while my maid stood staring in awed wonder.

But Paul wasn't done yet. Falling in with my own lascivious acts, he carried it a bit further. Picking me up in his strong arms, he carried me into the living-room and to the divan. Pushing me over on my back he kissed my breasts, neck and face like a madman, and all the while from the corner of my eye I saw the maid staring at us. I became more daring. Taking one of his hands in mine, I carried it to my cunt, patting the back of his hand as he fingered the naked lips, I, throwing my legs well apart and whispering into his ear.

Looking toward the door again, I noted that she had disappeared: the loving display had undoubtedly been a little too much for her sensitive nature. But our lovemaking went on until I thought I would surely lose the delightful load I had been saving for Paul.

The delightful fellow, while ardent in his attack, wasn't so foolish but what he knew when to stop, and as we lay there cuddling each other, I told him why I had adopted such an outlandish attire—and how he laughed. 'What you need is a more sympathetic maid,' he said, 'and I shall attend to it at once, today. I believe I know the very one for you.'

Rising from the divan, he called the maid. 'Here,' he said, handing her some money. 'This will carry you over until you find another place. You may pack your things at once.'

Though I felt sorry for her, I believe she was glad to go; such carrying-on as she had witnessed that day proved too much for her puritanical nature.

He kissed me and promised to return in an hour, and after he had departed I bid my maid adieu. I stretched out upon the divan to await my lover's return, and I couldn't help but think how happy I was. A position in the world of art, a splendid income from which I could prepare for the future, a splendid cottage to live in, and above all, a lover! Strong, handsome, young and animate and armed with the most noble prick with which to fuck me!

Paul found me radiant, indeed, when he returned, bringing the information that he had engaged the services of a charming maid and that she would report to me the following day.

'Oh, Paul, you darling,' I cried, pulling him down beside me, 'I love you so, I never want you to leave me again!'

'And I love you, too, dear,' he answered, kissing me again and again, 'and I feel that I never want to leave you again—even to sleep!'

There was plenty more said that afternoon, and it all ended by him taking up residence there with me. Then I told him of my conversation with the woman who had acted as housekeeper for me, and how she hinted at the necessity of my having a lover; one whom I could gamahouche (I used that expression to him, then) and the great good I would derive from it. 'Is that so?' I asked, looking him in the eye.

'I'm afraid it is,' he answered, smiling. 'At first I didn't want you to do that to me—'

'Why?' I interrupted.

'Well,' he hesitated, looking off toward the window, 'I realized, dear, that it was a dangerous thing for you to do, and—'

'Why is it dangerous?' I asked.

'Well, you see what happened—'

'And does that mean that every time I kiss you— like that—that you have the same thing happen?'

'I'm afraid so, darling,' he answered. 'It's a dreadful temptation to "come" when someone holds it in their mouth, as you did!'

'But I "came" in your mouth when you did it to me, didn't I?'

'I'll say you did, darling, and that's the way I want you to do, every time I caress you like that.'

'Is that a promise?' I asked, kissing him.

He nodded his answer—and five minutes later we were proving our promises to each other—and how!

During the night he told me it was necessary for him to be away for two or three days, and that he would spend his entire time with me. It seemed he owned some land in a distant part of the country, and as there were taxes and other things to take care of, he was forced to be away.

I wouldn't allow him to leave, however, until my new maid arrived, and I'll never forget the radiant smile that crossed her pretty face when she noted my scant attire. Not at all like the other country girl, who seemed frightened at my semi-nudity, but a pleased expression. She seemed to take it for granted, and I was sure she would be everything a maid could be . . .

My Secret Life

One night, being at the A*g**e Rooms, I saw a well grown, dark, sparkling eyed, dark haired woman, who looked four and twenty, tho but twenty-one years old. Her large breasts and general build, told me that her form would please me. I began the mercantile business, and having arranged that was going to leave with her, when a friend whom I had not noticed came up and said laughing, 'You've got the finest woman in the room again, you always do, I was just going to her—you took Miss***** away from me the other night.' I had never noticed him on either occasion, so we may be watched without knowing it. 'I'm not going with that woman,' said I lying—(she had gone out). 'Oh! ain't you,' said he and laughed again. I was surprised to see him there, but had heard he was going it fast. Shortly afterwards he was bankrupt and soon after that died, a fine fellow thirty-six years old and six feet two high.— Jessie C**t*s lived at W**t*n P***e in a house of her own. No lodgers were there.—I was very impatient to have her, and my delight was great on seeing her dark haired cunt. Rapidly I mounted her belly and inserted my prick.—'Ah! you lovely devil,' I cried, 'I am so sorry it's over, what made you fetch me so quick?' for I fucked like a hungry glutton, so impatient was I to have pleasure in her, to feel that we were but one body.

She was beautifully shaped, but with breasts like

those of a woman of thirty-five, they were very large, too large indeed, they hung down a much, tho they were not flaccid but quite hard like those of a quite young woman. She never had had a child.—All her sisters, she said, had large breasts quite early in life. Her thighs were superb, and she had the loveliest soft, dark hair, curling over her motte, and down the pretty lips below. Her ankle was disproportionately thin, and the foot a little long, all the rest of her form was lovely. Her face was charmingly bright, the mouth tho long and straightish, had splendid teeth in it. She came out very badly in photograph.—'Let me have you again,' said I, when I had paid her.— 'Come along then,' she said, 'you won't be in such a hurry now.'—We fucked quietly and then she spent with me, then I had her again, and stopped till three or four in the morning fucking her, which I rarely have done with women of late. But all the vigour of my youth seemed in me directly my hand touched her thighs.

I knew her for more than a year, took a great fancy to her, slept with her at times, and she got so friendly, that she as others have done consulted me about her affairs—I saw her own letters, and those she received at times from men. I visited her sometimes without fucking her solely for the pleasure of seeing her.—'I must get to the Duke's, are you going to have me first, and before I dress?'—'No.'—'Will you see me if I come home at twelve-thirty?'—'You may have a man with you.'—'That won't matter, I can come into the other bed room with you directly I arrive, he won't know, you shall have me before him'—or, 'I won't bring one home if you prefer it.' That was the sort of conversation, which sometimes passed between us.

Still more intimate, I used to dine and sup with her—one of the few Paphians I have dined with in their houses—I could do so, for like so few of the gay ones who are for the most part idle, and not too clean in their rooms, she was beautifully clean, and spent all her time when not with men in cleaning her house. The furniture was her own. Her kitchen was like a new pin, she only kept one servant but a good one, and had a charwoman. When I first knew her she had no lodger—afterwards she had one on the first floor. Her own bed room then was on the floor above. She only took a lodger at occasional times, and when they came from her own village. One she got rid of directly, the other stayed some time, leaving, just before Jessie left.

'You don't mind waiting half an hour do you? My dress maker has come.'—'All right go.'—After a time I used to say,—'No humbug, you've got a man—go and be fucked and get him away as soon as you can.'—I am now quite philosophical in such matters, have come to that time of life when men I expect usually are so under similar circumstances. 'Look—I've got a tenner,' said she to me one day showing a bank note after a friend had left her. 'And he's coming to morrow.' I could not afford to be nearly so liberal to her, but she was content with me. She had good friends and got much money without me. She dressed very handsomely but with a quiet style. I used to sit at times with her and—when she had one and her lodger a woman from Devonshire like herself, and one who came from the same village,—all three sitting round the fire one evening, they with their clothes up to their knees, I stooped and by the light of the fire peeped at the lodger's cunt.—'Show it him,' said Jessie, 'if he wants,' and she herself pulled the girl's petticoats up.—'Look his cock's stiff.' She unbuttoned my trowsers and pulled it out.—'It's a fine prick isn't it?'—Both women handled it. 'I'll fuck her,' said I, for this freedom excited me.—'I don't care if you do.'—But I saw that she did, so turned Jessie on to the sofa and fucked *her* before the lodger. I never had that lodger, who did not pay and left in debt soon. Jessie said she'd not have another.

But she did after two or three months, a charming, auburn haired, plump little creature whose name was Julia. They got on very well together. Before me, 'Oh, he's quite a friend'—and then they'd talk of their men.—Jess always asked the other how many times a man did her, it was quite the regular question between them. When I had slept there the same night and the lodger had a man, the lodger did the same—a charming frankness before me, a delightful intimacy for months which largely increased my knowledge of male strength.

This is how it ran. 'Who's your man?'—So and so.—'How many times did he do you?' —'Twice.'—'Do you like him—is he nice?' —'Oh never mind him' (me). This of course as said was when I had known her some time, and was often there and the lodger had seemed inclined not to answer.—Then Jessie would in her turn tell. She had met so and so, he wanted to stop all night, but she would not let him.—Indeed like most gay women I have known, she liked sleeping alone best, but after a time, she always wanted *me* to sleep with her.— When I did, I had to fuck her till I could do no more, and she left off jumping out of bed, and washing her cunt after each spend, as she did at first, when she knew I liked a smooth buttery cunt.

One night when I slept there, the auburn haired
Julia had a young man to sleep with her. He stopped
in his bedroom whilst she, Jessie, and I, supped in
the parlour.—Then we all went to bed.—It was in
the height of summer, heat and fucking made me
restless, and I could not keep from feeling and looking all over Jessie when not fucking. She got out of
bed just as the sun was just rising, saying, 'Julia's
awake, I can hear her moving.' Then on the landing
of the stairs she coughed significantly, and softly out
came Julia from her bedroom below, closing the door
gently. The two women went to the staircase window
on the landing between the two floors, which was
wide open on that soft balmy morning, and stood and
talked.—'What the devil makes you get up?'—I had
said to Jessie as she left me.—She wanted to ask a
question. 'I'll come too.'—I did, and stood in my
shirt with my arms around the two lovely women in
their nightgowns as they chatted in a low voice, and
looked out of the back staircase window.

Said Julia, 'He is spoony on me, I told you he was,
and wants to keep me, shall I go with him?'—'Do
you like him?'—'Not much, but he's rich, and he'll
allow me ten pounds a week he says.—He's an
Oxford man, quite a gentleman, and he is awfully
spoony.'—'How often has he done you?'—'Once
when we went to bed, and just now again, he's gone
to sleep now, he's not slept before to night, he's been
spooning me ever since we went to bed. I got out
directly he fell asleep.'

I was feeling both their naked bums at once, of
which they took not the slightest notice, then I began
rubbing my prick up against them, and both girls
laughed.—'Hish! don't make a noise, come to my
room,' said Jessie.—We all went there, naked footed

232

all three, and continued talking.—Julia had not spent with him. 'You don't like him much then,' said Jess.—No she liked a man whom she named and wished he would keep her, yet this man was rich and a gentleman—Jessie advised her to accept the offer.—She could have the other man for her pleasure on the sly. The man who was sleeping had a small prick, said Julia. They both laughed at that and so did I. They laid down and I said, 'Let me see you both naked together.'—Jess consented, they stripped on the bed, and were a lovely pair. I threw off my shirt and stood naked with a stiff prick.—'He wants *you*, look at his prick,' said Jess—I denied it but I did.—'You've made him stiff Julia, let him.'—Julia laughed—I saw Jess did not mind this woman, and turned on to Julia, who without persuasion let me mount her but resisted poking. 'Let him, I don't mind,' said Jessie—Julia's thighs distended at once, for she wanted me. Trying to feel Jessie's quim with one hand whilst fucking Julia, Jessie repulsed it, but she felt curiously about under my balls and frigged herself. We all spent together, all outside the bed, quite naked on that hot July morning at daybreak.

All three were still as quiet as mice, and we were enjoying the repose which followed spending, when a soft male voice below cried out, 'Julia, Julia.' We started up, Julia pushed me off of her.—'Hush! don't make a noise,' said Jess.—Julia called out—'I'm coming,' took a towel, gave her cunt a dry rub and left the room.—She had been to the closet, and went up to see Jessie, we heard her say to her friend.—'No, Jessie has no man with her, she's alone,' and the bed room door closed. We laughed. Jessie then told me a lot about Julia and her friend. Whilst doing so, we heard voices rather loud and

angry for a minute in the stillness of the morning.—
Jessie stole down stairs and listened, I stood on the
top landing looking over.—After a time she looked
up, smiled, nodded, pointed to the door and came
back to our room.—'He's poking her,' said she,
'but they have nearly quarrelled.' 'She has not
washed,' said I.—'No, but he won't find it out.'—'I
think I must have poked after him,' said I, after a
little reflection,—for now I recollected her quim felt
very nice and smooth. Jessie laughed.—'You have I
think, didn't she say he'd just done her and fallen
asleep?'—I began soaping my prick in a state of
anxiety, yet had at the same time, a voluptuous sort
of delight at having fucked just after him.

The man went off quite early to catch a train, and
Julia came to our bedroom at once.—The conversation turned on the occurrence and the man—I found
that his prick had gone into my spunk, but she would
not admit that mine had been in his.—'But I am sure
it has.'—'Well no one asked you to have me'—I was
in fear for some days about clap, but need not have
been.

I quite settled to this Jessie, and for a whole year
she was, excepting when I was out of town, the sole
woman of her class whom I touched. At times I
indulged in a few baudy freaks with her, but usually
fucked her in a husband-like style, tho with passion,
for I much enjoyed her. She was not a baudy talker or
actress, but we used to prolong our pokes, resolutely
keeping cock and cunt together without shoving, but
talking and endearing till we could resist movement
no longer—then sucking each other's tongues till our
mouths and chins were all moistened, restraining no
longer, and with a breathless, 'Fuck love'—our
backsides wriggled sympathetically till my sperm

swamped her love cage, and we died away into blissful sleep. She had the loveliest teeth and a full tongue, and used to like to lick my teeth when our mouths were close together, then my tongue met hers and that excited her.—She liked also my finger to lay well up her cunt, whilst we tongued each other before fucking, preferring that much to the titilation of her clitoris, which is the way most men play with a woman when side by side. But she was cool to me till I had known her some time and she began to like me.

'I am going home for a week,' said she one day, 'and want you to give me my railway fare.'—'You are going on a trip with a man,' said I jealously—and suddenly I found that I had an affection for her. I was astonished at myself, staggered.—Am I in love with a gay woman again, when there is one woman whom I adore? It was true. I was really loving two women at the same time. I loved Jessie, tho I would have slain her for the other.—What a psychological problem!—Her mother's letter, a badly written scrawl, asking her to go to see her as she was ill, was shewn me.—It looked genuine enough. She put on her plainest dress to go in, and took but little clothing with her, but had some fear of the honesty of her servant, there being then no lodger in the house—I suffered a good deal when she was away, and was savage with myself for being so fond of a gay woman, wrestled with myself, said I would never see her again, and indeed thought that nothing but harm could come of it. She was gone eight days and came home exactly at the time appointed. My heart beat loudly when I saw her, she kissed me, then rushed to her drawers and wardrobes (bonnet on). All things were safe as she had left them.—Then I closed on her, and threw her on the bed.—'Wait, wait till I take my bonnet off.'—The next moment I was up her.—'Oh I want it so,' said she.—No, she had never spoken to any man excepting her father and mother since she had left, they believed she was a dressmaker.—'Eight days without a poke, only think of that.'—Was it true?—It's just possible.

She went down stairs to cook the simplest bit of meat. I had taken lobsters and champagne there, and went down with her.—The meat was cooked, and we ate it in the parlour.—She rang for the lobster—the maid took the dirty plates away. 'I must fuck you again,' said I.—'Stop, Mary will be in with the lobster.' But I had been longing to be at her all the time we were eating, and said, 'I won't wait.'—On the sofa we fucked at once. Mary came in with the lobster but took no notice of our operations.—We sat down to table again, glorying in our moistened genitals and finished the lobster and champagne.—Then we went up to bed to revel in cunt plugging and a jolly evening and night that was.—A fuck with a woman whom a man loves, is better than the baudiest night with a chance woman, but both have their special pleasures.—A night with a baudy woman you like, one who will reciprocate any voluptuousness, beats everything.

We scarcely ever had an unpleasant word, but what annoyed her was my calling just as she was ready dressed to go out. I had a liking for having her just at that time, and used to call when the cab was at the door waiting for her. One night when I did, —'Mistress is just going out sir.'—'Any one with her?'—'No, sir.'—Up stairs I ran, she had her bonnet on.—'Now you can't have me, I'm in a hurry, have got to meet some one and am behind time.'—I would and we mingled.—'Damn it.'—She rarely swore. 'You do it purposely, as if you couldn't come a little earlier,' and she threw her bonnet off in anger.—'Don't be in a rage Jess.'— 'Fuck me if you're going,'—and flinging herself down on the bed side, she pulled her petticoats up to her belly.—She'd no drawers on, and there lay her sweet naked body on the diaphanous chemise, and a heap of flounced and laced petticoats surrounding her, from out of which showed the beautifully white belly and thighs, the lovely dark, soft, curly haired motte, and the small red split with the little curls round it. The combination of flounces, lace, silk stockings and boots, with thighs, belly, and cunt, is in some women more appetizing than nudity, and I gazed long, entranced with the voluptuous spectacle, then stooped, kissed, and smelt it.—'Make haste I must go.'—I plunged my prick in her glowing sheath, but took my time, prolonging my pleasure. 'Spend with me Jess.'—'I shan't, it will bring my poorliness on.' 'Do.' Then I probed and wriggled quickly, then slowly and in every fashion which I thought might heat up her cunt, stimulate her passion. I touched her clitoris, talked my baudiest, and at length succeeded. Her loins quivered, a tremulous shudder ran across her belly.— 'Aharr'—and with exquisite vibrations she spent, whilst a copious balmy injection issued from my prick into her. Then for a minute she lay gorged with prick and sperm, and was tranquil. Then her eyes opened. 'Pull it out dear and tell me what's o'clock.'—With prick still in her I told the time.— 'My God. He won't wait for me.' Uncunting me she gave her split a dry rub with a towel, put on her bonnet, and in a minute was at the cab door.

'I'm going your way and will pay the cab.'—

Jumping in, we drove to the A*g**e together.—On the road she told me who she was going to meet. He was so liberal, and twice she had disappointed him, so was anxious.—'Your cunt's full.'—'I'll wash it at the rooms.'—There was something in the affair which excited me. 'Let me feel your cunt.'—'You beast.'—But I did, and as my finger felt the mucilaginous moisture in her sweet temple, my prick stood hard, horny, almost inflexible again. We were just crossing the **** Road.—'Let me fuck you.' She wouldn't, how could she, it would make her in a mess, we should be seen.—I begged, insisted and had my way. She put her bonnet on the front seat, hoisted up her petticoats, and turning her bum to my belly, sat down on my hot stiff love pole—I clasped her round her hips, my fingers just touching the soft curly ringlets of her motte, and as the cab got to the bottom of R*g**t St. out shot my sperm, into her cockpit. She had pleasure with me, and in another minute had entered the A*g**e with her sperm filled quim. I satisfied, went to my club.

Gradually, we got from simple belly to belly jogging, to a few erotic pranks.—She protested, refused, swore that she had never done such things, and never would—I think she'd only been a year gay,—but in the end yielded. 'You're the most voluptuous fellow I ever knew.—No one man has ever asked me to do so many baudy things, scarcely any fellow wants to do more than poke either on the bed or at the bedside, not one out of twenty ever thinks of any other way, or talks as you do.'—But a Cyprian warms to her work, she likes the variety in time, takes pleasure in it, all human nature does, and after a dinner at her house, a dinner she'd cooked herself of a simple kind, and we had filled up with my

generous wine, our brains heated, excited, and suggestive, cunt and cock burning hot and demanding
their lewed pleasure, we used to set to work at erotic
whimsies.

Her big breasts excited me and one evening.—'I'll
fuck between them,' said I.—'You beast you
shan't.'—'I will.'—'You shan't.'—'Let me just
put my prick there then, only for a minute.'—'You
may do that for a minute.'—I had my trowsers on
which I pulled off in a jiffey, and tucking my shirt up
in a roll under my arm pits, stood between her legs as
she sat on a chair in front of the bedroom fire.—She
only had a silk wrapper and chemise on, the latter she
dropped down, and I laid my rigid pego against her
lovely bosom. 'Poke me properly first and do that
later, I want a poke so.'—'No now.'—In a minute
she had lifted up her great and firm white breasts,
firm as the udder of a heifer.—My prick was pinched
between them, and hidden all but its fiery tip which
just peeped out at the top, whilst my balls hung
rubbing against her flesh below. I thrust gently up
and down in the fleshy channel with a fucking
motion, she laughing, then looking down and trying
to see, which she couldn't well do, then looking up at
me.

My prick happened to be in the highly sensitive
state that night, to which I have alluded. The friction
on its gland against her dry flesh hurt me, whilst at
the same time it had excited and swollen it to the
utmost. 'Now that will do.'—'I mean to spend
between these lovely bubbies.'—'You shan't,' and
she pushed me away. But I was hot on my letch and
insisted, swore I'd go away unless she let me (I was
going to stop the night) so she consented. I took some
oil from her toilet table, anointed her breasts and my

prick with it, and resuming my position fucked till my sperm was nearly ejaculated between the bubbies. Now she took interest in the frolic.—I was sighing out my pleasure, when made lewed by contemplating me, by its novelty and already hot cunted by a good dinner, she grasped me by my backside, leaving *me* to press her breasts round my piston. She was again looking alternately up in my face, and down at her bosom as I thrust, and deliciously out sped my sperm.—As I gently moved up and down after I'd spent,—'You beast, the spunk ought to have been in my cunt,' said she, and rushed to the looking glass pressing her breasts together.—'Oh what a lot of spunk'—then laughing she restored her breasts to their purity with soap and water, whilst I did the same to my empty ballocks. She only used baudy words when lewed.

'You beast, you've made me so lewed, why didn't you poke me first,' said she again. When an hour afterwards in bed both stark naked, and entwined in each other's embraces, flesh greedy to meet flesh every where, my belly pressing hers as I lay between her thighs and fucked my second fuck.—Then as our mouths moistened each other, she gasped, 'Oh—what a lot of spunk was on my breasts.—A—ha—fuck dear—fuck me.'—'Ahar—yes—wasn't there a—har.'—Our soft sighs were coming, then our tongues meeting in liquidity stopped utterance; sighs and shortened breaths stopped speech in both, and told that our spunks were blending, that bubby-fucking had raised lewed ideas in her.—How they rush thro the brain whilst fucking.

She heard of this masculine whim, but no one had ever suggested it to her but me she said, when talking it over on another occasion. Whether that be true or not I cannot say.—Talking about it led to another whim.—What a fertile brain mine must be, for I declare I never had heard of such a pose as I'm going to narrate.—As she had already yielded up to me her breasts, she made no objection now to their use for a variation.—Both of us in a state of nudity, she laid on her back, I knelt across her breast, half lying half holding myself upon my knees and elbows, with my rump towards her face, and put my prick between her big breasts, which she help up and pressed together, making a comfortable fleshy channel round my pego, enveloping it nearly all around, in which I fucked, whilst she contemplated my backside and wagging ballocks. But cunt, that delicious, soft, red, pouting parting, even then had its irresistible attractions. My head was half way down her thighs which were closed. 'Open your thighs wide Jessie and let me feel your cunt—Ah—how I wish I could lick it.' She opened them. Leaning more on one elbow and hand than the other, I managed to put one hand, so as just to feel the clitoris and motte, and thus I fucked on and spent between her lovely hillocks, so soon as my fingers touched her cunt. But somehow this erotic whim neither excited her nor me, so much as the first bubby fucking, which was a complete novelty to her. No woman unless with very big breasts such as hers, could have made a nice channel for my prick as she did in the last posture. I have fucked between the breasts of perhaps a full dozen gay women, and of one modest lady, but it's not every bosom which rouses my lust in that direction.

That led to my using her armpits as a channel for my onanism, armpit frigging or armpit fucking, or whatever may be its right designation (I am not happy at coining terms) I have asked a hundred strumpets, and not one but owned that men had used her armpits as a cunt. I expect it is a common enough practice to entitle it to a distinct denomination like fist fucking (masturbation) or cock sucking (irrumination) or bum-hole fucking (buggery). [Yet in all my peeps at the happy couples thro holes in baudy house partitions and elsewhere, I have never seen a man doing it to a woman that way, or I don't recollect it.]

One evening talking about various fashions of sexual enjoyment, she consented. 'You've done it between my breasts, and I may as well let you do it once this way, you're a good old friend,' (I believe she then liked me much) and sitting on a chair naked in front of a cheval glass, she raised her arms for my operation. She had a good deal of dark hair in those valleys, which to me was one of her beauties.—I had used soap with the women I had enjoyed in that fashion, but now filled her thicket with cold cream, and putting my prick in its place commenced—but that lubrication or anointment seeming not to be pleasurable. I washed it off, and again had recourse to soap, which I rubbed in the hair till it was nearly a soapy paste.—'Now frig yourself, Jessie, whilst I'm doing it.'—She refused, tho I told her that most of the women in whose armpits I had fucked had frigged themselves at the same time. What a lovely thing it is that man and woman can frig themselves. It's a pleasure when had alone, is such compensation for trouble and misery, and a delectable companionship when tasted with others.

I thrust on steadily enjoying her, now looking at my prick which I pushed to and fro showing its rubicund tip near to her breast at each forward movement, now looking at ourselves reflected in the glass.—She sitting right facing it, her handsome haired motte and the beginning of the red belly slash between her round thighs, just peeping out.—It was her left arm. 'Push up your breast love, so as to touch my prick as it comes thro.' Up she pressed it well with her left hand.—It was a luscious sight, but I was not so full of sperm that night, so worked slowly.— Both were silent now till the first throb of pleasure made my frame quiver, and my love of cunt in which I know the supremest enjoyment of the woman is to be found made me stop.—'Oh! I'll fuck your dear cunt instead, it's nicer Jess,' I sighed and ceased thrusting.

'Oh—no—go on—finish there,' said she, for at the same moment she'd began frigging herself.— That completed the picture, and in silence I fucked on, saw her thighs widen, her hand move quicker.—'Keep your arm closer love and push up your breast.'—In her own pleasure, she had forgotten that part.—Her limbs obeyed, but with my left hand I pulled her breast still closer up to her armpit.—'Aha—cunt—fuck—I'm spending love.' I sighed, and seizing her head, pulled it back and kissed her face, still fucking on whilst she kept on frigging and spent with me in erotic rapture. 'My spunk's in your armpit love.'—'Ahar'—she sighed—'aha—aharr.'—Her hand ceased moving but lay covering her motte, her head she'd turned up to mine more, and our tongues were meeting as we spent.

'You frigged yourself after all Jess.'—'You baudy devil you'd make any woman do any thing I believe,' said she still sitting quiet with my prick still in her armpit. I pulled it out, and moving to her side felt up her cunt. I loved to feel the spendings of this woman, for I liked her, nay after a fashion loved her, for she was very charming. These were the only exceptions to the beast with two backs business which we did together. With belly to belly, after all, a woman is best enjoyed physically, the rest being largely imagination.

Altho I knew her some thirteen months, I scarcely touched any other woman during that time, and none of my Paphian regular acquaintances, so she must have given me intense gratification. The ten pounder came again and again, and she got from him lots of money. At length he was always there and much in my way when I called. He was spooney on her and said he would marry her.—What should she do she asked me—I was heart broken and cried like a child at the idea of losing her.—'Don't take on so,' said she. 'You are a good fellow and I'm very fond of you, but you are very much older than me, and *you* can't marry me I know.'—I told her that the very best thing she could do was to accept, if he really meant it.—After a week or two she said the marriage day was fixed, and their passages taken for Australia.—He had money, (tho only just of age) and thought it best they should quit the country, and in that they were wise. That night was to be my last poke, she had sworn she would let no other man touch her again after that day—I was to be her last free love.

Three days after I longed for her so that I took her a wedding present.—At first the servant said she was out but I refused to leave and after waiting half an hour saw her and gave her the present, which much delighted. She did not expect it. Then I begged her to let me have her.—No, she had sworn with the Bible in her hand not to do so—I begged again, prayed, cried, I longed for her with most furious desire. 'Once, only once and the last time.'—My crying upset her and *she* began to cry, did I wish her to break her oath?—every man who had called had been kept out but me. Mary had no business to have let me in.—Her mother had come up and was down stairs.—Would I go?—she hoped I would.—'Do. Go and see Julia R**l***s, she's fond of you and will be glad to see you tho she's living with a man now and hasn't seen anyone else.'

I kept on begging, entreating, crying and kissing her till she warmly kissed me.—'Don't be foolish now.'—'Let me feel your thighs—only that—let me get the smell of your dear cunt on my fingers, that I may take it away with me.'—With force I got my hand on to it. She had begun to cry, and now more than ever, and when I pulled my prick out, got angry; then tender.—'You'll make me break my oath and bring some misfortune on me'—were I think the last words she said before she fell back on the sofa. Then I saw her beautiful dark haired motte, the lovely red lipped cunt for the last time, and in two or three minutes we were spending together.—'My God,—don't—I won't come,—I've sworn.'—'Aha—my love, I'm spending.'—'So—am ahrr' —and her spendings mingled with mine.

When it was over she upbraided me, was sure breaking her oath would bring her some misfortune—her intended had said it would.—We parted in tears.—She was married a few days after, and in a week after that went abroad.—A fine vessel, whose destination was that of Jessie's, a month after was wrecked, all aboard drowned, and I have every reason to think that she and her husband were in that vessel.—No one ever heard of her after, I questioned dozens of women who knew her, and made other enquiries.

Early in November of the year when Jessie C**t*s married and left England, and at about two o'clock in the afternoon on a dull, rather muddy day, I was going along F***t Street, and met full face a handsome, fresh looking woman of about twenty-one or two years of age. I was struck at once with her great beauty, nothing sensuous for the moment entered into my admiration of her. Instinct aided by much experience makes me guess oftentimes rightly whether a woman feels lewed. Certainly I have been generally right, in judging whether they are voluptuous by nature or not. Our eyes met, and I thought that a full sized pego would just then please this lady immensely. She looked at me as if a man was in her mind, and as that passed through my brain, a voluptuous tingle ran thro my prick which began gently swelling. What sort of a cunt has she? next I thought. All these ideas and sensations, did not occupy more space of time than writing one of these lines does.— In a moment I was struck with her beauty, in the next minute cunt struck.

I was so smitten that I crossed the street, went back, and again crossed to meet her face to face. In doing so I saw she had a little foot and beautifully formed ankle, for she was holding up her petticoats from the mud. By that time my pego was stiff enough to be driven through a post, for I had been some days sleeping alone, and it had hinted to me that morning that at its roots lay a cunt lubricating essence which it wished to get rid of. The lady's eyes met mine, and again I thought that a good fucking was just then what her handsome body wanted. But who or what was she? Evidently not a professional of the *pavé* but a quiet, well to do one of middle class—I turned back and followed her, watching the lovely feet and ankles and undulating movement of her haunches, which I knew must be of ample size.—My prick was now throbbing and upright in my trowsers. She stopped at a watch maker's and looked long at the goods. She didn't look round till I went close up to her, and said, 'They are very pretty.'—She looked at me then for a second, and walked on without reply.

I had not been for some time in such a state of rut, I trembled with lust, and followed her longing for her, and wondering who she was, what sort of cunt she had, if it had ever had a pego up it, and the whole group of lewed thoughts and wishes rose which flood my brain when my prick is stiff. Just then she turned to cross the street, in doing she saw me, our eyes met and diverted her attention, an omnibus approached close to her, the driver hollowed out,—'Take care.'—She, scared at her peril, stepped back, and as her feet touched the greasy slippery mud of the foot-path, she lost her footing and would have fallen had I not caught her in my arms. 'I've saved you an awkward tumble.'—'Yes—thank you sir'—for a few seconds we stood close together without further word, till the vehicles cleared away, then she began again to cross, and had no sooner put her foot on the carriage way, than I saw there a small reticule which in her scare she had dropped.—Picking it up, without a word I followed her with it to the other side of the way.

She was there before me. In picking up the bag I lost time, and had to wait to let vehicles pass, and saw her standing and looking about, in the way people do who suddenly miss something—I put my arm with the bag at the back of me in crossing.—'Oh I've dropped my bag sir there,' said she in a tone of despair.—'Here it is.'—'Oh I am so *much* obliged to you, I should have been so sorry to have lost it.'—'Ah! I wish I'd looked at the love letters in it before I gave it you.'—'Not many love letters,' said she laughing.

Now we walked on side by side, chatting about her having been nearly knocked down by the omnibus pole, etc. 'I almost wish you had fallen, I should have seen more of those lovely feet and ankles, which I've been following for the last few minutes. I don't know what I wouldn't give to see them.'—'It's not very civil of you,' said she laughing, but she looked me full in the face, seemed pleased, and again I thought that her cunt was hungry, so went on chaffing in the same style. Suddenly,—'Are you married?' I blurted out.—She laughed.—'Guess about it—are you?'—'Guess about it,' said I.—'I'm sure *you* are.'—'What do you want to know for,' I asked.—'What do you, *you* want to know about *me* for?'—'Because I'm dying for you. I fell in love with you the instant I saw your lovely face, and since I saw your ankles I've been scarcely able to walk, I'm lifted off the ground almost by it.' This was risky, but I knew if she were virgin and very pure, that she'd scarcely understand my meaning; but if she'd handled a rousing stiff prick a few times, she'd guess what I meant.—She looked me in the face for an instant, and saying, 'I'm much obliged to you, but I'm going some distance and must walk quicker, good afternoon'—stepped out quickly. It was a plain hint that she wanted to get rid of me.

But I'd noticed that her face had coloured up, and

a look in her eye telling me that she knew my meaning, that she'd had the glorious life giver, working and injecting its balm into her; yes, she'd been fucked I felt sure. But was she married?

'I'm going this way too,' said I, still walking on by the side of her, and went on with my talk, making it warmer and more suggestive, but avoiding plain words, and at last asking her to have a glass of wine with me. She wouldn't, was much obliged, but surprised at my asking, and she stepped out rapidly and so did I. But she wouldn't tell me where she was going, and wouldn't meet me anywhere; if I followed her she couldn't help it, but it was useless.—These replies were made among many as we walked on together.—Then I left off suggestive chaffing for a sudden idea came to me. It struck me like lightning, it's wonderful it had not done so before, but now feeling sure that she'd been fucked I was nearly wild with desire, was in my rutting recklessness, and felt that I would give all I had to possess her for awhile. She had so enchanted me, that it seemed as if all the perfections of womankind were hidden under her petticoats, and then her face was so lovely.

I had a few years before given one of my sisters (she is dead now) a silver watch which cost ten pounds; and had that day fetched it from its makers where it had been cleaned. (Good silver watches were much more costly then than now.) 'Were you going to buy yourself a watch?' said I.—'No. I was only looking.'—'Where did you buy your own?' I asked with no other object than to keep up the conversation.—'I've not one,' said she. Taking out my sister's watch. 'That's a pretty one.'—'It is,'—and she half stopped to look.—'I'll give it you if you'll come and have a glass of wine with me.'—She stood quite still with astonishment, her eyes staring wide open, and then said quite softly.—'No thank you sir,' and resumed her walk.

Then I again begged her to meet me at any other time or place, said what I really then felt, that I was madly in love with her, that if she did not have a glass of wine with me now, I'd follow and would wait for her if I waited all night: that I would follow her home, and much of the same sort, all the time being at my wits' end to know where to take her to if she'd consented, for we had crossed the river, and were at a part of London but little known to me. I thought she would never get into a cab with me, for I'd already offered to take her in a cab to her destination, but she said she liked walking best, that she had that day walked from ****. About to name a place, she stopped short in her remark. I kept looking out as we walked along for any coffee house with the word 'beds' on the windows, and at length saw one, which was a chance, when just then she turned off to a side road, and after a few minutes, from one or two indications I knew we were going in the direction of the same main thoroughfare, in which I first saw Winifred a few years ago, and near to where I had found out a convenient accommodation house.

She had allowed me to chatter on after I'd shown the watch, but was herself silent. At length 'I'm going there, good afternoon,' said she.—'I'll wait.'—'You'll wait pretty long then,' said in a manner which stopped my hopes. She entered a largish house in a quiet respectable street, a house built evidently before the neighbourhood had become populous. She never even looked round at me as she entered the door.

Hope then nearly left me but my usual pertinacity

in amorous chases remained. I walked about keeping the house in sight for an hour. It grew dark but still I lingered. Tired at length of loitering, I felt my prick, thinking about her hidden beauties, and that if in the dark she would get into a cab with me to drive her part of her way back, I might get a feel of that adorable hirsute opening in her belly, a grope which is in itself a voluptuous lascivious treat with a woman not gay, even if a greater treat does not follow. She did not come out, and then in my lust I thought I'd frig myself. She had told me that her friend or one of her sons, would see her into a cab, and I had noticed one or two young men enter the house as if they were residents there. Still I paced about, thinking of her lovely face, then of her sexual treasure, wishing to possess it, and feeling sure that *she* was lewed, and dying for the luscious play as well as myself. The second hour went and it was quite dark when out she came alone. In another minute I was by her side.

She either felt or well feigned surprize. 'Pray leave me, I told you not to wait, why did you?'

'I would have waited all night, for now I can get a kiss at least.' 'Don't, there are people coming.'— Before the words were out of her mouth I'd snatched one, and she pushed me off. Then I offered the watch again, and pressed her, still not using the plain language of love to scare her, but she refused.—'Let me drive you part of the way home—you needn't tell me where it is.'—She at last consented to that, but no cab was likely to be in that quiet street, so I led her in the direction I wanted till I got one, then in it I pressed and prayed her to have wine with me.—The cabman stopped at the corner of a street I had named.—'This isn't my way home,' said she. 'My lovely girl come and have a glass of wine with me,

and that watch is yours.'—'I won't, I dare not'—
and so on for a minute or two.—Then 'I can't stop
long,' much more was said hurriedly by us both, and
in a fairly comfortable bedroom in three minutes
were we.

I ordered sherry expecting poor stuff, but
knowing there would be spirit in it to stir her lust and
heat her cunt still more, if that pretty slit happened
to be already yearning for a stretch.—Bacchus
always helps Venus. She took two glasses of the wine
which was very palatable, and then at my request
took her cloak and bonnet off. 'What for? I can't
stop long'—as if she supposed that I had brought her
into a bedroom only to take wine. 'You told me that
perhaps you wouldn't leave your friend before nine
o'clock.'—'Yes but her son would have put me into
a cab.'—'So will I when we have been on the bed
together.'—'Oh!—what next?'—said she hurriedly
and looking at me, then at the bed in a restless
excited way. Then she turned round, took off her
gloves, and put them into her pocket in a way which I
scarcely noticed at the time, but which occurred to
me afterwards. I produced the watch.—'There my
sweet girl,—what is your name? That's yours if
you'll let me.'—She took it eagerly.—It was in a
case, and whilst looking at it sitting on a chair close
by me, I suddenly put a hand up her petticoats,
and felt her naked thigh near to her motte, thro
the opening of her drawers which unfortunately
she'd worn.—'Oh—don't—you shan't,' said she
dropping the watch and case on the floor and standing up. I am a practised hand in assaulting cunts,
having done this to scores of women, and altho
surprized for the instant at her unexpected energy in
resisting, dropped on my knees, clutched her round

252

her petticoats with my left hand, and thrust higher that which had been dislodged, till the fore fingers to the knuckles were well between the ridges of her split. I felt its heat and moisture, as her thighs closed on my fingers tightly. The next instant she had got away from me, and we had knocked both chairs over in a scuffle. In half a minute all these movements were done and over.

It was no sham, her surprise and struggle, tho she must have known I'd brought her there to fuck her.—Our walk, talk, my delicate suggestions, the offer of the watch, must have taught her *that*. I expect she'd got her cunt heated, her lust set simmering,—and perhaps also I was pleasing to her—but hadn't counted consequences for she was evidently and truly scared. For the instant I thought her a possible virgin. 'Nonsense love, let me feel your delicious cunt.'—The first straight baudy word I had said.—'Oh! I must go, I don't want the watch'—I thought I should not succeed, for she moved off from me as I approached her, keeping her face towards me till her back touched the bed.— Now, wild with desire for her and reckless in my lust, I picked up the watch, put it on the table, and pulled out my prick, which was big as a rolling pin and ruby tipped.—'Don't be foolish my darling'—I tried to allay her fears.—'None can know, but we two'—and so on. A woman with a melting cunt can be talked into any belief which runs with her voluptuous desires. 'How lovely your cunt felt, let me feel it again—there's a darling—do feel my prick.—You knew now, don't fib, you knew when you came, that I meant to fuck you—don't be foolish.—I'm sure *you* want it.'—Thus using all the lecherous persuasions and endearments which nature taught me, which come to me readily and naturally at such times, and I suppose to other men—I went nearer to her pulling out my pego further and the whole of my ballocks, so that her eyes might be gratified to the full with the sight of the Priapean glory.

She stood with her bum against the bed, looking at my prick, then in my face, and then away as if ashamed at being seen looking at my tool—then again at the red tipped stiff stander, and so on; motionless, silent at first. Then in soft broken sentences as I poured forth my loving prayers, and lustful incitements.—'Oh—I didn't—no—I can't —I'm frightened.—I'm sorry I came,—I don't want the watch.—I won't let you—let me go'—and still her eyes wandered restlessly from mine to my prick. With male instinct, I felt sure that my prick was exciting her, and closing on her, I threw one arm around her neck and kissed and coaxed, in frank, strong, concupiscent phrases, no longer mincing words. Prick, cunt, fuck, spunk, and the choicest of the vocabulary of love, in undisguised carnal strength I uttered. She still refusing, but letting me kiss her, her voice getting gentler, fainter and fainter, as she said, 'No—I mustn't—really.'— Suddenly, 'Tell me the truth, *are* you married?'— 'My darling what does it matter whether either of us is married or not?—feel my prick, feel how stiff it is, it will spend outside unless you let me put it into your sweet lovely cunt—feel it.'

Taking her little hand, I placed my pego in it. Softly but modestly she held it in silence as I stood face to face with her. 'Let me feel that lovely cunt again.' She made no reply, and half stooping I began hitching up her petticoats, then letting go my prick, she pushed them down gently. 'Oh—no—don't'—

with a stoop and a grab I got my hand on to her cunt, my fingers well between the slippery pink lipped slit, and edging myself round to her side held her to me whilst I began titillating it. 'Lay hold of my prick— feel it love.'—Without relinquishing her notch, I took my hand from her waist, placed her round my swollen cunt rammer, and again she held it; and so we stood in lascivious talk and handlings, in all the quiet delight which the feel of each other's fornicating organs, give man and woman when under the influence of Venus. What luscious, heavenly play it was, by the light of two poor candles and a bit of fire. Gently I frigged her hoping to intoxicate her with passion till resistance was impossible. Sometimes my fingers slid back wetting themselves in her cunt, already self lubricated by its longings for the friction of the tool she held in her hand. Then my fingers titillated her clitoris again, till I heard the sweet significant murmurs which a woman gives, when her cunt insists on its full gratification, on that delight which a stiff prick and a scrotum full of sperm alone can give it. That soft murmur of pleasure accompanied by the delicate agitation of belly and thighs, almost like a ripple, which comes with it when the cunt sends voluptuous thrills thro the woman, and urges her to submit and let the prick up it—to let her cunt spend its juices, whilst the balmy liquid throbs out from the ballocks, and the prick with gentle thrusts mingles the love essences of cunt and prick together, in the lovely warm soft recipient. 'Come on to the bed darling, get on it,'—I knew that she now was filled with desire, unconscious almost of ought but strong sexual wants, ready to obey her eager cunt—to let me fill it.—'No—no—I'm frightened—I am really,' was all she murmured softly. Letting go of the moist, hot chasm of her belly and withdrawing my Priapus from her soft hand, I turned her round and gently helped her on to the bed. In silence she mounted it, and by her side I laid myself, pulling up her clothes to see her limbs, much hidden alas by the accursed drawers, then through the opening in the damned white linen, for an instant roved my hand over thigh, belly and motte, my fingers plunged up the lubricious avenue to her womb, meeting no obstacle and expecting none. Then twisting my fingers in the soft curls, then settling them on her clitoris, then rapidly running them over every part, in maddening excitement, endearing her in concupiscent language, talking of prick, cunt, and fucking, feeling her thighs and motte, then frigging her slippery clitoris again, and all in a minute; whilst she half lay with her face towards mine, eyes closed, silent, palpitating with expectant pleasure, overwhelmed with voluptuousness, her cunt wetting my fingers and hinting it was ready for its gorge.—What exquisite moments for us both!

Then fearing that still she might resist at the last minute—as I've had women do,—I pushed my trowsers down as well as I could (for we were both dressed) to give free play to my ballocks, pressing my belly towards hers and grasping her tightly, slowly I turned her over till she lay on her back, and I upon her, our bellies meeting. I grasped her bum (covered with the accursed drawers), her thighs opened and my glowing prick slid slowly up her sexual treasure, dividing the soft, full lips, stretching and filling the hot moist elastic avenue to her nest. A sigh, a sob of voluptuous delight escaped her as it reached the top. In sensuous delight her cunt responsively clipped my prick, as it felt its stretching, gripped it as if it feared to lose it.—'My prick's up your lovely cunt'—I murmured as I kissed her and sought her tongue with mine, but *her* lips were closed. So for an instant I rested triumphant up her, in full possession of her body— joined to it—being part of it—to do within it all that nature listed.—Oh mind and body, body and mind, will paradise ever give you greater joy than this?

But my glowing prick would not rest quiet long within her cunt, which hot and lusting for its libation, tightened and squeezed around its stiff possession. I thrust it to and fro in voluptuous friction, now its tip struck the portals of her womb, now drew back nearly to the entrance lips. Her lovely moist avenue closed up as my prick receded, its folds stretched out as it plunged back again. Then quicker I fucked as pleasure stimulated me. 'Aha.'—My sperm was boiling in my balls, my prick urged by them on to furious haste, now plunged frantically to and fro quicker and quicker, too quick alas, but *my* seething sperm would have it so, *her* thirsty cunt would have it so.—On it went plunging, searching, probing her lovely tube which now yielded, yet compressed it and more.—'Ahaa—ahar'—I hear her gently sigh, giving first signs of increasing pleasure, her pretty mouth opens, my tongue touches hers, it's the first wet kiss we have had.—'Aha—ar—a.'—My prick tip's found the nook of nooks close to her womb, it's lodged, it's buried there alive and keeps there nestling; the frantic thrusts are over, short pushes and nestling wriggles come now. 'Aha—my darling— I'm coming—I'm, ha—spending—my spunk's com—fuck—ahear—ah—ahr.'—'Aha,' she sighs, gently and sympathetically as she murmurs, her belly heaves, her thighs rise up, a delicate tremor runs thro her belly, bum and thighs, as a torrent of hot spunk rises up from my balls and thro my prick.—Its knob feels bursting with the throbs of pleasure, as it shoots the spunk into her cunt, whilst nestling its tip closer and closer to her womb. Sympathetically, greedily, her cunt tightens, grinds and sucks the tip of my hot stiff member, anxious to let her womb imbibe the balmy mucilage. Then our pleasure sighs and murmurs slowly cease, our bellies move with delicious tremors, but the climax of our sensuous joy is over, the delirium of the ecstatic gush is gone, the pleasure throes ceased. There, my prick still swollen, lays soothed and wallowing in its spermy bath. Her voluptuous cunt, gorged and flooded with the lubricious emulsion from my testicles, no longer closes energetically on my prick, but every second gives a gentle throb, and gentler squeeze, as if grateful to its pleasure giver. So we lay silent, tranquil in each other's arms, exhausted with our sensuous delights, faint with the joys of love, slowly dissolving the sweet junction of our bodies in lubricious liquidity, whilst luscious thoughts on love, prick, cunt, and fucking, float dreamily through our brains.

Her passions quieted, the lustful irritation of her cunt allayed by the soothing injection, now slowly absorbing the soft balmy fluid, she laid motionless, with eyes closed, her bosom yet gently palpitating. She looked so lovely, that desire awakened at once afresh in me. So exquisite had been my enjoyment of her, that as I now looked at her beautiful face, as my dwindling prick withdrew, and as her cunt gave an affectionate parting squeeze, that my lingering pego gave a sudden throb and ceased shrinking. Tightly I grasped her bum, squeezing my pego closer into her lubricated temple, and putting one hand between our bellies, felt the curls of our genitals twining together in the glutinous overflow of our spendings.—With sudden energy then she roused herself, like one just awakening.—'Oh!—get off— let me get up—do pray now—let me wash—for Heaven's sake do'—and she struggled to get from under me.

A pretty woman never looks more lovely to me, than when just fucked and I lay incorporate with her. The flushed face, the humid eyes, the recollection of the pleasure barely over which she has given *me*, and I to *her* endear her to me, filling me with a sense of love and gratitude. I feel this often with the ordinary Paphian, altho I know *she* may have gratified hundreds and perhaps I may not really have gratified *her*. Yet I have seen dozens of men spite of their sexual transports, when their pleasure was over leave the women as soon as possible, neither kissing, endearing, or scarcely speaking to them. The cunt had done its work and off they went. The woman was nothing to them.

So Alice looked to me more beautiful than before, and I held her tightly, hating to break our sweet conjunction, my prick enjoying its cuntal bath, and even swelling again in it at the idea of losing it. 'Oh! pray let me get up, or perhaps I shall be ruined.'— My selfishness struck me, I might have impregnated her, for never a hotter prick and cunt had spent on each other. So I rolled off, but as I did so grasped the whole surface of her cunt, lewed still, lasciviously delighted in covering my fingers with our spending. Then I lay handling my prick with semenalized fingers, it seemed almost like feeling *her* and watched her wash that cunt, which ten minutes before had been refused me, and yet had rapturously spent as it felt the emulsion from my pego. Not a word was spoken. She finished the rinsing, stood up, let her clothes drop, and stared at me. 'You've not dried it,' said I.—She stood looking ashamed.—'Rub it dry, or you'll wet your drawers.'—She turned her back and dried it with a towel, then turned round. 'I must go.'

Off the bed I jumped.—'No love, I'm going to fuck you again, you needn't go away till nine o'clock, I wonder if the watch is broken, it's yours.'—Taking it up I found it going, the case had saved it.—Giving her a kiss I put the watch into her hand. She looked long at it. 'I wish I'd never seen it and hadn't met you, perhaps I'm ruined through it—how can I account for having it.'—'We'll think of that presently—sit down and have another glass of wine.'—Saying that, I drew off my trowsers which were falling to my heels, threw off coat and waistcoat, and pulling two chairs in front of the fire we both sat down.

I put my arm round her kissing her, and for the first time got a kiss in return. No woman can refuse one to the man who has just fucked her. I talked about our pleasure in baudiest language, whilst she listened smiling, yet seemingly half ashamed and almost in silence. Then my hand sought her sexual treasure and her resistance was the merest sham. My fingers lodged between the pretty hirsute ridges, tickled by their curly fringe, whilst the tips rubbed gently the satiny nymphæ and little clitoris. Then it roved over motte, and belly and thighs towards the smooth haunches, where the infernal drawers caught my wrist and hindered its advance. 'Take off your drawers dear.'—'Oh no—I won't—I must be going.'—'Not till I've seen that lovely cunt—let me.'—Now she resisted, but a woman never long refuses a view of her cunt to the man who has fucked it, unless conscious of some defect; but few think that of their cunts. I'm sure that unless they be whores, that women don't know an ugly cunt from a pretty one, they haven't seen many full grown ones, and think well enough of their *own*.—Whores at times resist a close inspection of *their* splits, they know the difference in cuntal physiognomies for they've seen many cunts besides their own.

Irritated I pushed my hand roughly, the drawers hitched, stretched and tightened on my wrist.—'Oh don't'—I pushed harder, with a crack something gave way, the drawers loosened, and my hand slipped round towards her buttocks.—'There now—you've broken the string—what shall I do?'—She stood up half turning towards me and feeling underneath her petticoats. I gave a gentle pull, the drawers slipped down her thighs, that hand went round her backside, the other did the same, and they nearly touched each other on the slopes to the bum furrow, as they grasped two deliciously smooth, firm, hemispheres of flesh. By that time, through standing up and moving, the drawers had slipped down below her knees, whilst still I felt her delicious backside, holding her close to me as I sat. Then she sitting down wriggling her bum, and complaining of what I had done, I helped her to disengage her ankles from their linen encumbrance. One of the strings had come off.

(Several women's drawers I have treated in similar manner, once or twice have violently torn them off and rent them in doing so. It's the only way with a woman who won't remove the useless cunt wipers. Drawers are better not looked at when torn off.)

The field was clear, rapidly I knelt in front of her (always do this) and kissed her thighs up to her notch. What a delicious odour was around the spot; odour of cunt and sweetest young flesh combined. Grasping her buttocks whilst I kissed and inhaled spite of her struggles, the exciting aroma stiffened my pego. When I like the smell of the woman *there*, it always does. Rising and showing its rigidity, pulling back the prepuce to show its crimsoning plum shaped top. 'Look dear, it's longing for your lovely cunt.' I placed her hand around it, and as before, she held it till I sat down by her side. Then turning towards each other with my arm round her neck in silence kissing, we resumed feeling those blessed carnal implements of concupiscence, I gently feeling between the plump ridges of her cunt, she nervously feeling my stiff pego, with a soothing but not frigging motion; both now in silent voluptuous reverie.

'Let me see it, you must, you shall.' Vain refusals, words not meant. Gently I led her to the bed, placed her on it, opened full sized, handsome, well shaped, white fleshed thighs, and saw one of the prettiest cunts I ever set eyes on, smallish, youthful looking, with fullish ridges rather than lips, tho lips they were, with a well defined red coral line beween them, but without protuberances, and fringed with short curly chestnut coloured hair, which also covered slightly a fat motte. Praising it rapturously, she let me move her limbs to see this delicate bit of nature's workmanship; but saying, 'Don't—don't' (they always say that) yielding, pleased with my rapturous praises, proud of the admiration of her sexual charms. Then by her side I lay, our hands crossed each other's and we felt our sexual organs, till both were ready for another fuck. 'Take off your clothes

love, let's do it properly, my belly can't meet yours
with your stays on.'—Refused at first, yet I pre-
vailed. 'I'll only take my stays off.'—I helped them
off, and then off went one petticoat, for she was
warmly clad, and off I pulled drawers.

Then one hand on her cunt, the other round her
neck just touching with finger points one of a lovely
pair of breasts, talking of love and fucking, how my
prick throbbed as one hand roved restlessly from
thighs to belly, then to bum, seeking the furrow of its
cheeks, feeling her bum-hole, then up her cunt, and
into every crack and nook and cranny of her body,
kissing and smelling every where, where all was
beautiful and odorous even to her armpits, so
enchanted, enraptured, was I with her, so ruttish.
Then my fingers settled on her clitoris whilst her
hand still held my prick, and whispering, 'Let's do it
love.' She turned upon her back, and opened her
thighs. With one look at the red slit, its lips held wide
apart by my fingers; with one gentle lick of her pretty
clitoris, I dropped on to her belly now naked, clasped
her lovely ivory buttocks, my fingers meeting in their
valley, and then midst mutual sighs of pleasure, I
buried my glowing prick up to its balls, in her
thirsty, longing cunt.

I shall never forget with what delight I began the to
and fro friction, that oscillation of my arse, that
searching of my tool, met by the gentle heaves of her
soft belly. Our tongues now met, her bashfulness
was gone, lubricious felt her cunt as it yielded to my
thrusts, 'Ahaa, my love, my prick's up your cunt,
isn't it nice?' 'Ah—y—hess—ahaa'—quicker
moved my prick now stimulated by her pleasure,—
now I gave frantic pushes, as my prick got almost
painfully turgid—her backside heaved to me, her

thighs moved up round mine, as she felt the approaching voluptuous delirium of her senses— 'Are you coming love?'—'Y—hes—aher.'—Her belly is quivering, her thighs clip mine, my prick settles at her womb, our backsides, bellies and thighs, quiver together in our spasms of delight, we clasp each other tighter, her hand grips on my naked backside, my bursting prick shoots forth hot spunk with pulsating throbs into her cunt, which tightens, grinds, and sucks it with combined sensations of pleasure, intense, inseparable, indescribable, as the mucilaginous injection floods it, and the soft spendings come out from every pore of its lovely surface to mix with mine. Then again we die away in each other's arms in blissful, voluptuous silence. Ah! what a death to die, if death would come in such a shape.

I felt that I should like to lie within her for ever, but after short repose, whilst our wet lips were still meeting, she got off rapidly and washed away the evidences of our love. She piddled, and had not before done so, and now, our intimacy was complete, by fucking, feeling, cunt washing, and piddling before me. The joy of sexual partnership is only complete when modesty is gone.—Modesty!—a convention. There is none naturally either in man or woman, but the sham has its charm, for it gives the pleasures of destroying it, and yielding it.

Excepting in early manhood when my sperm reservoirs seemed always full, the second fuck tranquillized me, but my recuperative power always with a nice fresh woman, or one whose sweet body I much liked, enabled me to separate the soft lips of her belly cleft with a rigid pego, a third time within the hour, and then I needed longer rest. This vital power of fucking thrice in sixty minutes I still have (and have now, eight years later). The second combat I find usually tranquillizes the lady, the fucking fatigues a woman less than a man.—Alice—the name she gave me—seemed now quiet and thoughtful, as she sat by my side by the fire. I put her cloak over her, coals on the fire, got two more candles from the baud, took more sherry and gave Alice more. I had still strong desire for the beautiful creature, still had that sense of fullness in my balls, that redness, heat, and lustful voluptuous irritation in my gland; which foretold more fucking soon.

She took the watch off the mantel-piece after sitting silent for a time, looked at it attentively, and then at the fire. I guessed her thoughts. Said she, 'What can I tell about getting it?'—I have advised several of her sex what lies to tell under similar difficulties, and nearly always the same lie. The watch taken in a case, had been returned to my hands in a little wash-leather bag. Reminding the maker of that, he found the case, and I just then wanting a leather watch bag, put the one into my pocket.— 'Put the watch into this, then lay it in the mud, say you saw the handle shining and picked it up.'— 'That's what I have been thinking,' she rejoined. 'But if they don't believe me?'—'Stick to it and they will.'—With a sigh,—'I can't say anything else, but must keep it a few days first.—I'm frightened tho.' 'Name a spot where you found it.'—'I will.'— 'Your husband will be glad you've got a watch' (trying to catch her). She smiled, and said she wished she had never seen it.—'But I have, and there's no help for it, now I must go.'—'No dear, not till we've done it again.'—She shook her head. I wish I knew what passed thro her mind just then, but feel sure

265

that the desire for another cunt plugging detained her, tho she wanted to be off. The risk, the baudiness, the treat of the afternoon, the newness of the prick, affected her. In for a penny in for a pound perhaps. So we talked on, trying to entrap each other into telling who and what we were, but in both cases unsuccessfully.

I was going to my club when I met this fair creature, and having eaten nothing since breakfast, my stomach reminded me. I said I felt hungry.—'So am I, they did not ask me to stop and dine.'—Meat at an unknown baudy house was out of the question, so I sent for Bath buns, the only thing I could for the moment think of as likely to be good, and for more sherry tho the bottle wasn't finished. I determined to ply her with wine hoping to make her speak about herself. We stuffed ourselves with buns, she took more sherry, which perhaps added a little heat to her already hot lusting quim, but it never made her communicative about herself. We went on talking about fucking, she making few replies, but laughing and reprimanding me.—'What do you laugh for if you are offended?'—'I can't help it.'—Nothing is really more pleasing, more stimulating to modest women, than to have a man talk baudy to them.

Her petticoats now covered her legs, for she had again become as modest as she was before her quim had tasted my stretcher, but I could just see her shapely calves and little feet. The street mud, thickish and greasy, was on her boot soles, but had caused no splashes. I love to see a woman sitting by a fire, with petticoats so far up that the flesh of the thighs just shows, and I pulled them up so. Whenever I did she said she must go, but sat down when I told her that she must then go by herself. Some modest

266

women I have found, dislike much going out of a
baudy house alone. She hoped no one had seen her
come into the house, and if ever I saw her anywhere
again, that I'd take no notice of her. I promised, but
she must meet me again. She started.—'Oh *never*—
never—never,—oh! my God! don't ask me—*never
now.*'—She seemed horrified at the suggestion. Who
and what was she? Fucked she'd certainly been
before, but whether wife, widow, mistress or neither I
couldn't say (and never could). I am sure she wasn't a
gay lady. Perhaps she *was* married and coquettish,
and the offer of the watch had tempted her, just as her
cunt was hot and longed for a male, which conjunction
made her come to my arms. That is all quite probable,
for a randy cunt weakens a woman's moral force. But
women are inscrutable in their ways and lusts.

Then I put my hands on her breasts, a beautiful
white pair. I could see their upper half, but with
modesty still lingering (and certainly she was modest
spite of her yielding to me). She tried to hide them; it
was instinct, habit and not sham. But praising their
beauty rapturously as I did, and in my excited, lustful
admiration of her, she yielded, and quietly I handled
the firm globes, and felt the little bush in her armpits,
(which smelt as lovely as the rest of her body) talking
baudily all the time. Then I tickled her there, which
seemed to win her to me more.—Tickling increases
the lust of some women, when once their voluptuous
thoughts have begun, and the randy thrills are
attacking their cunts.—Then I sucked one pretty
small nipple, which I saw had never nourished an
infant, and told her so. Thus our loving familiarity
increased, she gradually surrendering to all my
wishes, silent, and seemingly reflecting.

As I spoke about suckling,—'Has she had a

child?'—passed through my brain. I had been too
excited before to notice her belly, so dropped on my
knees again, and kissed her thighs, and lifting her
clothes, saw her smooth white belly without a sign or
mark of childbirth on it. I don't think she knew what
I was up to. Then kissing, and sniffing the aroma
from that warm nest, stiffened my pego, and as I got
up I showed it to her. She laughed.

Sitting down by her side again, I pulled my shirt
well up to let my prick be visible, tho now drooping a
bit, and felt her lovely cunt. The fire blazed, the
room got hot, the food, the wine, my kissing, my
fingering her love trap, and baudy talk during an
hour which had run away, had stirred her passions. I
praised her cunt, its beauty and sweet odour, and a
desire to gamahuche arose in me, for hers was not the
cunt of a gay woman, and I wondered if a tongue had
ever given pleasure there. So I talked of the pleasure
of that lingual exercise and asked her to let me. She
refused—it was dirty talk—she wouldn't.— The
more she refused, the more I longed to gamahuche
her, begged, prayed, insisted, extolling the pleasures
it gave as higher far than those from fucking; kissing
and groping her all the time, till at length with my
ballocks in her hand, she listened quietly and ceased
saying, 'No—I won't let you.'

Then gently I led her to the bed, and tho she still
refused it she did not resist me, was passive in my
hands, and seemed ashamed and looked away, and
not at me whilst she yielded and I placed her on the
bed. Next minute I was kneeling on the floor, her
thighs laying over my arms were wide apart, my
hands clasping her lovely buttocks, her sacred sexual
gap, that temple of Venus and love was open wide,
and covered by my mouth which revelled in it. I

opened my lips wide, so that I could cover the whole of
the soft crimson surface of that entrance to her body,
for I felt madly in love with her, was beauty struck and
cunt struck as well, and delighted with the idea of
giving her pleasure. I licked, then sucked, then licked
again; from bum hole to her curly covered mons my
tongue played lasciviously, I licked her thighs. I
licked her navel, intoxicated with her sweetness, then
plunged my tongue as far up her cunt as it could reach,
and loved the taste, revelled in its odour, and in the
sweet salinity of its exudations which lust now caused
to issue. Then my tongue settled to the little clitoris,
and on it and around it licked, till with a jerk of her
belly she asked me to leave off. But holding her thighs
firmly, I played my tongue with the agility of a
serpent, and in a few seconds more, with a gentle
heave up of her sweet cunt, with a shudder of her belly
and a murmur of pleasure, she spent.

I arose, her thighs dropped down, the cunt ridges
slightly closed, but ridges, motte, and all their curly
fringe were soaked with my saliva, whilst opalescent
moisture issuing from the furrow between the lips,
shewed she'd enjoyed the lingual that I'd given her.
Then pushing her on the bed, feeling her lubricious
avenue, frigging her quietly so as to reanimate her
passions, and rouse again the lustful heat of her cunt,
making her feel my pego and talking my baudiest, for
several minutes I lay, whilst she quite silent submitted
to all, fatigued with pleasure, yet getting slowly lewed
in body again under my titillations. She must have
been like me on heat that day. Then when she drew
her cunt back with a voluptuous sigh. I knew she
would take it up her, and again fucked her. Ah! with
what delirium of sexual enjoyment, for I loved her.

It was approaching nine o'clock, she dressed in

silence, whilst for a time I tried to induce her to meet me again, but uselessly. Whilst listening to my advice again about telling how she found the watch, she put her hand in her pocket, took something out, put her other hand to it, and then with a start as if she had forgotten what she was about, put it back into her pocket. Then it came suddenly to my mind that early in the evening she put something into her pocket rapidly, and turned away from me as she did so.—'You were going to put your wedding ring on,' said I.—'I wasn't—I have no ring'—and she looked confused.—'Let me feel in your pocket,' and I tried to do so.—'You shan't—you've no right,' she shrieked out, and I desisted.—Then we joked once more about marriage, as to which, or whether either of us was married, and there it ended.

We left together. Before doing so I put my head up her petticoats, gave her cunt a parting kiss, and should have liked to have bitten her clitoris off and swallowed it, so madly did I feel in love with her. She had plenty of money (none from me). I put her into a cab, and neither listened to the address she gave, nor followed her—as I had given my word—much as I longed to do so, and have never seen her since.—She said it wasn't likely that I ever should, but not why (many a day since I've thought of and longed for her, and she is one of my most delicious reminiscences).

The watch had my sister's initials and the maker's name on it. I told my sister I had lost it and gave her a new watch. Alice was worth a dozen watches I still think.

She was of an uncommon type of beauty, had light chestnut hair which crimped naturally, blue eyes with heavy eye brows, and long eye lashes. She had beautiful teeth, a small mouth, was well grown, well formed, was neither stout nor thin, and in brief was in that perfect condition, which a healthy woman of about two and twenty years arrives at, after a year's fucking. Her cunt was small, youthful and pretty.— Neither nipple nor belly showed signs of childbirth, yet she'd been fucked before I had her.

[This narrative is almost word for word as I wrote it within a few days after I had possessed this lady. I was so delighted with the adventure that I could think of nothing else for some days, and walked over the same ground in the vain hope of meeting her again. Writing the narrative gave me the utmost delight, as I recalled each form and feature of the beauty, each voluptuous act, almost each sensuous word I uttered, acts and words I am sure *both* enjoyed.—Who and what was she?]